DETOURS

a Novel

Rosemary N. Gensler

Phyllis W. Hoffman

Marion S. Phillips

Nancy S. Sims

Ellyn Horn Zarek

Library of Congress Cataloging-in-Publication Data

Gensler, Rosemary N., Hoffman, Phyllis W., Phillips, Marion S.,
Sims, Nancy S., and Zarek, Ellyn Horn
Detours: A Novel

p. cm.
Paperback ISBN: 978-1-947708-94-5
Ebook ISBN: 978-1-947708-95-2
Library of Congress Control Number: 2021907958

10 9 8 7 6 5 4 3 2 1
First Edition, May 2021

 CITRINE PUBLISHING

Brasstown, North Carolina, U.S.A.
(828) 585 - 7030
Publisher@CitrinePublishing.com
www.CitrinePublishing.com

CONTENTS

CONTENTS

(CONTINUED)

FOREWORD

BY ROBERT WATSON, PH.D.

Writing is my passion. In fact, I can't imagine not writing on a daily basis. Often writing is a solitary pursuit—long hours of research and travel, pensive moments contemplating plots, characters, and the narrative arc, endless days (and nights) in front of a computer pounding away at the keyboards, and the difficult task of reading and critiquing one's own writing. That is how most of us write and how the public views the art. But, in *Detours*, a quintet of accomplished and experienced women writers have come together to pen an intriguing and inspiring story. Fittingly, their book is about women… and about women writers in particular, who are traveling to a literary event. Yes, I could almost imagine the five authors sitting together bubbling forth with ideas, experiences, and scenarios! What emerges from this collaboration is a compelling story of sisterhood—and of the unexpected challenges (or, as the title suggests, *detours*) that confront them. The sometimes humorous, sometimes profound plot keeps the reader on edge as these enjoyable characters experience changes in their lives and relationships.

Kudos to the authors, who good-naturedly refer to themselves as the "Inkslingers," on this highly readable and enjoyable novel. But, in a larger sense, I am both intrigued and inspired by their collaboration. Having written "young adult" fiction with my then-teenage son and worked with him on a project called "Let's Write Together," which encouraged children to write with their friends and family, I have always been interested in promoting the joy of writing and thrill of creative collaborations. The "Inkslingers" are on to something and, after their readers enjoy the book, I suspect many of them will become writers and co-authors themselves.

—Robert Watson, Ph.D.
   Award-winning author of many books including, most recently, *The Nazi Titanic, The Ghost Ship of Brooklyn, George Washington's Final Battle,* and *Escape*

PROLOGUE

Loneliness permeated the deepest corners of the old inn. Neither the changing seasons nor the glory of the magnificent grounds gave any relief to its crumbling core. Not that there wasn't life in abundance around it. Trees grew, their rings ever expanding, branching up and out, with housing fit for the small birds and rodents who sought refuge there. Saplings were consumed by families of deer, grazing unmolested in the lush meadows. When satiated, they would disappear into the waiting forest, almost as though they were never there, their white tails the only giveaway, if anyone was looking. But no one was.

Surely there was reason to be sad when the fall leaves were buried under the first coat of snow and the summer birds went their way. With no one to open its doors, make up a bed, or eat meals at its tables, the long winter brought more of the same weather.

Spring arrived, tulips peeking out of the cold ground, not having been told that their appearance would not signal anything here. Then came the daffodils, yellow and sunny, and finally the forsythia. The young, handsome resident caretaker, Jimmy John, didn't know what to do with them. He mowed the grass, replaced the slate shingles, hammered this, and soldered that—single-handedly keeping The Inn from falling apart. He merely accepted the blooms and weeds, however thick they grew, and went about his business.

Guests? Not lately. An occasional passerby might request permission to walk the grounds, perhaps picking some raspberries or gathering wildflowers that grew in abundance. The Inn waited in quiet solitude. Like unrequited love, the wait was both the challenge and the pleasure. Solitude was to be tolerated; expectation was its muse. The Inn represented tradition—and would not disappoint.

As time passed and summer waned, rain pelted its roof and threatened to strike down the slate shingles, piece by piece. Water whirled around and filled the roads with fallen trees and debris. The Inn stood at the ready. Yes, The Inn at Raspberry Hill would open its doors for any traveler. She held steady when anyone approached. The Inn would rise out of its loneliness to extend hospitality to those who needed it. And on this August eve, with nary a warning, a group of travelers arrived. The Inn shook with anticipation.

Guests?

⁓

THE TRAVELERS

The Washburn Writing Conference attracts hundreds of participants annually. The women in this story, having met and bonded at other writing workshops, have come together in Washburn, New York to celebrate the publication of Deidre's book.

Deidre Carr Darceau

Deidre Carr Darceau or, as she is known in real life, DeeDee Kandel, is a forty-four-year-old devoted tennis mom, corporate event planner, and newly published author. Transplanted from Chicago, she now resides in Florida. Prior to the events of this story, she had met and become involved with this group of women who'd agreed to travel to a writing conference in upstate New York. She plans, for the first time, to present her debut book, a short story collection, at a local bookstore. Having launched her children, a girl, Faren, and a boy, Greg, while being a supportive wife, she now intends for this to be "her turn and her time."

Mira Wells Lawrence

Mira is a proud native Floridian, a graduate of the University of Florida, and an avid Gators fan. She changed her major three times during undergrad, starting as a sociology major, switching to pre-law and then, finally, to journalism. Mira graduated in the prescribed four years by going to school two summers in a row. This was by no means an easy feat, given the heat and humidity of Gainesville in the summer. Her goal was to be an investigative reporter. She works as a freelancer for *The Miami Herald.* Mira is thirty-three years old and married, with an eleven-year-old child.

Ruth Ann O'Grady

The youngest of the group, Ruth Ann is twenty-eight years old, single, and a preschool teacher who loves her job. She writes mystery novels and has many manuscripts piled up in a corner of her apartment. Ruth Ann, who lacks the self-esteem to believe she is actually an author, has never tried to get her novels published. Currently, she lives in Florida and frequently visits her family and friends in the Berkshires in Western Massachusetts. Because of her modest attire and frameless eyeglasses, she appears older than she is. She has given up on love—almost.

Allison Rhoades

At forty, Allison is a newly divorced mother of three school-aged children and a writer of children's books, who hails from Petoskey, Michigan. She owns a catering business that features organic and farm-to-table foods. A nature lover with a penchant for the outdoors, she enjoys seasonal sports. While attending the conference, she hopes to meet potential illustrators for her children's books.

Roxie Ross

Roxie, a former model, is a classy fifty-three-year-old sophisticate. With her husband, Ben, she is co-owner of a real estate office in Palm Beach, Florida, where they are long-time residents. In addition to her successful real estate business, she is an enthusiastic cook, whose cookbook, *Staging the Kitchen*, is due to be published next May.

Joesie Wallis Walters

Joesie, known for never revealing her age, is married, childless, and a children's librarian with a passion for unexpectedly dressing in costume, especially when reading stories to audiences of all ages. She writes about women amidst the stimulation of Washington, D.C., cherishing escapes to her family hideaway along the Allegheny River in western New York State. Her military father began her austere upbringing by naming her Joesie, a forever reminder of his not having had a male heir. Her father also chose her middle name, Wallis. Reflecting his Anglophile obsession, he used the moniker of a woman, Wallis Simpson, who greatly influenced the course of British history.

~1~

ON THE WAY

Missed calls. Three in a row. The urgency of the fourth one vibrated through my pocket. I snuck a peek at my phone. "Roxie," I sighed, so loud that it caught the attention of the other participants gathered around the table.

The conveyor of the meeting peered daggers at me over his eyeglasses. I'd been determined not to display any anxiety: even though my heart was tethered to my writing career, I had resolved to focus on this venture as a corporate event planning consultant, and this meeting was important. My family's lifestyle was dependent on my separate take-home pay, as was marketing for my debut novel. The conveyor said, "Something you want to add, Ms. Kandel?"

"Please," I said, "it's DeeDee. And no…"

My phone buzzed again, now for the fifth time.

"Will you excuse me, please?"

I was eager to the point of fanatical to have my five favorite writing compatriots join me at the Washburn Writing Conference in Upstate New York. I wanted—no, *needed*—their support, Roxie's most of all. They were my emotional buffer against my family's disinterest and dismissal of my writing endeavors.

"I found an interesting writers' conference we all could go to near the end of the summer," I'd told them over video chat weeks ago, sharing the website and all that I knew about it.

The others had been fast all-in. But Roxie, my go-to person, had showed surprising reluctance. "How long will we be gone? How are you getting there?" She'd peppered me with questions.

Our group had formed when we'd met at a workshop years ago. Ever since then, we'd all made a concerted effort to remain supportive of one another. Our annual reunion, at one writing conference or another, always proved to be a confirmation of our encouragement and mutual respect. But this year was special. This year, I'd be attending as a bona fide published author.

"Sorry to dash," I told the leering conveyor. "Urgent call."

I hurried out of the room. "Ms. Kandel?" one of the participants called. It almost didn't register, focused as I was on reinventing myself as Deidre Carr Darceau, my penname. She said, "You left this." In my haste I had forgotten my sweater.

"Oh, thanks," I said, grabbing it, then blustering through a series of excuses as I took my leave.

I crossed the lobby, searching for a private location. I needed to speak with Roxie, as the number of calls from her concerned me. The phone went directly to voicemail. "Damn." What could have been so important?

Allison, Ruth Ann, and Joesie had each been an automatic "yes." Joesie, I mused, would need three rooms for all her belongings. That had left only Mira and Roxie. Mira wasn't sure if she could make it. She'd have to arrange for the care of her young son. Typical Mira, always hesitating. Still, I was confident she'd commit. But as for Roxie...

I had to reach her. She had only a few weeks left to register for the conference.

The weeks flew by. I worked and wrote. Roxie remained elusive, emailing me she finally had registered. Mira was coming, too. That's all of us. Six women, six writers, six different genres, each with a bond and a story. We were on our way.

Mira

The smell of him captured my every sense. It was Rico. But how, dammit? The dresser drawer was full of sweaters unworn in months, maybe years. I decided I needed an extra layer when the report predicted cool weather in New York. I pulled them out, throwing them on the floor until I came to the one—the one that was *his*—the one he gave me the last time I saw him. It was blue with orange UF letters. My knees buckled. My tush found the floor with a thud. No, it *can't* be—not after all this time. I squeezed the sweater between my hands, brought it to my face, and remembered.

The day we left Gainesville, after graduating from the University of Florida, he had come to my room to say goodbye. He just showed up without calling. My pillow and linens had been off my bed and stuffed in my laundry bag.

"Rico, I thought you were leaving early, I...." He pressed his lips against mine and pushed the door to my room closed.

"I had to see you one more time. Do you know how cute you are?"

"I'm not even dressed."

"All the better to love you."

We had learned how to touch each other. We knew the special places to kiss and caress. Every time we were the only people in the world and the world sang our favorite song. This time had been no different.

Eventually, sounds of people moving out had interrupted our afterglow.

"I have to go," he said.

"Yes, I know," I'd answered numbly.

"Here, take my sweater. Keep it. It's said, when you have something that belongs to someone you love, you *will* see that person again."

"Don't you forget that, Ricardo Monina."

My mother's reaction to Rico was worse than even I expected. Not that I thought she would approve of me marrying a non-Jew. But I at least held out hope that she would have been reasonable.

"You will not marry that man," she'd decreed. "You will never see him again. Do you hear me?"

I fled to my room. Before I could close the door, she grabbed my still-packed suitcase and purse. I became a prisoner in my own home. My father looked on with tears in his eyes. I was a grown adult with a college degree, acquiescing to my parents out of respect. But how could I ever let Rico go?

A month later, I was under the chuppah marrying Avrom Kohn, whom I had known since high school. He was shy and highly intelligent. Our families were close friends. My heart had throbbed with painful intensity as I walked the seven circles around my betrothed. What little time we had spent together before the ceremony had been closely chaperoned. As adults, we hardly knew each other. Avrom was tall. In high school, he'd had the obligatory long curls on each side of his short blonde hair. After the wedding, we agreed we would practice Modern Orthodoxy.

We spent the night in our new apartment, minutes away from both sets of parents. He was gentle, though he must have guessed I was not a virgin. "Don't worry," he said. "No one's going to check the sheets." I couldn't help but smile.

The next day we stayed at a kosher hotel in South Beach. We both enjoyed swimming in the ocean, picking up shells, and getting a tan. He rubbed sunscreen on my back and legs. I did the same for him. *Was I softening to his touch?* I wondered. We ate deli at Wolfie's and ended up at the Fontainebleau Hotel for wine and dessert. It was a warm, breezy night. We held hands as we walked in the sand to the ocean, took off our shoes, and let the warm saltwater wash over our feet. I looked up at the sky and wondered if Rico was watching the same stars.

Then it was back to reality. Avrom was highly organized; I was not. Avrom was an accountant whose clients were mostly Orthodox Jews. I told him I would respect his religious convictions though I would not share them. We agreed to compromise.

Over the years, I came to feel stifled. Even though he was a good man, treating me well, my passion had waned.

"Your religious convictions weren't why I married you, Mira," he had said early in our marriage.

"Why, then?"

"Let's go back to the beach; it's too nice a day for seriousness."

It wasn't long before I'd realized I hadn't had a period for months. The physician at Planned Parenthood told me she thought I was about three months along. Avrom was surprised at my news. We had only been married a few months.

The labor had been easy. Avrom would rub my back during occasional pains. He told me over and over that he already loved the child, who would be as wonderful as its mother. Throughout my labor, he remained at the head of the bed. When Dr. Break-stone came in she spread my legs and said, "You're ready. Here comes a head of black hair." One big push later, we had a son. His name would be Elijah. When I'd held him in my arms and looked into his brown eyes, I knew who his father was.

Avrom wouldn't think of my working outside the house. He said my job was to take care of our child and myself. I couldn't help wondering what he was thinking when he looked at Elijah, with almost sad eyes. As Elijah grew, I started writing again. I even wrote some children's stories that I read to Elijah while making funny faces and using animated voices. He always giggled with joy.

When we lit the Shabbat candles every Friday night, Avrom would take Elijah in his arms and dance around the room. The empty place in my heart was still there, yet my life was comfort-able. Avrom was a good man and a good father. I loved Avrom but I wasn't *in* love with him. After all, he was a kind, gentle person who loved both Elijah and me. How could I leave him?

When Elijah was five years old, we registered him in public school. I waited until he was settled and happy before deciding to take a creative writing class at our local arts center. Avrom was delighted to read my work. He was supportive and said I had a gift for storytelling.

I looked forward to the class as it gave me the opportunity to learn and get to know other writers. I started writing a book that

I threw away, deciding to stick with children's books and short stories. I sent an op-ed piece to our local newspaper, which was published. It opened the door for me. Soon I became a freelance contributor to the paper. I also continued with my personal writing, sure that one of these days I would have my name on the cover of a book.

I started to wonder why Avrom never spoke about having another child. Elijah was almost six. Our love life was satisfactory and unprotected. We were open about many things, just not this. It wasn't until years later I found out he'd had the mumps as an adult, before we were married, and suspected he might have been sterile.

When Elijah was eleven, my writing guru, Mirena, suggested a workshop in Upstate New York in the town of Washburn. Funny—she mentioned it right after Deidre had called me. The decision to go felt even better when I saw that Avrom was excited to spend a week alone with Elijah. They made a different plan for every day I would be gone.

They waved goodbye to me the morning I left. Though the conference was only four days long, I planned to be away from my husband for three additional days in solitude. As I checked in curbside at the airport, Elijah looked eager to spend seven days with his father. I was eager to spend seven days without Avrom.

The flight to White Plains, New York, promised to be smooth and uneventful. I could have watched something interesting on the screen in front of me. Instead, I ended up staring at the flight map. I closed my eyes to better concentrate on the production of my thoughts, and the rolling video behind my eyelids. My mother had not been enthusiastic about my trip. "Don't forget to print out Elijah's schedule," she'd said, and, "I don't want to cook if I don't have to. Have you been to the grocery store? Be sure to take your phone charger. You know you left it once and oh Mira, do you have your meds?"

"All right, *Mother*," I answered, feeling the pain of stress in my neck. "It's only seven days. There's plenty of food in the freezer and Elijah's schedule is on your computer. The charger's in my purse and *yes*, I have my meds." I might have added, "But I'm not going to take them. Scotch will handle everything."

Dreaming, at 20,000 feet, I pictured Ruth Ann to erase thoughts of my mother. I couldn't wait to join her. There she was, dear Ruth Ann, sitting in a large Adirondack chair overlooking the Berkshire Mountains. She had a book in her hands. Fifty Shades of—what? Maybe she was dreaming about her own Christian Grey. *Ooh! And she's a pre-school teacher!* What secret lives we live. Well, she *is* single, maybe not so beautiful outside, but certainly exquisite inside. With a little work, her pale green eyes and brown hair could perk up her round face. She's also busty, to say the least.

Ms. Deidre then entered my reverie. She was riding the train from New York with Roxie. She reminded me of a homecoming queen of the eighties. She had it all—brains and beauty. She'd married well, with the requisite two children. She was the organized one of us, a planner, a dedicated tennis mom, of all things, and a recently published author. *Good for her.*

Smelling coffee, I opened my eyes. "I'll take a cup with half-and-half," I said, smiling at the flight attendant. "And a biscotti too, please."

Suddenly, I heard Roxie's voice. "Hey Mira! How are you?" (I'd drifted off to sleep again.) There she was, dressed to the nines, as usual. *Oh boy, do I love her wardrobe. I should have gone into real estate instead of studying sociology.* And on her, the white hair is perfect. I thought about my hair, just colored at Mr. John's, a perfect red for me. Looking at Roxie again, I could see that sadness registered in her big dark eyes. Her phone rang. She turned her back to me. I couldn't hear her conversation.

The pilot's announcement brought me back to the reality of seat 12B. The aircraft had made a semi-circle and was now on a path to White Plains. It landed with a thud and shuddered to a stop. A woman who had hurriedly retrieved her suitcase from the overhead bin lost her balance and fell, spread-eagle onto my lap. She could not pull her heavy self, off me. The flight attendant made her way down the aisle, pulled the woman off me, and asked if we were okay. The woman apologized profusely, then sheepishly took her seat, leaving her suitcase to block the aisle. We learned there had been a plane barreling down the runway we were about to cross, thus the sudden stop. The pilot admonished everyone to be patient and to stay in their seats. No one else dared move, and I felt my heart racing. Was it from skipping my meds? Perhaps from daydreaming about Rico?

I collected my suitcase from the carousel and rolled it down the sidewalk to the rental car area. Grunting as I lifted it into the trunk of the Ford Taurus, I scolded myself for overpacking. Three extra outfits, four books, and a hair dryer weighed a lot more in the suitcase than they had in my closet. I found the buttons to set the seat the way I wanted it, looked at the unfamiliar dashboard to see where the lights were, and checked out the radio. I made sure my foot was on the brake and turned the key. The engine hummed to life.

My pills were in a special pocket in my suitcase in case I needed them. I felt totally okay, so why would I? Even so, something had told me to pack them, just in case. Even Avrom didn't know I'd stopped taking my medication. It had been over a month now and all was well.

I set the GPS to the address of the Abenaki Lodge and Conference Center in Washburn, New York, then took out the map and a set of written directions, just to be safe. I never was good at reading maps. I pressed the button. *Whoopee!* The lady in the box started talking and off I went. Thank goodness the air conditioning worked well. It had to be ninety degrees outside. I felt exhilarated by the thought of being alone on this beautiful day, on my way to an adventure with people I already knew. I envisioned the lodge as a quaint old building on a narrow tree-lined street.

The highway up to Washburn in the Hudson Valley of New York State was uncrowded. It was early Sunday afternoon, and the weekenders were going back into the city. I checked myself in the rearview mirror. My hair, which I had been letting grow, looked okay but my lips were chapped. I reached into my purse on the passenger seat, careful not to take my eyes off the road. Deftly, I found the container of lip stuff, opened it with one hand, and, with a free finger, rubbed the soothing softness on my lips. My stomach growled. I hadn't eaten for too many hours. This was certainly not like Florida, where every hundred yards billboards advertised fast-food joints. There were rolling hills and grasses of various shades of green. Cows munched contentedly, perilously close to the highway. Once in a while, I spotted a deer and prayed it would stay put.

I held the steering wheel tightly as I crossed over the Rip van Winkle Bridge. Heavy damp fog encased the high arches and the cars around me slowed. The fog persisted until I was away from the bridge and back onto the highway.

It had been at least a year since I'd been away with my writing partners. Allison was driving to Washburn from Michigan, by way of Pittsburgh, where she had visited her parents. Pittsburgh is an underrated city. I really like Pittsburgh. I like Allison, too. She is loving, gregarious, and intelligent. She's writing children's stories and is determined to get them published. Although the poor thing recently went through a divorce, we never heard her complain. Her blue eyes light up her olive complexion and black hair. It is so rare that olive-skinned people have blue eyes. Genetics are fascinating.

I wanted it to be my turn to present my book. Abigail Adams will come to life on my pages, just like she came to life in my mind. Maybe next year the group will meet in New York and Barnes and Noble will do a book signing for me. Dream on, Mira!

The lady in the box instructed me to exit the highway. I jumped a little. Why had her voice changed? *Dreamus interruptus*, I thought as I fought to bring my brain back to the present. There were no signs of civilization for as far as my astigmatic eyes could see. I heeded her directions and exited. After a few rights and lefts, I was completely confused. I was on the main drag of Washburn, supposedly on the Hudson River. Perhaps the river flows elsewhere? I looked for anything that resembled water. I did notice a bookstore, but I must have passed the lodge because the lady in the box kept revising my route: "detour, detour, detour."

I stopped the car and entered the address of the Abenaki Lodge on my cell. The friendly voice told me to turn around and turn right on Opera Place. After a questionably legal U-turn, I swear I heard a sigh of relief from the box as it announced I had arrived at my destination.

～2～

LATE FOR LUNCH

Joesie	Sunday 1:00 PM

I kept checking my watch. It was a two-hour ride from my mother's house in rural Maryland to the nearest Amtrak train station. Any delay would impact the time to park and get the multitude of possessions I might need for any eventuality in the station. I figured I could purchase the ticket and get to the right track. "If you have no negative issues in a day, Joesie, consider yourself lucky." That had been my mother's mantra, repeated all too often.

Why was I getting so many glances? Maybe because I was tripping a bit in my clunky red Western boots. They were fancifully embroidered with long branches of green leaves and red berries up each side. They complemented the black cowgirl hat trying to stay on my head of bushy red curls. Chaos, as always, seemed to reign. Yep, another good reason for my having been likened to an old girlie cowhand who, at times, thought she was reincarnated as, or at least related to, Annie Oakley or Dale Evans.

I *do* wear costumes when working as a children's librarian. It's hardly a chore. I've never wanted to do anything else. My husband Josh and I hadn't raised any children. That's another story and a secret we've kept close to ourselves and a few others. My borrowed children returned to their respective homes and families each day when they left the library. They loved witches, wizards, wands, and ghosts—anything unexpected. I dressed like the characters in the books. I read Newberry and Caldecott prize-winning stories to them, directing their book choices to well-written selections, as well as help their parents find stories. Of course, I have my favorite children but try not to show it.

This garb, however, was not a costume. I genuinely loved the western theme, especially after having lived in Texas. It was one of the places I liked to revisit and ride horseback through the open fields. When the tumbleweed blew in the wind, the landscape changed—as did my spirits.

I struggled across the intersection from the parking lot, gritting my teeth when the traffic light was not on my side. "Oh, no!" I cried out. "The station looks like it's been bombed!"

Inside it was massive construction: temporary narrow walkways, and neither the escalator nor the elevator up to my designated platform were working. Nobody with physical restrictions could have managed to get upstairs. Could I? I was towing my usual two large, overloaded, rolling suitcases. My shoulders proved especially useful with a plump soft-sided carry-on on one and my camera bag on the other.

After successfully fighting technology (with a credit card) I was able to purchase the train ticket. I was a lucky ducky as three young able strangers, with bulging Rocky Balboa muscles, offered to help me out. They were easy on even my tired eyes. Out of kindness (or perhaps looking for a tip) they took pity on me—a "woman of a certain age." They hauled my baggage, and those of other wannabe passengers, up the steep stairway. No doubt they'd have stories for a while about that dame who'd most likely had some fringe disintegrate from her brain matter. Eventually, my possessions and I were aboard the on-time train for a two-and-a-half-hour ride to New York's Penn Station. There I'd wait a few hours for the connection for another train north and west to somewhere in the Hudson Valley.

Despite the death of my father only a few weeks before, I just couldn't miss this conference. Deidre was presenting her new book. The two train rides would give me an opportunity to ponder all that was spinning in my head.

I hadn't wanted to leave my mother alone, but my husband, Joshua—Josh for short—had promised to keep checking on her. He no longer had to "fight the battles of Jericho" with his father-in-law, our own resident family's commanding officer, Dad. Whew! Joshua didn't want to appear *too* happy.

I needed to savor the joys of being away, surrounded by women I cared for. We were the same group of would-be authors, all trying to scale an increasingly taller barrier called *publishing* in a time of prevailing self-publishers. I hoped this would be a memorable time to take home ideas for our individual and group writing projects and carry them forward to publication. Mira and I were supposed to meet in the early fall to gather information for our mutual fascination with Abigail Adams. I couldn't wait to make those plans. But "plan" is increasingly a four-letter word!

Dad's death represented an end of an era. We had been a military family before I was relieved of daughterly duties by marrying a college economics professor. Down south in a peachy state, I was born pink from head to toe to a mismatched couple. My father was an incorrigible Anglophile, naming me Joesie Wallis Walters. And he called me Joe or referred to me as Wally Walters, sounding like "walrus" if said too quickly. Nothing was a consolation for Dad's having missed two opportunities: not being promoted to general in the U.S. Army and not having a prized male heir.

For too many years, army life was more of a hardship on Mother than on me. She saw no way out. An officer's wife since the fifties, she dutifully donned her own understood dress code, comprised of cute hat and white cotton gloves when attending the mandatory wives' events. After all, Dad kept trying so hard to get a promotion. He more than hinted that perhaps it was Mother's fault he was frozen at the lieutenant colonel level because of *her* lack of genuine enthusiasm. She carried many a burden of blame on her broad shoulders.

Following Dad's death, we'd tried to find moments of humor. After all, he was my father, for better or worse. Mom and I tried to conjure up the best stories of his career, mostly at his expense. We had a great laugh over his two left feet: one day he returned to our on-base house in the middle of his workday then shortly after, he went right back out the front door. Why? Because his "feet felt funny." He had realized he had put on two left shoes in his haste to get to a meeting with his commanding officer. He had grabbed the two identical spit-shined shoes without looking. He hoped his commanding officer hadn't seen his grimaces.

At the time of the incident, Mother and I got through his loud harangue of blame that moved from him to us. He walked out to return to work on the base. When he was out of sight, she disappeared into the bedroom without saying a word. When she came back, she had put her hat on backwards, wore two left white sneakers, and her gloves were on the wrong hands. We giggled about her surprising performance. She did another dress rehearsal a week after he died to provide us comic relief.

My transfer to the second train was far easier. There were porters ready and willing to gather up my belongings and wheel them to the next step of the journey. I was treated to a soothing, beautiful ride of contentment as the second train weaved in and out of the villages of the forested hillsides of New York State. A train trip was like safely canoeing or tubing down a calm river, not having to worry about falling out into the cold waters and quick rapids. I think I fell asleep from the soothing motion of the train and general fatigue. Tears were streaming down my cheeks and onto my lap. I struggled to figure out why—then an *aha* moment! I remembered dreaming about floods while asleep on the train only moments before.

We had lived in so many places—Dad's orders dictated where we'd go next—and through scary times when the gentle rivers reached out over their banks and became monsters in raging storms, with wild tentacles consuming everything in their paths of destruction. Despite the infrequent threats of hurricanes, our homestead retreat on the Upstate New York side of the Allegheny River was a stable getaway. No matter where the military sent us, it remained a place of solitude.

Suddenly, the train lurched to a stop. Through the static on the loudspeaker, we were able to hear that something got hit by a train and we couldn't move from the crime scene until the ME arrived. So close and yet so far! I had no cell service to warn the others who were probably drinking some good wine served with the dreaded cheese on top that would stimulate my lactose allergy.

Finally, after what seemed like another hour, I arrived at my intended destination—well, almost. I hailed what appeared to be a driver for hire without the usual markings—like "taxi." A woman behind the wheel of an old Buick clunker rolled down her window and claimed to be a driver. When I attempted to describe where I thought I was going, she'd never heard of the place, or she couldn't understand my lousy Spanish. After helping me swing my valises over the high bumper and into the trunk opening, she let me ride shotgun, windows open, to look for the right address.

Somehow, with combined efforts, I arrived at what would be my home for the next few days.

~3~

TOGETHER AGAIN

The town was old, all right. The absence of tree-lined streets was certainly not anything I had imagined. After our flight together from Florida, Deidre and I walked into the restaurant side by side to where Mira was seated. The delectable odors made my mouth water. Oddly, to our surprise, the management required a valid credit card before we could be seated.

We had just ordered lunch when a familiar face on a tall attractive body walked in—

Allison. Deidre and I greeted her enthusiastically; we all seemed relieved to have arrived at almost the same time. Our group had just finished exchanging greetings when Joesie, our favorite pack rat, lurched through the door to join us. Stifling giggles, we watched our friend negotiate the task of holding the door open while trying to get herself and her cargo inside at the same time. She needed a sherpa.

We should have taken a picture. Even though she's an amateur photographer, Joesie hated having her own picture taken. We didn't know why. She wore leotards, cowboy boots, a flowing printed top, a scarf, and a cowgirl hat. The scarf and hat were to tame her wild red hair—an impossible task. People are supposed to look like what they do, but not our Joesie. This army brat was a children's librarian.

Ruth Ann arrived from Western Massachusetts where she had been visiting family. Her smile lit up her pale face. We were all together now, full of anticipation. Everyone spoke at once. It was mostly, "How was your trip? How's your summer been? Any new writing projects we should know about? Isn't this exciting?"

"I'm trying my best. I hope you'll understand I can't get my father's death out of my mind," Joesie said.

We all watched as the tears slowly flowed down her cheeks.

Ruth Ann

I let the word "writer" twirl around in my head. Here, at this conference, I felt like a writer. Someday, I hoped to call myself an author, if any of my mystery books were to get published. In the meantime, I had been working on myself. I'd always been the shy one, the person in the group that's hardest to get to know. The first conference I attended with them was a turning point, albeit a small one. I had met a group of ladies who, for the most part, didn't notice my reticence or lack of social skills. Now, three years later, I felt like I knew each of them a bit better and I hoped they knew me.

I smiled, remembering what I was thinking when Roxie first approached me. I had had a lot of doubts. Would anyone care enough to publish the books I sent? Was that all we were, a bunch of words read in a huddle, taken to heart, loved first then lost? I had been immersed in negative thoughts when the voice of a woman boomed, "Which workshop are you going to?"

Startled, I'd hesitated, then answered in my boldest, yet still mousy, voice, "I think the mystery writers?" Gulp. It had been more question than answer, spoken like some California school-girl, not the adult woman that I was.

"Great, me too. I'm Roxie."

"Ruth Ann," I'd replied.

"I don't write mysteries, but I love to read them." Another woman had then rushed up beside us, petite and pretty in contrast to Roxie's more classic look. Roxie had said, "This is Deidre. She's going, too."

"Welcome," she'd said, offering me her hand, firm and warm. Then I'd recognized her.

"Wait," I'd said, "You're Deidre Carr Darceau. I love your writing. I've read some of your short stories in a southern anthology. So creative. I'm pleased to meet you."

"Yes, I *am* a writer. Hope to make some money someday soon. What do you write?"

"Believe it or not I write mysteries. Haven't sold anything yet or even tried," I said. At the workshop, Roxie had invited me to lunch. I'd sat with her, Deidre, and more of their friends: Joesie, Mira, and Allison. Amid munching on appetizers and sipping wine, I was ordained the junior member of this eclectic group, the little sister, the one they looked out for—and, I hoped, the one they would grow to consider a friend.

Now, here I am again, enjoying being with the group in Washburn.

Mira

Someone—I think it was Deidre—suggested we unpack and relax, then meet for dinner. We looked in vain for bellhops to help Joesie, after discovering her room was three floors up, basically in the attic. Of course, the one with the most to carry would be on the highest floor with nary an elevator. One of the employees helped Joesie bring up her bags, after which she finally made it to the restaurant. We checked the menu and found we liked the choices.

"Mira," Allison asked, "what about keeping kosher? Is there anything you can order from this menu?"

"Don't worry, ladies," I said. "This weekend I'm free. What happens in Washburn will stay in Washburn. I'm going to eat to my heart's content."

"That's original, Mira," Deidre said.

By the time we'd finished eating, it was getting too late to explore Washburn. We paired off according to which of the three or four buildings we were assigned to and went to our rooms. We had no inkling what lay ahead.

∽4∽

ABENAKI LODGE

The Abenaki Lodge and Conference Center was comprised of several small buildings, all old, well-kept relics of a bygone era. Entry to Allison's and my building required negotiating the narrow, uneven outside steps up to a locked door. The correct code in the entry box unlocked the heavy door, allowing entry into a narrow, dimly lit hallway. Allison turned and unlocked the door to her room. "See you at dinner, Mira," she said.

I climbed up the next seventeen steps and, with bated breath, opened the door to my room. Lucky me. Someone, maybe the perky receptionist, had put my luggage in my room. Nice touch. My room overlooked an alley where the garbage cans were located. Joesie and Ruth Ann were in a building down the street across from the Church of Perpetual Harmony. Deidre and Roxie were also across the street, overlooking the blank wall of the seemingly vacant Abenaki Opera House.

My room was spacious but sparsely furnished. The window air conditioning unit hummed, and the bathroom was clean and fairly modern. There was, however, no telephone. A sign on the mirror read: "In case of emergency call 555-555-5555." It did not suggest how we were supposed to do that, sans landline. Oh well, I had my cell phone and charger and I remained in good humor.

The sound on the old, small television was almost inaudible. No amount of jiggling the remote or turning the dials on the set itself could bring the words from the speakers to my ears. So, I puffed up the pillows on my bed and read.

I jumped when I heard scratching sounds. *Surely, they'll go away after a while!* I thought. But they didn't. I was convinced it was a mouse.

Slowly, I got out of the bed and found a broom in the bathroom, likely abandoned by housekeeping. I walked toward where I thought the noise was coming. The invader must have heard me approaching because it leaped from inside the closed curtains to the top of the desk. I smacked at it as hard as I could and missed. It jumped from the desk, scurrying to the bathroom.

I was hot on its heels. I heard screaming in my head as I lifted my weapon and walloped the creature. Red blood and still-squirming viscera splattered the black-and-white tile floor. I dropped the broom and ran into the bedroom, holding my ears and screaming aloud. I fell to the floor, sat holding my knees, and howled.

I don't know how long I sat that way before I heard the knocking on the door and the sound of Allison's frantic voice begging me to open it. I fell into her arms, crying. "Allison, my God, I killed it! I killed it!" She looked at the puddle of bloody death and led me away. Her mobile phone call brought a man who said kind words about my doing a good deed, then cleaned and disinfected the bathroom. After inspecting the scene, he reassured me this was a lone creature, but set a trap just in case.

I forced my shaking body to calm down and assured Allison I was okay. I told her I would see her later. Reluctantly, she left me alone. I found one of the miniature bottles of Scotch whiskey I had in my purse and poured it into a glass. After a sip or two, the burning sensation dissipated and the muscles in my neck and shoulders started to loosen.

When I was younger, I had always been the killer of insects and vermin that made their way into our house—palmetto bugs and the like. Recently, I'd become squeamish. Someone once told me to use hairspray if you don't have bug spray. It is quite effective. I'd catch lizards or chameleons too, setting them outside on the grass. I managed to keep one baby lizard alive in our bathroom for five days during a stormy stretch. I'd make sure there was water in the bathtub and a snip of lettuce on the floor. I learned afterwards that the lizard would have preferred an ant or a small beetle. It must have eaten something because it survived and that's what counted. When the sun eventually came out, I let it go.

I walked gingerly into the bathroom and climbed into the shower. The water on my back was warm and soothing. There was no hint of the recent carnage on the floor. I was able to smile as I toweled off and get ready for dinner with my writer friends. I drank the last gulp of Scotch, brushed my teeth, and walked to the restaurant, thinking about them.

I loved Joesie's sensitive writing skills, laughed at Deidre's connection with everyday objects in her short stories, and marveled at Allison's way of teaching through her writing for children. I wondered if the grownups who read to the little guys enjoyed the stories as much as their young listeners. I had commiserated with Roxie about her work and she empathized with my family struggles.

I was the last one to arrive at dinner. I hoped Allison hadn't said anything about my horrible experience of the afternoon. The looks on the faces of my friends told me she had.

"Oh, Allison," I said, trying to smile through gritted teeth, "what a big mouth you have."

"Don't be angry, Mira. I was just concerned. I don't know how you did that instead of running away."

Sweet Ruth Ann, in her own calm way, said, "Mira, we all hope it's the worst thing that ever happens to you."

Roxie chimed in, "Let's have a bottle of wine."

"Let's all toast Deidre," I suggested. "After all, she encouraged us to attend this conference."

"And we've become closer," Roxie said. "I propose a side trip. Deidre, didn't you want to see Astor Courts in Rhinebeck while we're here in New York? We might need a break."

"I heard it's worth the trip," Deidre said.

Glasses clinked. We talked about our lives, how women's roles and aspirations have changed, and how often we felt undervalued.

"Isn't it terrible what's happening to our earth?" Allison asked, changing the subject.

"One of my colleagues volunteers for disaster relief," Ruth Ann answered.

"The pictures of the aftermath of disasters are just awful. I don't know how people survive that kind of devastation, and all because of climate change," Allison lamented.

"My co-worker has been to New Orleans, Houston, Northern California," Ruth Ann said, "wherever she's needed, staying anywhere she can, even if it's in a tent."

"What gets me," Roxie interjected, "is when we send money and supplies to help after disasters, later we find out the supplies disappeared before they got to the people who needed them. It's really criminal. Corruption. Problem is you can't *not* give. Those poor people. We've been lucky lately in South Florida. Nothing major in a while. I pray for South Florida."

Another bottle of wine appeared on the table and our conversation drifted back to our first conference at the Sarah Lawrence Writing Institute, where most of us met. We continued talking about our own writing. Deidre said she liked Ruth Ann's style of writing her mysteries. Ruth Ann said she admired Joesie's vivid descriptions of places and people. Joesie confirmed she would be going to the history writers' workshop in Boston with me at the end of the summer. At that moment, Roxie's cell phone rang. She stood up and walked outside.

"What's going on?" Joesie asked. Deidre just shook her head.

Our conversation continued a bit less animated as a paler Roxie rejoined the table. No one commented on her expression. She moved away when Deidre tried to put her arm around her shoulders. There was silence.

"Goddamn it," Roxie said. "Why does Ben have to keep harping on this trip? It's like he didn't want me to come to the Hudson Valley. Wonder what he did when he was a realtor up here?"

I asked the server for our check.

"Oh no," the server said, "your meals have been paid for."

"Huh?" I asked. "Who do we thank?"

"Did you see that guy at the bar?" our server said. We turned to look just in time to see a tall man slip out the door.

Deidre asked, "Was that him?"

The server shrugged her shoulders.

"Gee," Mira murmured. "There's something familiar about him."

"Hey, everybody," Allison said, "Listen to what my sister Lexie just sent me on social media. 'True friends go long periods of time without speaking and never question the friendship.'"

"Like us," Deidre said. "It's been almost a year since our last conference and it's like we've never been apart."

"You guys have been together how long?" Ruth Ann asked.

"I've lost track," Deidre replied.

"It's got to be at least seven years," Roxie guessed.

"It's been three for me," Ruth Ann said.

"Really," Allison remarked. "With all our emails back and forth it seems like you've always been a part of our group."

"I second that, Ruth Ann. What does it matter? We're friends," I added, reaching around, and hugging her.

"Joesie, you look tired," Allison said. "How was your trip from Baltimore?"

"Thank God for the sherpas who carried my bags up the broken escalator at the train station."

"Who's watching your kids?" Joesie turned to Allison.

"The 'ex' believe it or not," she replied.

"Well, whatever," Roxie said. "Thank Lexie for the great quote, and so true."

The tension melted away. Without a word, we all held hands and smiled. We looked around and, finding the room almost empty, agreed to meet for breakfast, then walked outside.

The night air was cool and still. As Allison and I turned to walk to our building, we shivered as we passed the dark alley. We hurried along, looking over our shoulders. The door to the building creaked noisily behind us.

"What was that crash?" I wondered out loud. The goose bumps on my arms were still there.

Allison's face was ashen. "Probably just a garbage can."

I closed and locked my door quickly, looking around for anything unusual. Just to be safe, I put a chair in front of the door before climbing into bed.

∼5∼

WAFFLES

Monday morning, a wall of warm humid air enveloped us as soon as we exited the air-conditioned dark-paneled lobby of the Abenaki Lodge. We could have waited inside, but it wasn't that hot yet. The morning sun drew us like flittering moths, out of the dark towards the light. The six of us gravitated to the side of the door, to the right of the potted red geraniums. The sidewalk reflected bright white. Roxie and I rummaged through our bags to find our sunglasses. Each of our pocketbooks was adorned with scarves tied around the handles.

My scarf was tied on a Coach bag I'd found at a second-hand shop. The fabric was blue with a paisley pattern and swirls of indigo and white that coordinated with my solid blue linen dress. My dark hair was pulled back into a French braid, the way I have worn it since high school. As a child, I had always wished that I had been born with blue eyes instead of these bovine-browns. I was a homely teenager, dealing with acne and glasses. My grades had always been good, but the fact that I was average in height, looks, and popularity always made me feel as if I were lacking something. I had no idea what "it" was. I certainly didn't have "it."

As soon as I landed my first job teaching, right out of college, I went to check out the new colored contact lenses. When I slipped the free trial pair onto the surface of my corneas, and blue eyes blinked back, I knew that was "it." The contacts gave me a unique appearance, a look that set me apart. I hoped that people wouldn't discover my secret. Maybe they'd just think there was something striking about me—Allison Rhoades.

Each morning thereafter, I underwent a magical transformation: painting a little picture with foundation, blush, eye shadow, and mascara on the blank canvas of my face and popping in the blue lenses. Even during the worst days of the divorce, my ritual continued. My adult life included frequent trips to the hair salon and quite a bit of my salary was spent on projecting a trendy image.

On the sidewalk of the main street of Washburn, standing with this group of fellow writers, the soft blue of my eyes nearly matched the shade of my dress. Not one of the women had any idea that the color was fake. I hadn't yet revealed all my secrets.

"So, how did you sleep?" Roxie asked as she adjusted the red scarf tied to her beige bag.

She directed her question towards Deidre, as five women turned in Deidre's direction for the answer. She wore a fine-knit cream-colored sleeveless tank with navy slacks. She would add a blazer later. I wondered how it would feel to be the one who was going to present at the conference, the one who would be signing her book as readers purchased them, offering real money for words. This trip celebrated the first one of our sisterhood, Deidre, publishing a book. Was she nervous? Had thoughts of presenting her work kept her awake last night?

"Well, I only had two bathroom breaks instead of the usual four," Deidre said, grinning, "so I guess that wasn't so bad. It's really not such a big deal."

"Oh, but it is," Mira said, reaching out to touch Deidre's arm. People listened to Mira. She spoke with a quiet authority that was undeniable. "We are all so proud of you, Deidre," she said with a slight nod.

The rest of us murmured agreement. Deidre dropped her head a bit.

"I'm so relieved to have you all here. It hasn't been all that great, this book thing. The editing and last-minute changes have been surprisingly stressful. At least, here with you, my unshakable five fans, I feel like things will go smoothly."

I counted the group surreptitiously, with tiny—and I hoped imperceptible—nods of my head, a remnant of my years as a teacher. Six of us, all here. We were all adults, so there was no reason to do this. Still, it would be rude to leave for breakfast before we had all gathered. I just wanted to make sure. It made me feel better to check on things like this. I knew it was probably a symptom of my ever-present anxiety that had grown after the divorce and sent me into therapy. But nothing was wrong with a little counting and double checking here and there.

Joesie's trendy fuchsia top flowed past her wrists like little wings. She stepped beyond the geraniums in her matching cowboy boots and continued moving just past the group. Then, she turned and said, "What do you say? Let's get started. We can talk as we walk."

"Sure," Ruth Ann said as she moved towards Joesie. Ruth Ann wore jeans, a black t-shirt and ballet flats. I joined them immediately as there was just enough room for three of us to walk side by side.

"Yeah. I'm hungry," I said without stopping. "Let's get some food."

I had awakened early so that I could do my morning stretches, take my vitamins, pop the contacts in, and do my face. Normally, I would have still been asleep at this hour, and I told the women that I might not make it to breakfast, depending on how I felt. I hadn't slept well. My body ached from the drive. It had been a long trip from Michigan, and my mind refused to shut off. I really needed to find someone to critique my picture book manuscripts, and I wasn't sure how to go about it. Still, the more pressing issue was that I was the only divorced one of the group. The rest of them knew each other well, and I wished I could figure out a way to feel more involved. When I had rolled over to check my alarm at six, I decided that it was worth it to push myself a bit to make it to breakfast. I could rest when I got back to Michigan.

Roxie had read about a quaint little café the night before and we agreed to try it. The old storefront, between an antiques shop and a boutique, was roughly in the middle of Washburn's Main Street. It had been transformed into a "fifties" restaurant, and the owners had kept the black-and-white tile floors that appeared to be original, maybe from the earliest part of the twentieth century. Wood wainscoting shone with a newer varnish. Behind the bar, a young woman stood. Her hair was twisted into a perfect mess at the top of her head, and she wore deep-purple framed glasses. She mixed batter while simultaneously monitoring the grill. The scent of delicious baked goods and coffee teased our senses.

Roxie followed the server to a large table towards the back of the room. She turned to check for approval.

"Anyone object?"

No one did. We sat. Roxie at the head, Deidre, Mira, and I against the back wall, Ruth Ann and Joesie on the opposite side. There was no one sitting at the foot of the large table, leaving two seats unused. The menu featured their famous waffles.

"I'm having the waffles," Ruth Ann said.

"I think I will, too," I stated, folding my menu.

"And my order will make it three," Deidre added.

"May I have some raspberry jam?" Ruth Ann asked the server. Turning to the group, she added, "I know it's weird. I just like jam on my waffles."

"Any fresh raspberries?" Deidre asked.

"Coming right up," was the reply.

The woman took the rest of the requests for eggs, omelets, toast, coffee. Joesie's order took a little more time—the mushroom omelet with a small change.

"I need it to come without cheese," she said. "I have an allergy to cow's milk." The waitress took a note of this.

When she left, Joesie said, "Watch. It'll come with cheese. Never fails."

The food arrived on mismatched china. A slice of yellow cheddar peeked out from the edge of Joesie's omelet. She pursed her lips and handed it back to the waitress, who apologized.

"Typical. You called it, Joesie," Mira quipped.

"Go ahead," Joesie said. "Eat while it's hot."

The food looked like typical breakfast fare. Except for the waffles. They were darker than usual, spectacularly crunchy outside, and dense and nutty inside. I spread a hefty slab of softened butter over them, and it melted instantly. Then I poured thick syrup to fill each of the squares, cut a piece, and forked a bite. There were chewy bits of coconut and sweet pecans mixed into the batter.

"My God," I exclaimed, "Aren't these amazing?" Here was a start. I wasn't the only one who had ordered them, and I knew that good food had the power to bond people. Why not try to connect over the waffles?

Deidre and Ruth Ann also expressed their delight, and those without directed their attention towards the waffle plates with intrigue. Shared bites brought more exclamations.

The waitress, in her early twenties, responded, "They're wheat-free, too."

"How surprising," Ruth Ann said. "Typically, specialty foods are just things that people eat out of necessity. I've had other wheat-free things before, and they're usually bland."

"You're absolutely right," I said with a smile as I took another bite.

We continued to eat and talk about the upcoming events of the day. There would be opening remarks and then workshops later in the morning. After that, we would all walk to Deidre's book signing.

As we left the cafe, Ruth Ann, Deidre, and I commended the woman with the funky purple glasses. "The waffles were incredible," "Very tasty," and, "Delicious, thank you."

"And for the lack of cheese, I thank you," Joesie said with a little bow.

"Everyone just loves our waffles." She beamed with pleasure at the recognition.

"We need to do that," Roxie mumbled, "to create something that is outside of the ordinary." She peeked into a mirror near the door as she quickly swiped a muted shade of red over her lips that matched the scarf on her bag. She stepped out into the sun and flipped her sunglasses back over her eyes. Then, turning towards the group, Roxie continued, "You know, something that makes people stop and say, 'Amazing!' Don't you think that's what we're trying to do with our writing?"

"I think it's what every artist is trying to do," Ruth Ann said.

"And the trick is in figuring out *how* to do that," Deidre said as she turned, her blonde hair swinging over her shoulder. With a chuckle, she added, "If only it were as easy as making waffles. There are so many opinions in this world, so many likes and dislikes. If there's one thing I've learned, it's that all we can do is be true to ourselves."

"I second that," Ruth Ann said.

"Yeah, me too," Mira agreed.

"As long as it doesn't have cheese on it!" Joesie announced, index finger up in the air. She gave it a shake for emphasis.

"Here's to no cheese," Roxie said.

"Waffles, raspberries—a story," I said, glancing back at the door we had just walked through. "We all just want someone to stop and say, 'Now that was different.'"

Back at the Abenaki Lodge, after our detour to the Church of Perpetual Harmony, we broke up and headed to our rooms to gather our items for the Washburn Writing Conference. I brushed and flossed my teeth for the second time, then put a pad of paper into my book bag, with my glasses, contact case, and a small bottle of lens solution, just in case I had to remove the lenses. I'd had to do that in public once, years ago, at a party. I was able to go home immediately afterwards. Bringing these items was a sort of insurance policy, like toting an umbrella. If you had one, it seemed that you rarely had to use it. And didn't it always seem that on the day you skipped bringing it, the skies opened up in a downpour?

I also packed a miniature packet of tissues, two pens, and the manila envelope containing my picture book in case someone agreed to read it. I wanted to share it with the group but wondered if they'd be objective enough. It was only ten pages long, which was the benefit of working in children's literature. These manuscripts tended to be short, so they took no time to read. The challenging part was that every word had to be perfect, leaving no room for sloppiness. Children's books were the perfect fit for me. I hated being sloppy.

~6~

ANTICIPATION

Deidre	Monday 9:00 AM

After an invigorating walk back from the café, where we'd had the most delicious waffles, the group, minus Allison, took a detour. On a lark, we had entered the Church of Perpetual Harmony. I figured, what the hell? A little prayer no matter what the religious persuasion might help my book sales. Frankly, I was also nervous about reading my new work to a room full of strangers. Although most of the others seemed supportive, I detected a hint of jealousy among some of my fellow writers. Mira seemed to be off in dreamland and sometimes it was hard to read Joesie.

Ours was a loose group and clearly our passion for writing was the glue. I loved the variety of personalities but questioned if we would have bonded in the same way under different circumstances.

The Church of Perpetual Harmony, however, seemed to cement our commitment. From the minute we entered, a hush fell over us as we stared in amazement at the multi-colored pews. Each one had been adorned with notable quotes, not only from rock music, but revered literature as well. The psychedelic benches had been painted in dayglow murals depicting everything from John Lennon's and Richie Hayes' lyrics to the teachings of Mahatma Gandhi and Martin Luther King, Jr.

"Far out!" exclaimed Roxie.

"Is this from the hippie days?" Ruth Ann asked.

"Brings back a lot of memories," Joesie mused as she lovingly stroked the benches.

We bowed our heads in complete reverence, then created a semicircle around the altar and lit candles. It seemed like the only appropriate thing to do. Peeking sideways, I watched Allison and Ruth Ann silently mouth prayers. Roxie was staring ahead at the gigantic, gilded candelabra festooned with symbols from the world's religions. I stifled a giggle, not wanting to appear disrespectful. Still, I found myself drawn to the peace of the interior as soft-filtered light streamed through the stained-glass windows. It created a prism effect not unlike the one in the film *Pollyanna*. Were there spiritual forces working here? Who was I to really question?

As we left the church, we hugged as sisters would and agreed to save seats for each other at the conference's opening address. I headed back to my room to gather my conference material. I had shipped my books to the local bookstore to save time and energy. Not only did I have to present at the conference in a small workshop setting, but I also really had to sell myself and my book at The Bear Claw Bookstore. Anxiety and remnants of breakfast made my stomach feel a little unsettled. My only salvation was realizing my fellow writing partners would be there to support me. I was grateful that they were attending my writing workshop and my book signing. At least I knew there would be five friendly faces in the audience. As the signing was going to take place offsite at the bookstore, I felt like I needed to justify their expenditure of money and time for the conference itself. Roxie had stepped in as my cheerleader—if only I could be comfortable that I was fully hers. Guilt nibbled. I pushed it aside, waiting for the right time to deal with it.

For months, I had anticipated the Washburn Writing Conference at the Abenaki Lodge and our being together. It was going to provide me with the opportunity to not only hear from literary experts, but also to introduce my newly published book, *Overheard,* to an expanded audience. The book of short stories was my opus, fictionalized to "protect the innocent." It needed some traction. I had collected these vignettes over a number of years. Perhaps I could kill two birds with one stone.

Every time I thought about speaking, a knot would form at the base of my skull. I was used to presenting at events for my day job, but this was different. This event would be putting my work and my life on the line. My book was exposing *me*. I had taken a detour with this form of writing. I'd never been particularly good at talking about my feelings. Since my longtime friend, Amy, had died, I was even more reticent to overtly reveal my feelings. However, as I wrote the book, putting my feelings in writing felt therapeutic. Now, I would have to share my most intimate thoughts with strangers. Oh sure, I could gossip with friends for hours, even about my latest foible, but talking about myself to an audience was striking me at the core of my being. Would others judge me? It was not a comfortable thought.

⁓

We all hoped for that chance to encounter other authors and agents. In addition, we all hoped to land an important meeting with publishing houses. Roxie had said before the trip, "Give it a shot. Maybe someday you'll be coming to my reading. Stop stalling—it's your time now."

Roxie was my surrogate conscience. Her enthusiasm was often matched by her gutsy manner. That's why she was so successful in real estate. Buyers got swept up in her positive sales pitch. Houses that one might never have considered were sold one, two, three. She practically packed their boxes before they had a chance to say, "Maybe this would work." It was an art form in which she thrived.

We'd started out as just a cluster of women from different backgrounds and now we were slowly, very slowly, beginning to trust and share with one another. Some of us had come together sporadically over a period of seven years, peripherally sharing our lives and stories. Not all of us had melded, but again it occurred to me that it was significant we had bonded over our shared passion for writing. Perhaps within a more intensive environment we would grow closer. Perhaps, I really did long for sisters.

What had emerged over the years was a new appreciation for each other's styles and efforts. We had laughed and commiserated about each other's projects. I was hoping each of our unique experiences and perspectives could prove to be a source of humor and inspiration for all of us as writers.

The Washburn Writing Conference and its respective workshops had been billed as a "transformative experience." I hadn't recognized the names of most of the experts listed on the brochure, but the descriptions of their corresponding seminars were intriguing. I identified some areas in which I clearly needed guidance and was buoyed by the enthusiasm of my fellow writers. I didn't know whether we were all going for the same reasons. But it didn't matter. I had found at previous conferences that exposure to the most unlikely topics was often the most rewarding.

Even more gratifying was being given the opportunity to present. I had been asked to speak on a small panel. I also planned to throw in some pertinent information about the power of book clubs. It would be nice to expand my horizons, especially since losing my longtime friend Amy to cancer last year. We had shared so much. From teenage angst to parental challenges, she had been there for me. I felt a void and would often catch myself picking up the phone to tell her some silly thing that had happened that day. I longed to bounce a writing idea off her, but the receiver laid dormant in my hand. There was no one that could answer the telephone with the same lilt in their voice. That was what I missed most, not her smile, which had been captured in pictures, but her voice. Her irrepressible giggle always seemed to bubble up from deep inside. It was gone and so too, some of my humor. My husband said it takes time to heal, but I think some wounds just fester.

Enough! I shook off my sense of gloom and doom and thought about how proud Amy would be if she knew my book had finally been published. The dedication of my book to her would remain just one of her legacies.

I had prepared as much as I could. No one could accuse me of traveling light. I had two suitcases packed tightly with extra books, pashminas, and sticky notes. My shoes took up most of the room. Even though I knew the conference was in an informal setting, high heels gave me confidence. They were a staple even though I knew the more practical walking shoes would be more *de rigueur*. I hated the look of them, but I figured my knees would thank me for wearing them. No use suffering all the time for the sake of beauty. I could always run back to the room and change before I spoke. No use looking too out of place.

I intended to get the most out of the other speakers. I thought an agent or two might consider my future work. Independent publishing had been an entrée into the literary world, but I was not satisfied. I wanted real recognition and crossed my fingers that I would get lucky.

I smiled, thinking of how some of the others had packed. Some came with barely a backpack and others, like Joesie, with what looked like a caravan. She was noted for a wagon train of her "necessary" items. The image of her lugging her essentials required me to bite my tongue. What happened to the days of throwing everything in a weekend bag?

I often wished I could be a minimalist, internally and externally, but it wasn't meant to be. Or perhaps, I reserved my minimalism for my writing. Short stories were my preferred form of communication. In my daily existence, I spent half the day attempting to sort through the clutter of my life. My intentions were good. For example, while I attempted to clear the accumulated detritus from my kitchen counter, I'd find myself randomly engaged in another activity. Perhaps I had adult ADD. Nonetheless, my desk was my kingdom, and I made numerous piles in an effort to organize my writing and my thoughts. The sight of my multiple containers of colored felt pens lined up on the edge of the desk seemed to center me. It was my visual "zen" cue.

My husband just shook his head at my new writing career. He was relieved when I adopted a *nom de plume* for my first published work. The name "Deidre Carr Darceau" seemed as removed from real life as I could get. My family called me DeeDee. I had always planned on using my given name. Strongly, they objected—and convincingly. As I often did, I put their needs first and used a pen name.

Although I thought a part of him was proud of me, he frequently called me "his charming dilettante." I tried to laugh it off, but it grated on my nerves. Throughout our twenty-five-year marriage he had frequently traveled for business, and I was the partner who stayed at home, minding the store, so to speak. Not that I hadn't been productive. After the kids were of school age, I returned to part-time work. I clearly stated to my whole family—the two dogs, a histrionic bird, a husband, and my grown children—that this would be *my* time. They needed to respect my priorities. That fantasy had lasted about ten minutes. Just last week my eldest child, Faren, had called with a typical request.

"*Mom*," she'd started—the "m" was elongated so I knew I was in for it. "My car insurance is due, and I don't know whether to renew it or go back on your policy."

I'd counted to ten in silence. "Faren, how old are you? At twenty-four, don't you think you can figure this out for yourself?" is what I'd *wanted* to say, but what came out of my mouth was, "Well, have you analyzed your budget? It's not really in your best interest to be on our policy."

"Oh." I could hear the dejected tone in her voice. "Okay, I just thought I'd ask."

"Nice try, Faren. You wanted a car in the city. You'll have to sacrifice somewhere else." And I quickly changed the subject. Tough love isn't so tough sometimes, especially when you know you are right.

My son, Greg, always tried to be cute and made me feel like he was my buddy, not my youngest child. He is, in fact, his father's son. When they stand shoulder to shoulder, from the rear, it's hard to distinguish them. Their erect, athletic posture and dark curly hair belie their ages. My husband has only a hint of gray around his temples, much to my consternation. I, on the other hand, have to spend untold funds on my prematurely silver locks.

"Deeeeds…do you need to go away next week? The qualifying finals for the tennis tournament are in Orlando and I thought you would come." Translation: he thought I would drop everything, fly to Orlando, and pick up his hotel and restaurant tabs.

"No can do, hon," I'd replied. "Besides, didn't you ask to use my points last week?"

"Uh, I assumed I could save them for a trip down to Cancun in the winter with my friends."

"Greg, that's not happening. One, Mexico is too dangerous, and two, you don't need another vacation. You just got back from France and the qualifying rounds there. End of discussion." And it was.

Yes, this was going to be *my* time. I'd reflected upon that before the cab had deposited me at the airport. I was distracted during the flight from Florida, trying to appear outwardly calm for Roxie's sake, even if she'd noticed that the incessant leafing through my book was a sure sign of my anxiety. I'd perseverated. What if we didn't find a cab? What if we got lost? What if we went to the wrong lodge? I'd been committed to this new endeavor, having double and triple checked my notes for the signing at The Bear Claw Bookstore, as my heart beat a little more rapidly.

My time, with my friends, and my future fans. What heady and liberating thoughts.

7

AT LAST

Deidre	Monday 10:00 AM

My mind kept wandering to the upcoming book signing and it was difficult for me to concentrate. Prior to the keynote speaker's presentation that morning, I had tried to introduce myself to my fellow participants. I'd passed out the flyers and bookmarks I had prepared to notify them of my upcoming appearance, all the while gauging their facial expressions and body language. Some smiled warmly at me as they received my materials, others just moved them to the side or pushed them under their pile of notes.

"Oh, thanks," said one puffy-faced participant, which was either a dismissive or sarcastic tone.

Talk about an ego deflator! I'd retained my game face so as not to discourage anyone who might have changed their mind about coming to my signing. It was clear that all the attendees were preoccupied with their own work. We were all in the same boat, budding writers with one thing on our minds: validation. The need for approval is powerful, perhaps even primordial, and truthfully, I was as much a sucker as anyone else for recognition.

So, catching the eye of the person doing the introduction at the podium, I'd slunk back to my seat and sat with my familiar group members. Mira and Allison were fiddling with their respective pens and notebooks.

"It's so good to be away from little ones," Ruth Ann said. "I just know I'll get something out of these workshops. How great it is to carry on an adult conversation."

Joesie nodded in agreement as she removed her hat and shook out her hair. "This is a great escape. I think I even brought enough stuff with me to carry me through the conference." She smirked as she rummaged in her oversized purse, eventually lining up a packet of Kleenex, a water bottle, three pens, a notebook, and a computer on the table in front of her.

"What else do you have in there?" Allison snickered. "Are you planning on staying for a month?"

Joesie just smiled benevolently as we settled in to listen to the keynote speaker. Our personalities were so varied. I could always count on them for everything, from comic relief to a sense of pathos. That suited me fine. I was tired of all the tennis moms who seemed preoccupied with their highlights and workout routines. Over the years, as I had accompanied my son around the country, cheering him on, I had identified less and less with their harping about the humidity, conditions of the courts, etcetera.

The keynote speaker went on too long. I noticed that the others were equally bored as I tried to stifle a yawn. I sat more upright, eager to figure out what he was doing wrong, so I didn't repeat his mistakes. I wanted my small presentation in the bookstore to capture the attention of the audience. The rustle of papers, assorted coughs, and water glasses being filled were clear indicators that the speaker had overstayed his welcome. With a quiet nod from the coordinator, he concluded, picked up his notes, acknowledged the lukewarm applause, and exited the stage. To my right, Roxie let out a big sigh and mouthed, "Thank God."

Oh, cripes! Please don't let me crash and burn like him. What a disaster.

I was called up next to participate in a panel discussion. They had only allotted twenty minutes for what they called "mini presentations." Before I could even blink, my session was over. What a crock! I felt cheated although somewhat relieved, as my real anxiety was over presenting at the bookstore. I shrugged off the supposed slight and decided to concentrate on what I could learn from the longer workshops. They were led by noted lecturers, so I couldn't really complain.

The breakout sessions held later that morning were more worthwhile, limited as they were to eight people. I made sure Roxie and I sat together. That way we could pass notes and make comments back and forth to one another. We had developed a comfortable nonverbal means of communicating that sometimes bordered on the mischievous. Her sense of humor was notoriously wicked; she could be counted on to lighten any situation. She would do it in subtle ways like doodling funny faces in the margins of her notebook, gently sliding it closer to where I was sitting. Today was no exception, as an oversized head, bubbles spouting from its pouty lips, emerged on her paper. It took great willpower to suppress my laugh.

My breakout session was about character development. The first few participants had compelling stories which they read aloud. A professor from Vassar gave some insightful commentary. I was a little nervous to read my new work out loud but was encouraged by his warm smile and gentle suggestions. Roxie winked at me as the woman in a blood red, low-cut, draped polyester dress read aloud from her piece about arriving in New York City for the first time. It was difficult to temper my critique while still being constructive when the story was clearly a rip-off of *Sex and the City.* Another guy in his twenties spouted off some sci-fi drivel. It was all that Roxie, and I could do to stifle our giggles.

"That's crap!" said a young woman. We turned to who had spoken. Her spiked hair was tinged with blue and the tattoo encircling her neck read S-K-Y-E. The gasps of the other participants didn't change the author's demeanor. In fact, the reader became more defiant, until the professor intervened, trying to neutralize the unkind remarks.

"Now, let's respect everyone's work," he said. "We're here to *constructively* comment and help each other out. No one's piece is perfect." All one had to do was look at the flush on his face and the set of his jaw to know the professor was quite displeased.

Roxie and I exchanged sideways glances and shuffled our papers. I hesitated, racking my brain for something kind to say. At last, it came to me.

"Perhaps you could have the alien fall in love with the human," I suggested. "And make him more likeable? That way we could root for him as the main character."

Dead silence from the author, nods from the others.

"Yeah, yeah, I like that idea," added the woman dressed in red.

"Well, it is a consideration," the professor said. He impatiently tapped his watch, glanced at the clock on the wall, and surreptitiously checked his cell phone, clearly indicating that our time was running short. I wondered if he was thinking of his snack or a bathroom break.

By this time, I had had enough mental exercise and all I wanted to do was seek a quiet corner and gather my thoughts before I needed to head to the bookstore. I shook my head to clear my mind. My turquoise drop earrings jangled and drew the attention of a few of the other participants. While their stares made me uncomfortable, I was aware my own anxiety level had elevated. I mouthed, "Sorry," to the instructor as I slid out of the swivel chair and made a beeline for the ladies' room. I figured that would kill a few minutes. The stall door next to me opened and closed. I noticed familiar footwear under the partition beside me. Roxie seemed to have had enough, also.

"A cappuccino sounds good right about now," she said. "I've heard enough about aliens. Besides, what time do you have to be at the bookstore? I'll gather the others. Roxie to the rescue."

I could count on her in the most unlikely situations. Could she count on me? I chuckled and said, "Oh God, one more minute of aliens and horny women, I would have gone mad! I can't wait to hear what the rest of the group encountered. I'm sure Joesie will have some unique take on her session."

"You can bet on it," Roxie said. "We have a break until tomorrow morning. Didn't you mention going to Rhinebeck after your talk? I could use a good old-fashioned ride in the country. It's been ages. The hedges in Palm Beach are so high, you can't see anyone's home. I think that's one reason why I became a realtor. I like to view other people's lives. We could pretend your daughter is getting married and we want to size up the place."

"That, and you can't resist a good story. I love hearing how the other half lives." The words flew out of my mouth faster than I realized. I checked Roxie's expression to see if she had interpreted this as an insult. She apparently did not, as she laughed.

"That's me," she said, "Roxie the raconteur. If only my stories reflected all that I've seen." She winked and moved to the sink. Did I note a slight shadow cross her face? Was it my imagination or were there dark circles under her eyes?

Frankly, I was more interested in my friends' feedback than that of the workshop participants. I also hoped that Allison and Mira had made some good contacts. Their work was percolating along, and they deserved a shot at publication. As the reticent one of the group, Ruth Ann seemed to be finding her footing. Mysteries were her interest. I was sure it gave her a break from the little ones. Perhaps she would get lucky, too.

While applying an extra coat of soft peony-pink lip gloss and fluffing my hair to give the illusion of more height, I commented, "This is harder than I thought."

"Oh, you'll be great," Roxie said. "Everyone will love your book. Besides, Allison, Joesie, and Mira have been encouraging the people in their sessions to come. You know you can count on Ruth Ann. I overheard her telling guests in the lobby this morning about your presentation at The Bear Claw Bookstore. You've got a built-in fan base. Relax."

"Still," I said.

Joesie stumbled into the bathroom as Roxie and I were exiting.

"Are you okay?" Roxie asked.

"How was your workshop?" I asked.

"Ghastly boring," Joesie replied.

Roxie said, "Come to ours. You don't want to miss the rest of the aliens."

Breathe, I kept telling myself, *breathe*. There was a lot riding on this book signing. I had sunk a small fortune in this creative enterprise and was now wondering if it should have stayed just a hobby. But no more self-doubt. How much had I invested in

Greg's tennis lessons or Faren's flute lessons? Not to mention the golf outings that my husband claimed were crucial to his business. Why was I so conflicted? *Well, there's material for you, girlie,* I further ruminated.

Fortunately, by the time Roxie and I got back from our restroom escape, the professor was summarizing the session. He gave us a sideways glance, and I mouthed, "Sorry," once more and sat down quickly.

"Our final presenter will be Skye B. Blu with her essay on family," the professor announced.

Skye, the one who had exclaimed "that's crap!" read a gut-wrenching story about being raised by a single mother, expressing her sense of loss at not knowing her birth father. I glanced sideways and noticed a teary Joesie. Roxie sat stone-faced. We joined in the loud applause, a contrast to that earned by previous presenters.

"Thank you for your poignant essay, Skye," the professor commented. "Now, any last remarks?"

Roxie's hand shot up. "You are all invited to The Bear Claw Bookstore. At one o'clock, Dee Dee—I mean Deidre Carr Darceau—is going to present her book and it's terrific." Her voice was strong, emphatic.

Good old Roxie, I thought. I felt the heat rise to my cheeks as I said, "I'd love to see you all there. They are serving refreshments, too. It's free." Maybe that would entice them.

I was too nervous to eat lunch. I told Roxie I needed to scoot down to the store, which was fortunately only two blocks away, to make sure everything was set up. When I arrived, I was glad I did. Of course, no table was cleared for me.

"Where do you want me to set up?" I asked the woman who had identified herself as the assistant manager. Her pendulous breasts and long gray braid made her look like a refugee from the hippie era.

The store was a throwback from another time. Crammed bookshelves, some teetering and looking like they were an accident waiting to happen, took up most of the space in the front. The varnished oak counter housed an old-fashioned cash register that made a shrill ring when its oversized keys were pressed. I had found the independent bookstore online and contacted the owner weeks before.

A café had been set up in the back. The aromas of coffee and chocolate croissants were enticing. I wondered what would keep customers there—me or the pastries? I only prayed they had baked enough to keep them satisfied.

"Oh, just push some tables in the back together," the assistant manager told me. "You can put your books on one and tell them I said to give you a cup of coffee. What did you say your name was again?"

"Deidre. Deidre Carr Darceau. That's my penname."

Darn! I can't even act like a professional author at a provincial bookstore. How am I going to get a big-time publisher to promote me? Maybe my fellow writers addressing me as Deidre would reinforce the image I wanted to project. They seemed to have fallen into that pattern already. I switched to my "honey" method. "It was really kind of you to give me the time and space to present," I said. "I think a lot of people from the Abenaki Lodge are going to come today. We tried to spread the word to support your store. I know independent bookstores are a dying breed and I *really, really* appreciate your efforts." Damn, if it didn't work.

"Well, if you think it would be better to move to the center up front, I'll tell Al, the waiter, to help you."

"Oh, that would be great. Maybe front exposure would be better."

Within fifteen minutes, my faithful writing partners, Ruth Ann, Roxie, Mira, and Allison appeared—all except Joesie. Roxie took a front and center position and gave me a thumbs up. Twenty-five minutes later it was still just us. After a while, a few stragglers from the larger session arrived. By the time a half an hour had passed, everyone was getting antsy, so I decided to start. I kept glancing at the door, anticipating Joesie's arrival, and found myself tapping my foot when she didn't appear. *Where the hell is she?*

The presentation was a blur. I began with a joke, read a little from my book, and took questions. A few patrons from the upstairs café came down to the front and joined in. I signed a total of nine books and wanted to crawl under the table. So much for my publishing debut. Still no Joesie. When I was done, I gathered my notes, headed for the checkout counter, and practiced my apology to the hippie lady.

"Sorry, I didn't sell many books." My head was bowed, and I bit my trembling lower lip.

"Are you kidding? That's more than usual. Last week someone sat here for two hours and only sold two books. Leave six more copies that are signed, and we'll see what happens." Why hadn't I noticed the delicate lilt to her voice before? It was as comforting and maternal as my friend Amy's had been.

Just as I was getting ready to place the books on her counter, there was a crash nearby. Wanting to appear accommodating, I bent down to gather the books that had fallen for no apparent reason. Picking them up, I was taken aback when one of the titles struck a chord: *Where the Past Begins* by Amy Tan, a provocative title to be sure. I picked it up gingerly, realizing that it was a notable author's memoir, an author I had long admired, ever since she had published *The Joy Luck Club.* The book stood out among the other brightly colored jackets as well. Was it a sign? It felt it was cathartic that the author was an "Amy," like my friend, and the title related. I vacillated between purchasing the book or placing it back on the shelf. I was awash with guilt. Had I been a good enough friend to Amy? And was this "Amy" an omen to be a better friend to Roxie?

I was conflicted. How could I bring up the secretive phone exchanges I knew she was having with Ben without damaging our relationship? What should I do? Should I leave it alone, just play the distracting ally, or interject my opinions? What would Amy have recommended? I missed her so. She would have put a humorous spin on the situation. Still clutching the fallen omen, I proceeded to the counter, still unsure of what tack to take with Roxie.

At that moment, Joesie flounced in with none other than Skye in tow. Joesie's hat was askew, her face flushed, obviously from rushing to arrive. She was of course carrying bags from various stores in the area.

"Where the hell were you?" Mira demanded. "We were worried. And who is this?" She pointed to Joesie's new partner in crime.

"This is Skye. She was showing me around town. Did I miss the presentation?"

"You certainly did," I said in a sharp tone and turned back to the manager. I was hurt by her apparent disinterest in my debut. *Wait until she publishes.*

"Sorry. Skye and I got to talking after her workshop presentation," Joesie replied. "We hit it off and got waylaid shopping, and guess what? Skye is going to read to the children at my library. I'm hoping the library foundation will subsidize her trip."

"Sorry, my bad," Skye added, rolling her eyes.

"I take full responsibility," Joesie said.

The manager patted the copies I put down by the register and asked, "How long are you staying?"

"Three more days, why?"

"Stop by before you leave. There's supposed to be a big group of ladies from New York City coming here. If we set you up again, maybe a few more people will attend. Check with me tomorrow."

I felt my body relax. "Sure. I can't thank you enough. Your store is charming." With that, I purchased five pens, notebooks, and bookmarks. Mementoes for my buddies. I figured it was good-will. To my utter amazement, the previously silenced piped-in music resumed, and "Once in Love with Amy" could be heard all over the store.

Heading out the door, I glanced back at the "Amy" book. Would my late friend haunt me if I didn't buy it? Was she sending a message from the beyond? I realized I had probably just spent more than I had made. *What the hell!* I had done my first book signing. To celebrate, I bought the book and took Amy with me.

～

~8~

DESTINY LIFE
INSTITUTE

Roxie	Monday 2:30 PM

After a morning of listening to tales of aliens, horny women, and Deidre's presentation of her book, *Overheard*, at The Bear Claw Bookstore, we were finally ready to leave in our two cars. We were headed toward Rhinebeck, in search of Chelsea Clinton and Mark Mezvinsky's wedding site. One of the clerks at the front desk of the Abenaki Lodge had suggested we stop at a "marvelous bookstore in a nearby town." We agreed to do that first, since it was on the way.

Still no return call from Ben. I was glancing down at my cell phone so often, I thought it might reject me all together. For God sakes where—I stopped dead in my tracks as someone tapped me on my shoulder and asked, "Can I go too?" It was Skye. Taken aback, I tried to think fast, and mumbled, "Sorry, we're full up." *God, what striking blue eyes she has. They remind me of Ben.*

"No worries," Skye said. "Let me give you a short cut. It's a little complicated to find."

Skye

I was disappointed the women didn't have room for me on their trip to Rhinebeck. But seriously, I had enough to worry about now that my DNA results had come back. My mother had always been evasive about answering why she was a single mother or who my birth father was. I knew she had been married and divorced but was that man my father, or someone else? Her former husband's name was Jonathan Dexter Corkerin. I didn't look a thing like him. I am fair and have blue eyes; he's dark-haired with brown eyes.

We lived in Syracuse, New York, back then. When I was fourteen, I used to go up in the attic of our home to be alone. It was dimly lit so I would sit by the window, reading my sci-fi books and writing in my diary. My mother hadn't forbidden me from going through her things, but I had a feeling she wouldn't like it. One day, I had finished a book I had been reading and made my daily entry into my diary. I sat cross-legged on the wooden slats and began opening boxes. The first one offered nothing. The second also failed to deliver. Box three really piqued my interest, though. It held my mother's college memorabilia, her framed diploma, some legal paperwork, her parent's wedding album, and a bunch of miscellaneous pictures. Each time I saw a picture of a man, I wondered if that guy was my dad. In a moment I would never forget, I found the first clue to my true identity—a book of potential sperm donors that included pictures with numbers but no names. None was circled or otherwise distinguished from any other.

My heart was pounding out of my chest. I wasn't sure if I was going to hurl or run away but that booklet hit me at a place in the depths of my soul. Who was I? Who was my father? One thing I did know is that I hated my mom for withholding information on my genealogy. I would never forgive her.

I immediately called my friend Carla, who rushed over. Our yards were kitty-corner to each other so we could get together anytime, for any emergency—and when you're a teen, you have many emergencies. She had to squeeze through the broken slat of the fence behind my garage, climb over the lower fence, and then go through my yard, to get to my house. She and I had been BFF's since the fourth grade. We had been in theatre together, so I guess you could say we were "dramatic." We shared everything; I mean *everything*—from braces to sleepovers to boys. No matter what, we were loyal like only tight girlfriends can be.

To my disappointment, Carla didn't agree with my assessment of the situation. I was angry. Carla was sensible. "Look Skye, your mom's really cool. You wouldn't even exist if she didn't really want you, right?"

"No, I'm a freak. I don't even have a real dad. Ewww. Sperm donor. Is there anything worse?"

"First of all, Skye, you don't know anything yet. Maybe your father was a sperm donor, maybe you're adopted, or maybe he's one of the guys in these pictures."

"Adopted? You're a big help. I'm dying over here. I never thought I was adopted but you could be right. Anything is possible. Why didn't my mother tell me the truth?" I melted into Carla's shoulder and cried my eyes out.

"Girl, calm down. I'll come back over when your mom gets home from work and we'll talk to her. She can't keep this secret any longer. Let's go get a Slurpee and forget about all of this for now."

Funny, I remember that my Slurpee was blue raspberry, and Carla's was cherry. Carla mentioned that I had an affinity for blue. By the time my mother got home from work, I had clammed up, and told Carla never to mention the "sperm" thing again. I went on with my life, though it gnawed at me.

I didn't find out or pursue the truth of my existence for ten more years.

Roxie

"Rox, you okay?" Deidre whispered as we headed to our cars.

"Not sure," I replied. "Just missing Ben."

Leave it to her, my sympathetic friend, to always be intuitive when it came to me. We had become instant friends in our first writing conference together, seven years ago. We'd navigated through life's cycles together. Our husbands had bonded; dinners out with them became a monthly ritual. She was my rock. I supported her in every way possible. Deidre's book being published was the highlight of this conference for me, too, as I shared in her joy.

I felt a little guilty about brushing off Skye. We all assumed we were going to a store similar to Barnes and Noble. In my mind's eye, I envisioned walking among the best sellers, touching, browsing, and finding some new juicy novel to read. Or perhaps, I'd indulge in my second passion, cooking, perhaps finding a new, stimulating, or exotic cookbook. I have loved bookstores since I was a child. The bright covers and the rows and rows of books still beckon me. I could never get my fill of them. I still steadily maintain a pile of books to be read on my night table, reading whenever I have that rare free moment.

Our first clue that we were *not* heading toward an urban mall should have been the meandering roads with the horrible switchbacks, which made even the most experienced of us nauseous. We persevered, ever reliant on our GPS. Through the car windows, we viewed partially broken-down billboards advertising food spots, motels, and gas stations, all resembling vestiges of the past. Rambling farms and their adjacent fields, tall grass, corn, and lush green rows of plants and vegetables lined both sides of the road. For a change of pace, we opened the car windows. We observed swaying old trees and felt gentle breezes blow as we chatted and questioned where we were headed. How could there possibly be a bookstore in the midst of all this? We started to get anxious. Would we ever get to our destination? All we could see was more farmland and some apple groves. Our GPS just kept telling us which way to turn.

All of a sudden, our GPS stated with authority, "You have arrived." There was no sign of Rhinebeck, only a dirt road leading to something called the Destiny Life Institute. But wait! This was surely not the place—or was it? As we pulled into the parking lot, we couldn't help noticing the tennis courts on the left, and a group of cabins on the right. We stepped out of our cars into what looked like a scene on a post card. It was so picture-perfect—too perfect. Maybe it was the silent children, all lined up, dressed in white.

I blurted out, "Where's the Kool-Aid?"

"Joesie, are your kids quiet like that in the library?" I asked.

"Hell, no. Normal children make noise." She added, "Lots of noise, and even laugh about it." I began to feel creepy, as if I was in the midst of a cult-like atmosphere. Why did I sense that?

We came upon a woman sitting cross-legged on a bench, her upturned palms resting on her knees. Unfortunately, our chatter broke her trance, and she opened her eyes, smiling sweetly.

"Excuse our interruption," Ruth Ann began. "We are looking for the bookstore."

"This is the Destiny Life Institute, a retreat for spirituality and personal growth," she said. "It is Family Week this week. That is why you see so many children. Normally, it is an adult-only complex." She droned on in a strangely hypnotic voice, "The bookstore is up the hill to your left and around the corner. Easy to find. You won't miss it."

We continued up the incline, not feeling particularly welcome. Nonetheless, we persevered and climbed the hill. We noticed a low wall, upon which was perched a male statue. The figure was clad in black and stood in the reverse warrior position. Our unrelenting noisy chatter caused said statue to lose its balance. He unfolded his limbs and stretched.

"Oh my God," a blushing Mira sputtered, checking him out, up and down. "He's real!"

"Mmm, I'd like to see my Ben in a position like that," I added, wondering for the umpteenth time why he hadn't called or texted lately. "Whew, is that sexy or what? Or, should I say, is *he* sexy or what? Of course, now I'd like to see him in any position. Will I?"

Deidre turned to Ruth Ann, "You are as red as a ripe tomato. That is some blush."

Ruth Ann kept her focus on "our man," tall and lithe in his black yoga attire. Seemingly undaunted by the six of us staring at him, he deftly repositioned himself into his former pose. Collectively, our voices oozed deep admiration. After we reached a safe distance, we marveled at his physique and abilities with "oohs" and "ahs."

Continuing on the path, we noticed low wooden buildings, denoting various courses of study. Finally, the elusive bookstore, housed inside a worn, red-painted, rustic cabin, came into view. Outside the door was another clue that this was not a big city bookstore: the rickety steps to the aging porch, which tested our balance. A short metal rack on the porch held peasant blouses in a variety of colors, tie-dyed skirts, and yoga apparel. The site beckoned us to browse, touch, and perhaps buy.

"Well," Joesie said, "Barnes and Noble, it ain't."

Fingering one of the skirts was our new writer friend, Skye. Her spiked blue hair stood at attention. I couldn't help but notice the tattoo on her wrist: a bright red raspberry.

"Oh hi, everyone," Skye said. "I see you made it here, too. My directions were quite good, weren't they? Look at this skirt. Just so perfect for me, with all the shades of blue, don't you agree?" With her barb-like hair, long flowy skirt, slouchy sweater, and the *piéce de resistance*, black combat boots, Skye was a throwback to "Hair," Woodstock, and the grunge phase, all at once.

Allison smiled and said, "Skye, that skirt *is* you. Perfect for your long, lean frame, and the colors match your hair and eyes. Buy it! What a bargain."

"I don't know," I whispered into Deidre's ear. "She wouldn't be able to wear it in Palm Beach. Why is she following us, anyway?"

"C'mon gang, we're here, so let's at least take a peek inside," Mira said.

"Yeah, what do we have to lose?" Deidre asked.

"Ladies," I said, "I don't know what anyone else expected, but seeing the interior of this store reminds me of the day I got off the train in Geneva, Switzerland for the first time. I thought I would see snowcapped mountains, rolling farmland, and lots and lots of cows. Where, oh where, were Heidi and her grandfather?" But to my surprise and chagrin that day, I'd arrived in the center of a chic, cosmopolitan city.

We entered the store. The strong aroma of incense floated around us, causing Ruth Ann to pinch her nose with a "pee-yoo!" She began sneezing as Joesie raised her eyebrows, gesturing to us to look at the people stretched out in front of the bookshelves, reading. In addition to the pungent incense, the tinkling of wind chimes rang in our ears as we walked along. Maybe I'd find some interesting ones to add to my ever-expanding collection. None of us had anticipated seeing Buddhist flags draped over racks of pashminas, wooden drums with skins pulled tight, and other percussion instruments. Yoga outfits made from bamboo, CD's of New Age music and meditation, and shelves with books on religion, nature, and self-help dominated the inventory. I started tapping each of the drums, listening for different sounds. As Allison fiddled around with some mechanical dancing frog, it was so hard to keep a straight face.

Skye came over and started banging a small snare drum, Mira began tapping her foot, and I shook a maraca in time with Skye's beat. Deidre picked up a marimba and Joesie pulled Ruth Ann and Allison into the center of it all, dancing and swaying to the music. Mira joined them, as readers gathered. Was this the right setting for our joint frivolity? Who knew? It was quite possible, even probable, that the store had never witnessed such a scene. Everyone twirled and swirled as the music reached a crescendo, then softly came to its end. We hugged each other as if we had each been forever friends, and then went back to browsing and reading.

"Not bad ladies," I said. "We put on a good show. Wonder what trouble we can get into next?"

As I ambled along to the pace of a dancing frog, I spied a book with a nun, cigarette in hand and dancing in the street, on its cover. The book was aptly titled *Nun Fun*. Within its pages were pictures of nuns in other atypical poses, cute quips underneath. I carried the book to my cohorts, showing them each a picture of a "nun" in a weird position, doing something completely un-nun-like, causing us to burst into gales of laughter. Was this blasphemous, or were nuns ever this free, this rambunctious? What about the other religions? Could one be pious or observant and at the same time be happy-go-lucky and silly? This might be a great topic for conversation over dinner tonight.

The problem with laughter is that once you start, you can't stop. It is a freefall. I'm the master and ringleader of it. I just keep going and going like a hamster on a wheel.

Oh, Roxie Ross, you led them right into temptation, I thought to myself, and I had. I walked by the colorful scarves. As I fingered them, Joesie whispered into my ear, "Stay away from those scarves. You'll be buying them all." Unfortunately, she was right. I had at least two drawers of scarves that needed weeding out before I purchased any more of them. However, a scarf with a bright red raspberry on a white background caught my fancy for some reason. I waved it at Mira, as if to say, "How about this one?" *Why was the raspberry scarf so intriguing to me?*

Exploring further while trying not to step on the people ensconced on the floor meditating or reading, I signaled to the group to come over so I could show them my next illustrious find. "Look guys," I said. "I found the perfect gift to bring our spouses or significant others." I pointed out the shelves filled with books about sex. Some discussed sexual relations, others, how to have good sex. And of course, there was the big one, the *Kama Sutra.*

Would this entice my Ben? Would *anything* entice or interest him? He'd bought me that beautiful blouse before I left. Yet, he seemed so distant in many ways. Was it a guilt thing, or was I just imagining things? Would he be receptive to any of them?

I grabbed a few books, dancing and waving them in the air. I set off another big round of laughter and giggling. Perhaps this was not the best way to act in a meditation bookstore, but oh what fun we had! All of us were surprised by the bookstore and its contents. It was not particularly big, though it was charming, holding a lot in a small place. I ended up with a beautiful new Asian cookbook, while Deidre succumbed to one describing other ways to be happy besides eating chocolate, one of her favorite pastimes. I looked over my shoulder and glimpsed at the title of the book Mira was holding: *Surviving Depression Naturally without Drugs.*

As a result of our raucous performance, Ruth Ann had crept out to the porch, looking straight ahead while trying to avoid the people meditating. The rest of us noticed the "why don't you leave" looks from two salespeople. We walked slowly out the door, heads held high, carrying our biodegradable bags. As we went down the stairs on our way out, we caught a glimpse of Skye's blue hair as she placed a helmet on her head, straddled a motorcycle, and raced off.

"There she goes," Joesie said. "Didn't even say goodbye."

While we agreed it was no Barnes & Noble, The Destiny Life Institute Bookstore sure had created some moments of delightful fun, bringing "the sisters" closer.

～9～

RHINEBECK

| Ruth Ann | Monday 4:00 PM |

After our detour to the land of the cult, a visit to Rhinebeck promised normalcy. We hopped in our cars, continuing to Astor Courts, a popular venue for weddings.

"Wow!" Allison remarked on speaker phone from her car to ours, "To have been here the week of Chelsea Clinton's wedding! I'm sure we would have seen a gaggle of celebs."

"Right now, I would love to just walk around inside," Mira said. "Too bad it's all locked up."

"Didn't I tell you?" Deidre said. "I called and made an appointment... said I was looking for a place for my daughter's wedding. She *is* getting married. I just don't know when. Not like I lied." Deidre grinned, leaned out the car window, pushed the intercom, and sure enough, the gate opened. *So self-assured, that Deidre. Not me, the ultimate doubter. But who could blame me?*

The thought of visiting Rhinebeck, particularly Astor Courts, both thrilled and depressed me. As a fifth-time bridal party member, and two-time Maid of Honor, I was the quintessential "always the bridesmaid, never the bride." Visiting Astor Courts conjured up my most brilliant wedding fantasies. Within each part of the property we planned to visit, I would envision myself the bride.

The thrilling part involves this fantasy wedding of mine. I am both shy and exhilarated to be "on stage," as the bride. I'm in an exquisite—of course—white mermaid gown with just enough bling to sparkle. I'm served by a court of sherbet-clad colors. My Matron of Honor, probably my sister, is in raspberry. My one friend from high school is in pale pink. Next comes my two friends from college, Jessica in a light cantaloupe color, and Jodie in a complementary lemon yellow. The Best Man sports a raspberry-colored boutonniere, and the groomsmen follow with their boutonnieres matching my bridesmaids' dresses.

Young. Demure. *My* wedding.

The depressing part was that I didn't have a boyfriend. Insert sad face emoji. "Never the bride."

I'd asked the universe numerous times to please explain why a nice, caring girl, with nary a parking ticket, had not had a date in years. I knew I wasn't the cream of the crop or the girl everyone wanted to date. I'm a bit too thin. I admit my hair is "mousy." I have a cute face, or so they say, but I've also been told I have a standoffish attitude. *That* I deny. Still, the perception is apparent. I am often asked questions such as, "Are you okay? "Is anything wrong?" Why? I'm not sure. My look is my look. My look, I guess, is my downfall.

My sister married right out of college. I was in high school at the time. I made a lovely Maid of Honor—if I do say so myself. Usually, I don't like my looks. For her wedding, I had my hair in an elaborate updo that included beautiful but itchy extensions. Her black wedding dress was the talk of the town, not only because it was unconventional, but it also had a full ball gown skirt, lace everywhere. She chose a hideously unflattering pumpkin-colored gown for me, which made my skin fade. Still, I felt beautiful. The theme of her wedding was macabre, to say the least, with the wedding cake decidedly Halloween-esque. What else does one do for an October wedding? The glaze on the multilayer cake was black and orange. If you could get past the color scheme, the cake tasted delicious. At least I got to wear the orange gown. I would have truly disappeared in the black gowns of the other bridesmaids, as I'm far too fair to pull off wearing black. Yet, despite the color of the gown, I primped at every opportunity and was determined to be the life of the party—and I was.

I danced with a bevy of eligible bachelors. Each treated me like what I was: the kid sister. I twirled the night away, feeling like Cinderella. One of the groomsmen swept me up in an elaborate spin, fueled by Long Island Iced Teas. He had a clean scent with a subtle yet noticeable woodsy fragrance that spoke "man." I swooned under his tutelage. When he whispered that he'd ask me out if I wasn't so young, I nearly fainted right there on the dance floor. We danced and danced to the guests' approval until the next man tapped him on the shoulder for a chance turn with me. I dreamt about him for weeks afterwards. Then, reality set in. I have, since that night, been on exactly nine dates—and one technically doesn't count, as that was my high school prom. He was an acquaintance whose mother had set us up. The next three were real: first dates in college that never led to a second. I tried and failed at small talk. I'm sure each guy felt he could do better than date an early childhood education major with conversation issues. Next came my one and only first date that led to a second. Sweet guy but he failed to see why a third date wasn't in the cards for him. This was a time when I was open to another date, but he didn't brush his teeth properly, which was a giant turn-off. Why the next three dates with other guys didn't work out, I will never know.

Four or five years ago, I'd signed on to a dating website. Instantly, there were fellows who wanted to date me. My pictures were very appealing. It's my "in person" that needs polish. Just ask my mom.

"Ruth Ann," she'd say, "do something with your hair." Or, if we were going out somewhere, she has actually said, "You're not going in that, are you?" How can I have positive self-esteem when the person who should love and accept me the most, doesn't?

My next date, after I'd started working, was with a great guy named Trent. We had a fabulous "day" date, walking hand-in-hand around town, eating at food carts, and generally enjoying the day. He mentioned that he had work out-of-state that would take him away for several months. That day was his last attempt at fun.

We kissed at parting and vowed to keep in touch. Unfortunately, he went off to Northern California, never to be heard from again.

Then there was the awkward dinner theater episode. My date and I went to a funky black box theatre. He appeared to know what was going on in the play. I was completely lost. He kept putting his hand on my bare knee. I kept pushing it back to his lap. I couldn't wait to get home. He held my hand. His was as soft as a girl's who had just gone for a manicure, not to mention a bit sweaty. No thanks. I guess he felt the same way. Another first and only.

Finally, I had a date with a doctor, my mother's pride and joy. "Marry a doctor and you'll live in health and wealth," she'd always say. Well, a marriage was not to be. I fell asleep during his monologue, subsequently canceling my dating membership.

⁓

We parked in the visitors' area at Astor Courts in Rhinebeck.

"Good afternoon, Ms. Darceau," a man greeted us. "My name is Franklin. I see some of you ladies are wearing comfortable shoes—good for walking our acres." A collective groan filled the room. "Let's begin inside." Relief.

Joesie was wearing a new hat which she'd let fall to her back, held at her throat by a bright yellow ribbon. Her hat, trimmed in the same yellow, coordinated perfectly with her floor-length summer dress. She looked like a southern belle. Stunning. I looked around. The rest of us were dressed a bit more casually. Roxie was in navy slacks and smart white Converses. Allison, in blue, showed off her dark hair and gleaming white teeth. I had on capri jeans, the kind with the permanent crease, and a white Oxford blouse. Deidre wore a classic wrap dress with an over-sized "summery" bag, fashionable slip-on sandals that looked comfortable. Mira wore a sleeveless print top, solid navy slacks and boat shoes. We really looked the part, a bunch of women looking at a wedding venue for our friend's daughter.

Franklin started his lecture while we were served tea and finger sandwiches. "This isn't just a wedding venue. Astor Courts once had over two-thousand acres. Now, even the fifty remaining wooded acres seem huge. One would have to imagine what it was like as a farm and a sports arena. Astor Courts had many guest bedrooms. It held the first indoor pool and tennis courts at a private residence in the United States. It was built for Jacob Astor IV and his wife Ava."

We took in the marble floors, grand ballrooms, and guest suites. Deidre, our wedding maven, asked the appropriate questions. "Do you have written information on Astor Courts?" she asked.

"Ma'am, I have a whole packet with the price list, contract—everything you'll need to help you make a decision. We're conveniently located, only one hour from the city."

"How many guests can you accommodate?" Deidre asked, winking at me. Franklin answered each with knowledge and grace. Outside, the grounds were life in bloom. What a beautiful place! The flowers rivaled Longwood Gardens in Pennsylvania. Beautiful day and night water lilies decorated the ponds. Water fountains sprayed effortlessly as we imagined the most beautiful wedding pictures—at least *I* did. Would I ever get married?

Walking around, we saw everything from roses to pastures of wildflowers. I was struck by their delightful aroma, even though my allergies were kicking up. I rubbed my eyes, sneezed a few times, hoping my colleagues understood that it was allergies, and I wasn't actually contagious. They seemed to, as we made the decision to end the tour and head back to Washburn.

Deidre hopped in the passenger seat and declared herself the navigator of our car. "I'll be in charge," she said, grabbing the GPS, typing in our next destination.

⁓10⁓

BRIDGE OUT

Mira	Monday 5:00 PM

Ruth Ann started to sneeze. I guessed that she was affected by some of the blooms. It was sad that someone could be allergic to such beautiful things. I appreciated the beauty of nature but couldn't identify any flowers except roses and orchids.

We got into the same cars in which we had travelled to Rhinebeck. It reminded me of my carpool children who would call, "Same seats!" as they got into the car, especially if they had been sitting in the front passenger seat. I smiled and dutifully sat in the back. I wondered if I should take my meds when I got back to the room. Maybe I'd sleep better tonight.

Allison and Ruth Ann, the drivers of the two cars, chatted back and forth about the gardens at Astor Court over the car speakers. Since I had visited Longwood Gardens in Pennsylvania, I didn't feel left out, but had to lean forward against my seatbelt to hear the conversation. All in all, so far, it had been a good day.

Imagine Chelsea Clinton getting married in a small town like Rhinebeck. Yes, it's lovely and all that, but she could have chosen anywhere. She must be very unspoiled. I liked that.

By and by, the talk slowed down. We settled into a comfortable silence. Visibility became difficult as the light drizzle we'd driven into turned into a downpour. Between the rain and the unlit country roads, driving was a challenge.

"OMG Ruth Ann," Allison brayed over the speaker, "are you sure you know where you're going?"

"I think so," Ruth Ann said.

Before long, it was clear we were lost. It wasn't as if we didn't know where we were headed. We approached a sign in front of us.

"Ruth Ann slammed on her brakes. "Detour!"

"Hold on everybody!" Deidre exclaimed. "Brace yourselves!"

"Now which way do we go, Ruth Ann?" Allison asked.

"Not sure," Ruth Ann replied. "I know these roads, but I can't see a thing." She skidded to a stop in front of the Detour sign.

Joesie screamed, "Allison, you almost hit Ruth Ann's car! What are we going to do?"

"Whew!" I yelled. "That was a close call. I can't get out of the car. It's raining too hard."

From Ruth Ann's car, Roxie piped up, "Joesie, do you have an inflatable raft in that bag of yours?"

"Everything but. Will an umbrella do?"

"Yeah, but I'm not getting out in this storm," Roxie said.

"Where do we go?" Deidre asked. "That was *it*—the sign didn't say *where* to go. No arrows."

"I've got this," Ruth Ann said. "Here's another sign. *Bridge Out. Barricades*. We need to turn around. I don't want to end up in the river."

"Good thing we didn't follow the GPS," Joesie added. "It kept telling us to go straight, right into the river."

"Thank heavens we saw the barricades and signs," Deidre cried out.

To the left and right of us were narrow country lanes. Lightning filled the skies. The rain poured down, sounding like stones hitting our windows, filling us all with fear—at least filling *me* with fear. Trembling, I said, "I remember as a child, sitting under an umbrella in Miami Beach. I saw a man struck and killed by lightning. I have been terrified of electrical storms ever since."

The raindrops pelted the car windows. Rain came from all directions, making visibility nearly impossible. I gripped the edge of the back seat, trying to keep calm. Allison tried to call Ruth Ann's cell phone. It was that small, powerful device, equipped with an up-to-date GPS, which finally found a road that would take us somewhere other than where we were.

The car with Ruth Ann, Roxie, and Deidre made a sharp U-turn. The car with Allison, Joesie, and me stayed close behind. Although it was only late afternoon, the sky was black. Allison kept Ruth Ann's rear lights in her sight. She thanked the technology which had developed her contact lenses. They remained clear, as contact lenses do, in spite of the fog outside.

We all remained quiet. No one wanted to say, "What if?"

"What if we hadn't seen the barricades?"

"What if we didn't have a working GPS?"

"What if someone had to pee?"

I saw Ruth Ann's right signal light start blinking. "Look, she's turning!" I yelled, as if Allison hadn't seen it. We didn't know where she was leading us, but we followed like lemmings.

Then we realized that Ruth Ann had spotted a half-broken sign, swinging from a crooked post: The Inn at Raspberry Hill. We were on an unmarked road. The cars dipped, sloshed, and slid as we turned, then proceeded slowly.

The panic eased. Suddenly, there were audible intakes of breath as our car sank into a huge mud puddle and careened sideways. Allison's foot eased off the accelerator, allowing the car to find its balance. The wipers smeared splashing mud over the windshield. Still, Allison was able to keep Ruth Ann's car in sight. I closed my eyes tightly as claps of thunder and bolts of lightning lit up the ground around us.

Allison's cell phone connected as we pulled up beside their car. Someone said, "Thank you God, it works." I think it was me speaking.

I could hear Ruth Ann's voice say, "Let's make a run for it. We'll see if the door is open."

"We'll have to do this quickly," Joesie said. "But be careful. It might be slippery out there."

"Let's wait 'til the next clap of thunder and lightning. After that we should have a minute to make it to the porch."

"Oh goodness, Mira, you're so knowledgeable," Ruth Ann said. "I wish you could have predicted this storm."

At that moment, the car lit up with a bolt of lightning, quickly followed by the crash of thunder.

"Let's go now!" I shouted. "Come on!"

~11~

THE INN AT
RASPBERRY HILL

Nothing was visible. I could only feel the car lurching and turning, grateful not to have been one of the drivers. The wheels crunched and splashed until the car came to a sudden stop.

"What the hell happened?" I said. "I can't see a blasted thing. I hope everyone in the other car is okay. My cell phone won't connect with anyone. No service right now."

Allison rolled down her window, letting in a stream of water. "Hey, Joesie," she shouted, "that was Ruth Ann. She's found an inn. See if we can make it to the entrance. Be careful!"

It was as horrific a storm as I'd ever seen. I struggled against the pounding rain to get out of the car and used my tush to close the door behind me. With one hand I clung to my oversized purse with a useless umbrella inside, as well as a bag of fruit from a local farm stand. With the other hand, I held onto my hat, fighting to keep it atop my head and doing little to protect my hairdo. I could see practically nothing ahead. Blind trust catapulted me forward, following the faint figures ahead. My sandals were squishing in the mud and no longer gripped my faltering feet. I had an eerie sense of loss of control as though a magnet was pulling me forward.

"It's pitch dark and still afternoon," I spoke to myself out loud as I stumbled under a stone archway. I could see the sign for The Inn at Raspberry Hill. Six rarely speechless women huddled together, first hugging then laughing in a cacophony of high-pitched giggles and squeals. Hands wet from wiping faces celebrated the latest victory lap to safety with hearty high-fives, followed by a cheer.

"I was sure you ladies in the other car would think I was crazy," Ruth Ann exclaimed, "to pull up to a driveway of someone's house, uninvited for sure. A driveway usually leads to shelter. I thought I made out the word "Inn" on the sign at the end of the road. This seems to be a cross between a manor house and the Addams Family hideaway. At least we found somewhere to land."

"Ruth Ann and Allison are our heroes," I chimed in. "Driving us to a new destiny. What a miracle! What a detour! Perhaps it was the prayers of the worshipers at the Church of Perpetual Harmony that had saved us. Without divine intervention, we would never have found it."

Ruth Ann added, "We're not intruding at all. It's an *inn*. What a perfect place to wait out the storm." With those words, Ruth Ann tripped on the threshold as the large door opened. A small, almost munchkin-like female peeked out. She wore a crisp white apron around her plump form. Strands of her salt-and-pepper gray hair peeked out of the bun on top of her head. She uttered welcoming instructions.

"Come in, come in, come in. Wet, wet, wet. Off, off, off," she said as she pointed to a mat on the floor and a coatrack beside the door. Drenched and dripping, we trusted, following the woman's directions without hesitation. I was delighted to leave my soaked sandals behind. I hated the oppressive heat of summer but wore filmy long sleeves to cover the sagging wrinkles of my no-longer-supple arms. I peeled off my sopping summer-weight sundress, which left me in a damp airy sports bra and stretch capris. Renewed comfort it was! Once inside, my usual paranoid survival instincts were replaced by safety concerns and fear of the unknown.

We stood in the reception area of a grand home. Our greeter held a flickering lantern in her right hand. At her side was a fluffy white cat. Beside her, the much larger shadow of another older woman appeared, dancing on the wall. The woman came into focus. She was slightly hunched over, wearing slippers, wrapped in a faded pink chenille robe snugly tied around her waist. She was welcoming, smiling as she gestured. She shouted above the chatter and clatter of weather.

Once we were all settled inside, our accidental guardian angel, wrapped in pink, continued, "Welcome! Please call me Eve. Are you ladies okay? I heard voices above the noise of the storm. It's been a while since I've enjoyed the pleasures of the company of younger women. I haven't had many visitors lately. Our Inn is for sale and closed for business, hence the plethora of white coverings on the furniture. A bit eerie, wouldn't you agree?" I nodded. Those in the front, better positioned, peered into an inner room. It was other-worldly—beyond eerie.

"It makes it easier for Hazel, our resident housekeeper. It seems you've already met—she opened the door for you. She's a wee bit daft," Eve whispered. "The covers keep Merlin, her cat, off the furniture." Hazel put some towels down on the floor. "These are to wipe your feet," Eve continued. "Be careful not to slip on the wet floors."

I held onto the wooden reception desk in front of us, stomping to dry my feet. Lights from candles added ghostly shadows as we followed Eve farther inside. We walked through a more formal living space where white sheets covered the furniture. Supposed wall decorations, paintings or whatever, were not readily visible in the low light. I screamed as I felt something brush my neck as my hat fell to the floor. "What happened, Joesie?" Mira asked.

"With my luck, it was probably a black widow spider."

Eve stopped in the doorway between two rooms that faced us. "Oh, Hazel," she said. "These ladies are stranded. The bridge is out."

"Not again," Hazel said. "Shh, Merlin." She stroked the white Persian cat in her arms.

"I'm fine," I said. "What's a little black widow among friends?"

"Righty ho! You are welcome to stay the night," Eve offered in proper polite British fashion.

"The night!" Deidre exclaimed. "*I'm* planning on leaving. I'll wait for the rest of you in the car."

"Oh, Deidre, that's not safe," Roxie said, following her, hoping to dissuade the determined Deidre, who headed right back out the door while the rest of us stayed put to discuss our serious dilemma.

"They'll be hit by lightning," Allison said.

"Fools," I said.

Crash! We jumped at the clap of thunder. *Boom!* We huddled together as the deafening thunder boomed and the lightning flashed.

"Oh my God, are they okay?" I ran to the door and wrenched it open, pulling Roxie and Deidre back inside.

"Gee whiz, Joesie, I'm sorry your umbrella blew away," Roxie said as I hugged each of my companions.

"Are you okay, dearies?" Eve asked again.

"I'd be fine if the tree wasn't blocking the roadway," Deidre said.

"My, my, my…tree down, tree down, tree down," Hazel mumbled. Merlin the cat was nowhere in sight. I raised my eyebrows at Hazel's odd phrasing.

Eve went on, "The bedrooms are made up to look perfect at a minute's notice for any potential buyers of our Inn here at Raspberry Hill. So unfortunately, we can't use those bedrooms, but you are welcome to spend the night here in the parlor or sunroom—minus the sun, I'm afraid."

"Really?" Allison said. "We can't stay in the actual bedrooms? We can pay."

"No need for that, dearies," Eve responded.

"Wait, Allison." Turning to Eve, Roxie said, "I understand completely. As one who stages houses, we call that 'realtor ready.' Besides, with the power out, we wouldn't want to burden you or Hazel."

"It doesn't matter to me," Mira said. "I don't sleep much anyway."

"Well, at least it's dry," Ruth Ann said.

"Leave it to Ruth Ann to be our own Pollyanna," Mira said.

"Some hospitality this is," Deidre said under her breath. "Sleeping on a sofa is not the same as a nice comfortable bed."

"Oh, Eve," I said, "on behalf of all, we are thankful for the dry shelter and gracious welcome. I'm Joesie." As I introduced myself, I couldn't take my eyes off Eve's striking steel-blue eyes, deeply set into her lined face. No doubt she had been a raving beauty in her younger days. Her warm smile put us all at ease.

"Well, Joesie, you might not thank me after a night sleeping in a chair or on a sofa." Eve's voice was soft and strong, her lilting British accent comforting.

We now stood in the hall between two rooms that faced each other. There was a stone fireplace at the far end of one room. On the opposite wall was a woodstove. Both were alive with fire. Floor-to-ceiling drapes were drawn over the windows, but they did not silence the sounds of wind and rain that persisted. Plush, comfy sofas and stuffed armchairs were revealed as we removed the coverings in each room, the candles flickering throughout the rooms and lighting our way.

Eve asked, "How did you find Raspberry Hill? Had you seen it advertised somewhere?"

"We happened upon you by avoiding a disaster," Allison said. "We had to take a detour. The road was out, and our lead guide Ruth Ann saw the detour sign in the nick of time. She managed *not* to dump us into the raging waters. We're thrilled to be alive, standing here to report this after she found your sign."

At length, Mira, Allison, and Deidre introduced themselves. We managed to be silent for a moment to hear Eve say, "We've had some terrible storms here these past few years. Not-so-subtle warnings of global warming. The bridge has been out for some time, and they failed to add more signs for the unaware."

I wondered how such an elderly woman managed, especially when the electricity went out. I noticed a ring on her right hand—European style, indicating marriage or widowhood. So, was there still a *Mr.* Eve—or a Mr. *Adam*, in fitting with Ruth

Ann's assessment of the house? I didn't want any more data pushing into my failing internal memory chip. Though it was only late afternoon, what I really wanted to do was to stake out my spot for the night with a soft throw, a glass of wine, and some pigs-in-a-blanket or some other "wicked" hors d'oeuvres.

"We had planned to add a generator," Eve said, "but we never did. With a well in the back, you can pump water manually, but neither the toilets nor the showers would operate. Although Raspberry Hill has been for sale, our troubled economic times have not been favorable for potential buyers. Lots of compliments, but no offers. Our only hope is that our nephew, Jimmy John, will be interested. On the days when the house is scheduled to be shown—not often lately—we hide the sheets of course."

More nods of agreement. With or without offspring, there seemed to be a unanimous appreciation of the next generation's perceived, often obtuse, priorities. Roxie blurted, to the chuckling of all, including Eve, "If your nephew can afford it. The new generation doesn't save like we did."

"You're so right, dearie. Well, I should stop my incessant chin-wag," Eve continued, "and allow you to relax and dry off. All should be dry by morning, especially if you hang your clothing on a drying rack near the woodstove fire."

We thanked her, and Mira and Allison retrieved our footwear and whatever else we had discarded by the door on our way inside. I desperately wanted to warm my wet, shivering body. "Perhaps we could make some tea if there is a kettle to put on the woodstove."

"Of course, Joesie," Eve responded quickly, finger in the air. "Let me get the kettle while I gather the towels and robes. I shan't be more than a few minutes. If someone could please come with me into the linen cupboard down the hallway, we can gather what you might need."

Our Mother Superior, Roxie, followed Eve toward the back of the first floor of the house. Deidre brought up the rear, muttering to me as she passed by, "Do we really have to spend the night? I stopped camping out a long time ago. I'd rather stay in the back seat of the car since I usually fall asleep there, anyhow."

"Nonsense, girl," insisted Mira. "We don't know how much this rampant river will rise overnight. We almost ended up swept away. Once was enough."

As they left, Allison managed a muted murmur, "Not a five-star hotel, girls!"

Roxie and Deidre related our day's events to Hazel, who had followed us to the back. "Not many exciting things happening here anymore," Hazel lamented, stroking Merlin. "I wish I was young again and could have been with you."

I wandered away from the group back out into the hallway to touch the walls. The candlelight reflected dark mahogany expanses that seemed to go up an endlessly wide staircase. Beautifully framed closed doors were the only interruptions of the panels of wood. I always appreciated carved wood. I wondered how many floors there were and what the rooms looked like. Too many *Nancy Drew* mystery books as a young girl had put ideas into my suspicious, nosy nature. Maybe there were even hidden rooms! My curiosity was countered by not having enough nerve to explore freely—yet.

Just as Eve had promised, the three reappeared with an assortment of robes, all of which had seen better days. We listened as Eve began her instructions, which sounded a bit like a stream of consciousness, of which I am eternally guilty myself. Allison said, "Here Eve, let me take them from you." She stumbled forward and almost fell into Eve.

"Are you okay, Allison?" Ruth Ann asked.

Like a puppeteer, Allison whispered through clenched teeth, "I'll tell you later."

Eve continued as though nothing had happened.

"It doesn't matter to me. I don't sleep much anyway," Mira said.

"I must have had a sixth sense that you were coming," Eve said. "I collected pots and buckets of water which you'll find in the kitchen. Bad storms cut off the electricity, hence, no power to the well."

"Eve, I wonder if there's a way to use a bathroom?" pleaded Allison. "It's getting critical."

"The door next to the kitchen is the loo. Please use the buckets to pour water in the tank to flush. I shall leave you all to settle in. I'm sure you're quite exhausted from your ordeal."

"Please excuse me," Allison managed as she rushed to the bathroom.

"There is water still fresh and cool in a pitcher in the ice box. I may sleep in and shall not likely see you in the morn. I'm sure you will want to leave early to get back to your quarters to freshen up. I'm a wee bit tired from having worked in the garden earlier today. You can see an assortment of my beloved roses from my own, albeit petite, Queen Mary's Garden. By the way, I picked some raspberries, which are in a bowl in the kitchen."

I couldn't help stating the obvious. "You come by the name 'Raspberry Hill' honestly. Where are the bushes?"

"Oh, goodness gracious, behind us, interspersed throughout the property."

"You must make wonderful desserts," I said.

Eve beamed a grin from one ear to the other. "I used to be quite a good cook. I had to turn it over to Hazel, who lives in a cottage behind us. A pity we don't have much in the way of left-overs. Lots of jars of raspberry jam in the butler's pantry to satisfy a sweet tooth though. We all have a hand in the canning."

I saw Ruth Ann's eyes light up at the mention of her favorite jam.

"Let's make the best of this," I said. Deidre just groaned.

Eve directed us to the registration desk I'd leaned on earlier in the front entranceway, to obtain a printed brochure with instructions of how to get back to town. Eve was truly our guardian angel. She continued on to the last of the list of her caring suggestions, "Wrap up. Don't catch colds. Help yourselves to whatever you find in the kitchen. Too bad no more kidney pie left, just bits and bobs. I'm afraid there aren't any more mashed neeps and tatties left, either. What a pity if you've never had them."

"What a pity, Eve," I managed politely with the fingers of my right hand crossed behind my back. "Besides seeing you, another good reason to come back here again."

I, for one, knew the food reference from my travels to the United Kingdom. I couldn't resist a smiling peek at the not-so-subtle horrified faces of my companions. Eve continued, smiling broadly, "*Haggis* for us is a tasty Scottish dish made with mashed turnips, carrots, even potatoes—and quite good, if I might be so bold. Many Americans say it tastes odd. If you're a vegetarian, you wouldn't have to eat the kidney pie. If you want, I'll cook you some if the power comes back."

Rolling her eyes for my benefit alone, Mira politely added, "What a lovely offer. Would have loved to have enriched my palate. Maybe another time."

"Thank you for your cheerful company." Eve faced us with a single large tear glistening in the candlelight. "Oh, yes, forgive my husband, Charles, for not having descended the stairwell to greet you. He's a bit under the weather. Dampness worsens his rheumatism. Certainly, I should expect you can return to your lodge when the water recedes. Hopefully for you that's tomorrow. God Bless."

"Lady Eve" seemed deserving of a proper English curtsy. Instead, I gently hugged her frail figure as an expression of our gratitude for welcoming us into her world. With her final swift nod goodbye, Eve disappeared up the stairway, as though floating into another world I hoped we'd get to see.

"There was nothing to her," I said to the group.

Before settling into the sitting rooms, Roxie added an interesting observation, "Eve is so light on her feet."

"Somehow I feel safe now." Roxie's words seemed comforting to me.

I wondered if the rest felt the same.

The Inn

The travelers had arrived—a bit wet and scraggly but settled in nicely. They seemed to have awakened the belly of the beast. I was doing my level best to accommodate them. Eve had stepped up to do what she has always done: take care of people. Even Hazel seemed a little brighter, helping here and there, tidying up. What now? Will they stay a day, or two, or three? Will they overstay their welcome? If they stay out of my business, all will be well.

～12～

HUDSON
VALLEY VOICES

We settled down on the overstuffed sofas and chairs in the double sitting rooms. Curling up there would be doable for one night. I was especially grateful we weren't suffering by sitting in anything resembling my aunt's décor, remnants of the French Provincial furniture craze of yore. Sitting in such discomfort was intensified by her heavy plastic, zippered slipcovers—ugly, in my opinion. Getting up was so embarrassing. How could anyone gracefully extricate sweaty underwear that had found its way into forbidden crevices?

When she came back with a kettle and matches to relight the stove if necessary, Hazel said, "Just in case you want to make hot tea to warm up. Tea, tea, tea!" She was right. The house was surprisingly cool for not having any functioning electricity for air conditioning, if it even existed in older houses. No lights. We were lucky to have the candles and lanterns in abundance. I had never seen so many candles outside of a church. It reminded me of the Church of Perpetual Harmony that had dominated the view from my window back at the Abenaki Lodge. If someone was praying for our safe return, at least part of the prayer had been answered thus far. We were still alive.

"Thank you, Allison," I said, "for putting the kettle on the woodstove." I gave her a big hug, adding, "Luckily there's plenty of wood to stoke the fire. It'll cut the dampness from chilling our bones. I'll search for some cups and teabags. By the way, what happened with Eve that made you so jittery?"

Allison said, "I'll tell you over tea."

Roxie returned from the kitchen, carrying a tray of successful finds. I joined the spontaneous purse-emptying frenzy to reveal something to share. To everyone's delight, I pulled out a couple of tea sandwiches from Astor Courts. Our salvaged booty became a plentiful, unexpected pile.

Mira the magician pulled out three miniature bottles of Black Label. "Never leave home without my Scotch," she said. "Tempers the terror."

"Better than pulling a rabbit from a hat for some," I said, "but none for me, thanks. A whiff will do the trick." I managed a sniff, smiling to be polite—not my favorite drink, even in a pinch. We took a quick inventory of our additional treasures: from the kitchen wanderings of Deidre and Roxie, a sumptuous selection of raw vegetables, a bit of leftover brie cheese, a few soggy crackers, a basket of raspberries, and my added bag of apricots.

"I can't stand this anymore," Deidre moaned. "I'm hungry, I'm wet, I'm tired. I've had it. I don't even know how many books I've sold."

"Cut it out, Deidre," Roxie said. "Chill out. You'll find out about your books. Just be glad we're safe."

"It pays to have been a girl scout with a gazillion merit badges," Ruth Ann said. Compliments of her small cooler, along with a knife, Ruth Ann cut and somehow stretched a few succulent chicken salad finger sandwiches into hors d'oeuvre-sized pieces for each of us, saved from Astor Courts. In addition, she pulled out a miniature jar of jam from the restaurant in Washburn. "Thank goodness my mother sent me with the cooler," she added.

"Food for our bodies and marvels for our souls," Allison said. "I would have eaten more of that delicious Italian food last night, if I knew it was going to be our *last supper*." Allison always had something positive to say to make everyone feel good. We had inadvertently shared a nearly tragic experience. I felt the bond with my would-be sisters growing stronger.

"Aha, look what I found!" Deidre said. "Eve said to help ourselves—so we did." From behind her back Deidre produced a bottle of glorious merlot she had unearthed in the kitchen. She had also, thank goodness, located a corkscrew. Maybe this would help us forget about our predicament.

"Check this out," Allison responded with a coy grin. She withdrew yet another bottle of wine, discovered behind her chair. "Eve is certainly full of surprises."

Roxie found some Waterford stemware for a touch of elegance. She apportioned the remains of the luscious carbs, mostly muffins and doughnuts, she and Deidre had brought.

On an end table lay a map. We agreed that we were a hop, skip, and a jump from where we began in New York State. We were somewhere in the southern Berkshires, according to the map, and closer to Washburn than we had thought. Ruth Ann guessed Cheshire, Massachusetts. I mused aloud, "What if we'd been swept into the raging river?"

"Incredible that Ruth Ann spotted the sign," Allison said with raised glass in hand. "I am so thankful for a place to bed down."

Ruth Ann was giddy with excitement. "I started to think about supper last night at that splendid Italian restaurant. We can't duplicate it here. What an unexpected dining experience at this inn-of-surprises. It's like being marooned on Gilligan's Island."

"As long as we're not here for years," I moaned.

"Amen," Deidre said. "How did we get so off course?"

"As the lead driver, by default," Ruth Ann said, "I was sure you all would think I was crazy to pull up into a driveway uninvited." Ruth Ann continued on as if she were confessing a sin or apologizing, neither of which was necessary. "But I knew it had to be a haven when I thought I saw the word *inn*. It was barely visible during a flash of lightning. Perhaps we were meant to find Eve and our temporary Eden. Raspberries are safer than finding apples. No sin after a bite."

"How succulent," Mira added. "These raspberries are gifts. The mix of rich colors—raspberries with apricots—couldn't be lovelier."

"Succulent, such a twenty-five-cent word," I added, ever the children's librarian.

"Only because we have no Adam to tempt us to sin," Ruth Ann remarked with a blush.

"Oh darn," Allison said, eliciting more giggles, "like manna from heaven."

I was still anxious from the experience, grateful to be safe, dry, and consuming food and wine. *Not worth further silly discussion of the fruit's identity*, I thought. I raised my glass, proposing a toast. "Never mind any *if*. We made it, thanks to you wonderful drivers. In deep gratitude to Ruth Ann and Allison, a toast. Here, here!"

"How unbelievable that Eve so welcomed us into this Eden," Roxie said. "I hope that she still feels that way after we leave in the morning."

"Oh God, you're such an optimist," Mira said. "What if we can't?"

Deidre frowned a bit, looking down at the English bone china plate and dessert forks that she'd unearthed in the kitchen. "At least we're living in style, like The Breakers in Palm Beach, right Roxie?"

"Hardly."

It was a refined bacchanal. We devoured, savoring our spread; glasses clinked and clanked. I could see our group relationship definitely changing—for the better. In just a few hours, a camaraderie had grown out of circumstance. We were experiencing an altered reality, captives with an unknown fate. We had the good fortune of knowing one another in different ways, individually and now as a group.

And what an unlikely bunch! Minus our planned wardrobe for a normal retreat, we were on an unplanned journey to an unexpected destination. I imagined a gathering of college sorority sisters—like I never had.

For a while we ventured into "safe" talk: aging, travel, the weather. Eventually, we began tackling hopes and dreams, including more serious topics. Each was expressed freely with unwavering trust. The rest of the evening was not a blur. It was a frenzy of chatter. We should have been exhausted. We were revved, revived, and talking like engines that wouldn't quit. At one point, we each reflected on a loss which had changed our lives. Some shared health issues that added to life's vicissitudes. I felt compelled to ask, "Is all this reflection what happens when women are stranded?"

"Yes, but…" added Mira kindly, "both my father and mother would repeatedly bring the past into the present."

"In our house, too," I said. "We heard the same stories over and over again."

Then Roxie jumped in. "Add to that all the falls—you know, fallen boobs, drooping excesses of the neck, withered brain cells."

"Come on, guys!" Allison said. "This is what I have to look forward to?"

Ruth Ann nodded. "About the only topic which consistently aroused humor from my father was hair loss. It was always the same quip, 'Nothing stops falling hair except the floor.' Regarding his short, stubby military cut, he would bellow, 'My crew bailed out a long time ago.'"

Giggles could be heard above the sounds of wood crackling in the stove. Rain pelted the windows. "What will our kids say about us?" Deidre brought it back to reality.

"I don't have any children," I reminded the group.

"Me either," Roxie said.

"No husband, no child waiting for me," Ruth Ann offered. "Would anyone miss me? If we'd gone off the bridge, who would have left purple plastic flowers for me or a roadside marker that would say, 'In memory of our beloved Ruth Ann?'"

"It's talks like this that scare me about the future," I added. "For better or worse, no kid to call me crotchety. I was pregnant once. She would have been my daughter." Surprised looks from the others did not deter me. Perhaps my frank revelations were due to having come within inches and seconds from having our two carloads of unassuming victims careen into a raging river.

"Oh, Joesie, that's so sad," Allison said.

"I feel comfortable with you, our group of survivors," I said. "Coming so close to disaster created a spiritual bond. It reminded me of the ritual of becoming 'blood sisters' we foolishly practiced as youngsters—making cuts in our fingers, then forming a circle to blend into one gory family of friends. But no spilling any blood today."

"We never did that!" exclaimed our younger Allison. "That certainly was an original BFF thing to do. Back then, it must have been easier to believe in 'forevers.'"

"Ugh!" Ruth Ann said. "Too many diseases now, for sure. And what's this about an 'almost' daughter?"

"So, true confessions," I said. "Such a long story. I had met Josh, a graduate student, while on a break from college. It was near my family's summer home. I had discovered sex and its consequences—pregnancy. That's all I'm going to say about that now. Sometime later, I ran into him, my 'older man.' We reconnected, ran off to Elkton, Maryland, the eloping capital of the East Coast. No more pregnancies were in the cards."

"I know it wasn't easy to tell us that." Mira cut to the essence. "And your father?"

"Don't ask. I'll save the rest for the next detour. Today we almost died!"

"Not again, Joesie—but we didn't. Get over it. We're all alive. End of discussion. Move on."

"Roxie, you are always so sensible," I said, "but I can't let it go. We *almost* became a sad bouquet of artificial flowers. An ephemeral monument at the edge of a bridge on this God-forsaken remote road to nowhere. It would have been the end of trying to write the next best-seller. Maybe we'd have to have given up sex in whichever world we'd have gone to next."

"Joesie, where is this going?" Deidre interrupted. I ignored her, continuing in a stream of consciousness.

Returning from the bathroom, Ruth Ann stood with her mouth open and managed in a squeaky voice, "Needing the loo put me out of the loop. Did I catch the word *sex*?"

"Afraid so," I replied. "The devil made me say it. Sorry. I was just thinking of life after death. Who really knows? Maybe we go somewhere idyllic and have *another* first time. For the right man, I'd get dressed in a mink coat. Naked underneath."

"I'd just wear an apron," Roxie said.

Mira said, "Just think of me as Mira on the Mountaintop." We all chuckled.

"Been there, done that," Allison smirked.

I said, "As I saunter to the door, my dream guy would say, 'Let me help you slip out of that animal skin and let's have a drink.'"

"Oh, I can't believe this," Ruth Ann gasped. "What does he say when he sees you *naked*?"

"Not a word."

"And then what?" asked Ruth Ann, her eyes bulging.

"Simple, my dear Ruth Ann. They 'make love.' Right?"

"Right, Roxie. Madly and passionately."

"Yeah, but what happened to your shoes?" Deidre was, of course, worried about the shoes.

"Shoes?" Allison asked. "What shoes?"

"Wouldn't you be wearing stilettos?" Mira answered. I tried to answer but Mira filled in for me. "She kept them on, or she'd have had to jump onto the table. Could possibly fall, break a hip and end up with all kinds of complications."

Ruth Ann seemed astounded. "Naked except for shoes—and wearing a man across your naked body? Holy cannoli! The closest I ever came to that was this blind date that left a paper bag on the credenza by my front door. We *were* going to dinner."

Deidre looked puzzled. "So, where's the sex?"

"On our way out," Ruth Ann continued, "after he helped me with my coat, a navy-blue pea coat, no mink. I reminded him about the bag he left. He told me that inside were *two* chocolate croissants for 'our breakfast in the morning.' Can you imagine such nerve?"

"I call it chutzpah," said Roxie.

Allison piped in with, "*And*? You did it? With that guy?"

"Of course not, Allison," answered Ruth Ann with a triumphant grin. "I knew that 'Mr. Presumptuous' would *not* be my first lover. He was such a creep."

Roxie jumped up, spilled her wine, and burst forth with, "After so many years married to the same man, I think we've done it all! I'd vote for a whipped cream party."

"We could all write our own version of that red-hot trilogy and begin with *Red Hot Sex for Writers.*"

I added, "What about introducing a line of lingerie? I sometimes love to dress up—before I undress. Red lacy panties so thin they get stuck and matching bra tops sound so sexy. And they hide a multitude of sins, especially as we get older."

Roxie's voice sounded distant. "I just wish Ben would stay in bed a little longer."

"If you tied him to the bedposts, he wouldn't have had a choice but to stay beside you," said logical Allison.

Suddenly there was a loud clap of thunder. Ruth Ann's look had turned to horror. Mira tried to come to our rescue. "Now, if that thunder were not an omen to quit, I'm a monkey's uncle. It's late. This *wasn't* our last day on earth. What if we revel in the conversations we've had and can still have? Let's call it a night."

Roxie mused, "When we return home, will we all be changed by our experience together? Or will we fall back into arguments over anything, like emptying the dishwasher or trash? Which restaurant doesn't serve bad food? Come on, let's celebrate *us.*"

"Thanks again, Roxie, for bringing me back from 'Dreamville' to enjoy the moment."

"Damn, my cell's not working," Roxie exclaimed, looking at her phone.

"Mine either," Deidre said. None worked.

"No matter what our persuasion, we are safe tonight and blessed to have each other," Mira chanted in a pastoral tone.

"And may we escape tomorrow," Deidre added.

"Amen, amen, amen," Allison and Mira said in unison.

"Whoever said that must have eaten the same food that Hazel ate," Ruth Ann said, smiling.

Without another word, we each settled into our personal spaces. What an assemblage of bodies! We were leaning in every direction. Just when a really bad day was settling into group harmony, I couldn't hold it back. The devil made me do it. I stood up and announced to mostly sleeping bodies, "This camping on chairs in a musty old house is no paradise. This *is* an inn. What about the beds upstairs? This is all bullshit!"

Mira's was the solitary voice. "Joesie, can't you just relax, enjoy the moment? Settle down."

As the wind and rain continued, we faded like the smaller candles, extinguishing one at a time.

~13~

MIRA FINDS
A FRIEND

Mira	Tuesday 1:00 AM

What a night! The number of words we spoke could have stocked enough books to fill a library. At least a small one. I found a woven rug to curl up in, but my mind was going ninety miles-an-hour. *Where are we? I'm still hungry.* Well, at least it stopped storming. I don't like lightning or thunder, but rain is fine with me. *Wow, that was scary! Close your eyes, Mira.*

Despite the chairs and sofas, I chose to sleep on the floor. I couldn't find a comfortable position that would allow me to relax. Sleeping was always hard for me. To sleep on the floor, albeit a carpeted one, wrapped in a large musty tapestry, made it even more impossible. After what seemed like hours, I knew that falling asleep was not in the cards.

I heard night sounds coming from the others: soft moans, a light snore, quiet sounds of light breathing. I was wide awake, my heart beating in racing-car mode. Carefully, I unwrapped myself from my rug and rose from the floor. Carrying my shoes, I tiptoed past my sleeping friends and crept out the back door.

I emerged into an eerily magical scene. The sky was brilliant with stars. Bright flashes of heat lightning, horizontal remnants of the storm that brought us to this place, lit the clumps of trees surrounding the house. Animals screeched, birds called, the hair on my arms prickled. My eyes adjusted to the available moonlight. Off to the right of the porch I saw what looked like a path, so I decided to see where it led me. My other self, the reasonable one, couldn't believe what I was doing. I felt a strange kind of peace. Though I wasn't afraid, I should have been. I had no idea what I was looking for and felt compelled to explore the night. The path had changed from wet to a walkable muddy slosh. The elevation out back was higher than the front. My cell phone's light, though dimming assisted in showing the way.

My jacket snagged on a thicket of bushes filled with small berries. I shined my light on the bush, saying aloud, "Of course Mira, you fool, those are the raspberries. *Raspberry Hill*. Duh! I think I'll try a few to see if they are as tasty as they look.

There were some cleared areas with what looked like a garden left unattended. I bent down and picked up a pod of small peas. They were delicious, filling my mind with memories of helping my mother shell fresh peas, eating them before she ruined them by cooking. It was at that point I knew we were all here for a reason. Maybe we were supposed to find the answer to an unsolved mystery. I said a silent prayer to keep me safe and trudged onward.

"Klutz!" I yelped as I tripped over a large rock, landing ungracefully on the ground. I examined my scraped palm and bruised ego, but I wasn't seriously hurt. The beam of my light revealed a small headstone. I had tripped over a grave. There was a date and a name:

BABY LOUISA BROADHURST

1974

I had stumbled into a cemetery. Around me, I could see two other mounds, new graves with no headstones. I shivered with fear. Then, out of the darkness, I heard footsteps and a voice.

"What in bloody hell are you doing here? What in God's name brings you out on a night like this?" The glare from his flashlight prevented me from seeing him, but I did recognize a slight accent.

I squinted my eyes, trying to make out his image. Before I could see him, his strong grip pulled me upright as I tried to explain. "I'm... I'm Mira. I'm at The Inn. M-m-my friends are, are—we're stranded. The storm. No bridge. I couldn't sleep. Who... who are you?" I sounded like a blithering idiot. His flashlight blinded me, washing out his face in the darkness.

"Don't be scared," the faceless one said. "I'm Jimmy John, Hazel's nephew. I look after the place. We don't get many visitors nowadays."

I was smiling when he put down the flashlight. He grimaced and seemed puzzled by my humor. "Please," I said. "Your accent just doesn't seem to match your name, Jimmy John. I mean, two first names is so southern. You are so obviously not." Now that my eyes had adapted to the darkness, I could not help noticing how handsome this stranger was. I quickly quashed other ideas as they crept into my mind.

"Oh that," Jimmy John explained. "My parents came to the US from the UK when my mum was pregnant with me. Her story is that the first Americans she met were from South Carolina. The man's name was Bobby Ray, thus my two first names. She thought it was very American. I'm used to it, of course."

Neither the starlit darkness nor the dripping trees deterred our conversation. I followed him to a bench beside his small cabin. How had I not noticed it before? "What did your parents do? How come they came here?"

He told me that his family was part of the Society of Friends—the Quakers—who believed that quarrels between people could be settled peacefully. Their beliefs prescribed that war was wrong. Though the Quakers were founded during the 1600s in England, current day Quakers have expanded, including to the United States.

"That did not make for good relations with the Church of England or the British military. Father joined the British military, despite his beliefs, because he couldn't make a living on blacksmithing alone. Once in the military he wanted a position that didn't require him to carry a gun. As a result, he was branded a coward. Luckily, he was able to improve his farrier skills.

He and Mum eventually lost their livelihood and decided to move near a horse farm in Kentucky. They were both creative artists. He was a blacksmith, she a weaver." I thought of the tapestry I had wrapped around my body earlier and wondered if Jimmy John's mother had made it. He paused as though to make sure I was listening and went on.

"Hazel came here to New England to live with Eve and Charles, who had agreed to sponsor my parents and Aunt Hazel, their niece, from the U.K. Father found work at the horse farms. My mother made beautiful shawls and our clothing. Hazel was my father's twin sister. They were the babies of the family. Originally, my parents moved to Kentucky where I was born."

I was more curious with every word. "So how did you get here?" He looked into the distance as if trying to find words that would tell the story. I studied his face. He had a light complexion, large green eyes, a chiseled nose, a jaw with a full mouth, and thick, black, wavy hair.

"There was an outbreak of influenza when I was eight," he said. "Mother died. Father and I became desperately ill as well. I survived. My dad died before my eyes. Neighbors helped me bury him beside Mum. My parents are resting together in Kentucky. The neighbors kept me until Hazel could come for me more than a month later. She brought me back to the recently renovated Inn and raised me like her own. I've never left here except to attend culinary school. I'm used to being alone, although…" He stopped, his dark eyes looking away for a brief moment. We sat in silence, listening to nature's concert. Finally, I stood up to go.

"I should get back," I said reluctantly. "I just have one more question. Who was Baby Louisa Broadhurst?"

"Hazel's baby girl, but that's another painful story," Jimmy John answered. "I'm so happy to have met you, Mira. Perhaps some time you could tell me the story of your family and how you got here." He pointed the way back to The Inn. "Here's a flashlight. Be careful. Follow the path. By the way, how many of you are there?"

"Six of us."

"Six? Okay. I'll bring you a basket from my garden. Come daylight, I'll check the property and get you ladies on the road. Don't worry about me. I know my way around here. Be safe!"

I wanted to hug him. Instead, we shook hands and nodded. I pointed my flashlight downward to keep from tripping when it started flickering. Unfortunately, it left me as much as in the dark as I was about Hazel's baby.

Neither it nor my cell phone flashlight worked. My body stiffened, shaking with fear. I closed my eyes and prayed. I heard what sounded like hundreds of buzzing bees. Still shaking, I opened my eyes as the path lit with hundreds—no, *thousands*—of fireflies. Suddenly, all was silent as dozens of them made a solid circle, almost like a headlight, in front of my shirt. The others flew just feet ahead. Did I imagine the buzzing or was it the noises in my head?

"This can't be real," I said to no one. Like one large army, the swarm started to move ahead like a guide. When I stood still, a horde of them flew back to me and motioned, as if to say, "Come on, Mira, we haven't got all night!" Minutes later The Inn appeared. The fireflies formed a circle around me. I stood still, silently praying, "Thank you." I watched as my rescuers flew away into the darkness surrounding Raspberry Hill. It became apparent to me that I had no idea how long I had been walking. Time seemed irrelevant in this place, at least to me.

The door opened soundlessly. I removed my shoes and tiptoed around my sleeping sisters. My rug was there as I had left it. I curled up, feeling as if I had experienced something otherworldly. Would anyone believe me? Despite my surroundings, I fell into a deep sleep.

Jimmy John

Mira seemed like a nice lady, albeit a little strange. I wondered about the others. I should have asked more questions. Who were they? Where were they from? How long will they stay? Could Hazel handle taking care of guests? After all, The Inn was essentially closed. My Aunt Hazel was getting on in years. She had been experiencing some memory loss. Hazel puttered around and tried to keep up; however, she was starting to need some help herself. I didn't know if I should worry or not, but I did.

Hopefully, there was enough food in the house. I stayed pretty stocked up myself, as a chef, but Hazel was one of those "daily" shoppers. She liked to look at the produce and meat, selecting items based on freshness and price. She even shopped like that for her pets, buying only the best for them. She and I shared a love for animals. I always wished that The Inn at Raspberry Hill could have a petting zoo, full garden, and more. I envisioned growing pumpkins, with children running around picking their favorite ones. In the spring, we would have more than raspberries for the picking. Dreams, I guessed—and so far, unfulfilled.

With the storm nearly over, I pondered what I would be doing over the next couple of days. It would be left up to me to clear the road once the water receded. Hopefully, the power would come back on. I had gas-powered tools, regardless, so I would be able to cut up the fallen trees. I liked physical work. It kept me in shape.

I headed toward my humble abode to get a good night's rest for the work ahead.

~14~

MORNING COFFEE

Ruth Ann   **Tuesday 6:00 AM**

Not having slept in my clothes before, I felt less than clean and a little disoriented when I awoke. I put on my glasses and saw the others still sleeping. I wished I could be that way. The first glint of light made me pop up like a baby bird. I was aching for a coffee and a shower. Not wanting to disturb the others, I rummaged around the kitchen as quietly as I could but caused a pan cover to ring against its pot. I winced at the sound, so penetrating that I had to cover my ears until the ringing quieted. I've always been sensitive to sound. The thunder of the night before had unnerved me. It was amazing that I had slept at all.

I tippy-toed around the corner, peering into the main room. Thankfully, my friends were still undisturbed, despite my clumsiness in the kitchen. *Much better to awaken to the smell of coffee*, I thought. Finally, after opening many a cupboard, I acquired the necessary ingredients: coffee maker, drip coffee, glass pot, coffee scoop, and a bunch of assorted coffee mugs. I turned on the water, but nothing happened. The tap was dry. How ironic: no water after a storm like that. I couldn't help but recall a part of the poem "The Rime of the Ancient Mariner."

Water, water, everywhere and all the boards did shrink.

Water, water, everywhere nor any drop to drink.

Eve had left some buckets of water in the sunroom, but I might've awakened the ladies getting them. I decided to keep looking elsewhere. The sunlight filtering through the windows provided plenty of light. I needed to see if the power was back on to use the coffee maker; that is, if I could find some bottled water. The huge industrial refrigerator held nothing. *What kind of place is this?* I wondered.

I flipped a few switches, to no avail. The power was still out. I groaned at the prospect of morning without coffee. Feeling a bit hopeless about the failed coffee mission, I slipped out the side door onto a wraparound back porch. The porch held rocking chairs, a chaise, and a full bench swing that was hanging from the solid rafters. There was also a large gas grill. Great! If my friends were awake, I could use the wood stove inside. Maybe it would be better to use the gas grill out on the porch so I wouldn't awaken anyone.

Everything was wet, with a rising dank smell. I was taking it all in when I noticed an old-fashioned well with a hand pump, just as Eve had mentioned. Next to the well was a tin bucket. I clambered down the small bank of stairs.

The bucket was partially filled with rainwater. Some dirt and debris had settled at the bottom, but the top water was clear. I reached in and found the water surprisingly warm. I splashed some on my face, instantly feeling refreshed. Could I use this water for coffee? As rustic and tempting as it was to make rain-water coffee, I decided the sediment was too risky for human consumption. I went to the well, and pressed the handle down, gingerly at first, gaining confidence with every push. Sure enough, water flowed out of the pipe. Grabbing the bucket, I swished the water around and dumped it on the ground, where my feet were sinking into the muck. I rinsed the bucket a few more times before filling it halfway with well water.

Can you boil water in a tin bucket? My next step was to light the gas grill. The automatic starter actually worked, unlike mine at home. The gas flames lifted above the grill and licked around my bucket. Perfect. I sat in a relatively dry spot on the built-in bench seats that lined the porch. The sun warmed me and though they say a watched pot never boils, I had piping hot water in no time.

Back in the kitchen, I placed a filter in the coffee maker, removing the hopper to the top of the coffee pot. I poured the boiling water onto the coffee and it dripped obediently. I recalled in my early days having a fancy brand-name coffee maker that worked on the same principle. "Coffee's on!" I said.

Mira was up moments later. "Coffee! Wow, I need this after the night I had. I went for a walk, found a cemetery, and met the caretaker, Jimmy John," she exclaimed, and padded over to the counter to fix herself a cup.

"Caretaker? Where the hell is he?" asked Joesie, appearing behind her. "How 'bout some tea?"

"I'll check." In the same cupboard where I'd found the coffee was one box of English Breakfast Tea.

"How do you take it, Joesie?"

"With lemon."

"Sure, you do, Joesie, but I need milk," Deidre exclaimed, popping in behind Joesie.

"Damn," I said out loud, but opened the massive door of the refrigerator and looked out of habit. I pulled open a drawer and saw a few large shiny lemons. Had I missed them the first time, as I had the small pitcher of milk?

Once everyone had their tea or coffee, we made our way out to the front porch to contemplate the day. Next to the porch swing was a round cedar table between two Adirondack chairs. On the table was an assortment of breakfast pastries, including biscuits, and a glass canning jar of raspberry jam. There was an assortment of real silverware and small breakfast plates. Where had they come from? Hazel or possibly Eve?

"Must have been Hazel," answered Roxie, except I hadn't said a word about anything. I shivered at the strangeness of the appearance of milk, lemons, and pastries. I had been out on this porch at least twenty minutes ago and I had not seen any pastries. I'd have to check later to see if there was another entrance to the porch.

I had been by the kitchen door and no one had left prior to our going out together.

"Look, no mystery here," Mira interjected. "Jimmy John must have left us the pastries. He promised me last night."

"Mira, can you tell us more about your walk and Jimmy John?" I asked.

"Well, some of it was fun. Jimmy John's a hunk, no doubt. The fireflies led me back through the darkness."

I looked over at Allison and Joesie, who were rolling their eyes. Deidre twirled her index finger at her temple, raising an eyebrow at Mira. "A hunk? I don't care what he looks like. Can he get us out of here?" Deidre demanded.

"No doubt he can," Mira chirped.

Putting the strangeness of everything aside, I gazed at the scenery. I hadn't noticed the glorious mountain views when I'd first ventured outside. The mountains were still green but would be turning to remarkable oranges and blazing reds in less than a month's time. Although I had never been a hiker, much less a mountain climber, the rolling hills made me want to explore. I walked to the edge of the porch, sipping my coffee, and feeling at peace. The hills unfolded into grassy mounds until they reached the higher mountains, which looked to be almost within walking distance. It was clear that we were in a valley. I sighed deeply and walked to the railing. I looked beyond the well to see beautiful deep green grass almost under water. To the right, where we pulled into the driveway last night, it was even more flooded. Tree branches lined the driveway's end, resembling matchsticks beside what looked like a felled giant oak.

"You have to admit, this has been fun," Mira chimed in. "Like summer camp. Come on girls, how often do you get to be away from it all? The kids, husbands, et cetera?"

"Summer camp this ain't," Deidre responded with a laugh. "But I appreciate the company."

I lowered my eyes a tad, not really feeling like talking about kids or husbands, not having any of my own. But it sure was nice to be away. Some of us had slept well. We were enjoying the piping hot coffee and certainly the company.

"Try your cell phones now," Roxie suggested to everyone.

I removed my phone from my purse. I didn't have an iPhone like the rest of my friends but at least it was a smartphone and usually had good reception. *That's strange, no bars. I swear, when I get back to civilization, I will switch to a service that gets reception everywhere.* Though I am not one to panic, I felt jittery, like at any moment something was about to happen and I would have no way to contact anyone. The others were digging in their bags and announcing things like, "Mine will work," and "I have T-Mobile," or "Verizon," or "AT&T." What was really strange was that *none of us* had a signal.

"What? Are *all* the towers down out here?" Deidre asked. "I have to call my publicist and my daughter is going to be worried sick."

Again, I lowered my eyes and felt slightly out of place. Truth is, I didn't have a significant other or anyone, really, who was going to miss me. I was on summer vacation from my preschool job and had just left my mother's house. Maybe if two weeks went by and I didn't show up for work for the start of the new school year, someone might notice.

We started to shuffle around, looking for Eve, who was nowhere in sight. Perhaps she was still sleeping.

"Allison?" I asked, "Want to take a walk out to the cars, see what we're up against here?"

"We'll need hip boots," she answered.

∽

~15~

KNOCK KNOCK

Despite having had a few sips of Ruth Ann's much-welcomed coffee along with some nibbles of our mystery pastries, I was nevertheless still hungry. I knew myself and those rumblings from my stomach were just crying out to me to eat more. This was a bit strange for me, as I often skipped breakfast, in a hurry to get on with whatever I was about to do for the day. *Should I be thinking about food, or the phone calls I was missing? Is the real estate office trying to reach me? What about Ben? Has he tried to text or call? Does he miss me at all? Was he so absorbed at work or with something else that he hardly noticed my absence? Should I care? Where are my friends? Are they missing my calls? And why am I so wrapped up in all of this?*

I opened the screen door to the porch. "Hey, guys," I said. "I'm going to see if we can attempt to get out of here. Anybody else want to take a look?"

No response from my new "sisters," so I ventured out by myself.

Looking down the road, I knew we were doomed, at least for another day. Water was everywhere, and the potholes in the road were still filled to capacity. The deep ruts on the driveway from the tires appeared to have less water but were still too wet to get out.

How did we get here at all? How had we found this driveway with all the tall grass and stones obliterating so much? This couldn't be. I took out my phone. No bars, no nothing. *Why? Still? How will I ever know what is going on?* I turned around and went back into the living room.

"There's no way we're leaving yet. It's a bit better than it was, but there's just too much water around, and the cars will never make it to the road. Sorry. It may be possible later if the water keeps receding. Guessing it will be better by late afternoon. We could leave except for that giant tree blocking the road."

"Oh, for God's sake, are you kidding me?" Joesie shouted. "For sure I don't want to stay here another night. I hope Jimmy John is working on getting us out of here."

"Yeah, me neither," chimed in Allison.

"Crap, crap, crap," piped up our so sarcastic Deidre.

"You know what?" said Mira, "With such a mess, we're damn lucky to have found this place. Calm down, and like the Serenity Prayer says, 'accept the things you cannot change.' Let's just get on with it."

"Well, in that case," Allison said, "Ruth Ann and I are going to go for a walk, anyway." "We are convinced we'll be able to catch some fish for lunch."

"You never know," I said.

Deidre added, "Joesie and I were on the back porch, and our cells didn't work either. Someone has to tell Eve we're staying a little longer and that hopefully we'll leave in a few hours. What do you think, Mira? Want to go up and tell Eve?"

Mira, looking askance, asked, "Me? You want *me* to go up there? No way. Someone else can do it—not my style at all." We finally decided I, Roxie Ross, would brave the steps and talk to Eve for all of us.

But where was Eve anyway? Certainly, by now, she had heard us moving around. We debated her whereabouts and came to no conclusions. Boldly, perhaps even brazenly, I headed up the winding staircase.

I took each step slowly, listening for a creak and hoping I wouldn't hear one, as I admired a wall of what seemed to be old family portraits done in oil, framed in gold. Who had taken these stairs before me? Family members, as well as guests, travelers, families? It was an inn, after all. Just who had stayed here before? Had Raspberry Hill been full and thriving? No doubt it had been, but I wondered—had ghosts walked the halls in the wee hours of the night? Did former guests share stories in the dining room at meals? Oh, if these walls could talk! Thoughts like these ran amok in my mind as I went in search of Eve.

At the top of the stairway, I admired the long hallways going off in opposite directions. The walls were covered in faded silk, once shades of blue on a now-yellowed background. There was, however, a certain dignity about it that brought a smile to my face. Directly in front of me were two magnificent mahogany doors heavily embossed with hand-carved angels, their mother-of-pearl wings shimmering in the early morning sunlight. Surely this must be Eve's room. I was about to knock on the door when I heard movement in the room. I knocked anyway, waiting for a response that did not take too long in coming.

"Yes, who is it, please?" I recognized the voice as Eve's.

"Eve, it's Roxie Ross. The ladies and I would like to thank you in person for your kind hospitality. Are you coming downstairs?"

"Oh, no my dear," Eve answered through the closed door. "Perhaps later on, I'll see. And I hope you're not planning to leave yet. I've been through these storms before, and I can tell you the roads are washed out. It will take at least one more day for any semblance of normalcy. I'm sure Jimmy John could help. Have you met him yet?"

"No, I haven't but hope he can help us," I replied.

"Make yourselves at home and feel free to roam the grounds and house," Eve said. "By the way, if you lift the rug in the kitchen, you'll find a trap door to the larder below. It's well stocked and there should be a variety of foods for you to choose from. I don't know why I forgot to tell you that yesterday. Enjoy yourselves and eat well. I may join you later. By the way, Roxie, you may want to speak to Ben."

"How do you know my husband's name?" I couldn't help but wonder if she'd been listening through the walls. I waited for a response; there was none.

Baffled by Eve's remark, I returned downstairs to the others to relay our conversation. They too, were puzzled by Eve's comment about Ben. *What did she know about Ben?* I'd call him if I could, but the damn cell phones weren't working, and the land line was equally dead. I wondered why the water didn't recede here as quickly as it does at home in Palm Beach.

We were disappointed we could not leave The Inn. Why was Eve not coming down to see us? Was she busy tending to other "mystery" guests? Of course, the bright side was the hidden larder, and the thought of having real food for dinner. What wonders lined the shelves, bins, and barrels below? If Eve's larder was well stocked like those of the olden days, surely, we would hit pay dirt. Allison, our capable caterer, and I would look for ingredients we could prepare together. We were, after all, the cooks of the group, and hoped to find some morsels to create a dessert as well. I wondered if Eve would join us for dinner and if she did, what was her preference in food?

In time we might know.

~16~

GONE FISHIN'

Allison	Tuesday 10:00 AM

Ruth Ann and I stood on the back porch, sipping our second cups of coffee. "Just a minute," I said to Ruth Ann. "I'll be back outside in a bit." I went inside to look for my glasses and the small travel-sized container of contact lens solution in my purse, just in case I had to remove the lenses in an emergency. When I squeezed the bottle, it spit and sputtered. A moment of panic hit me. There wasn't enough fluid to put them in, and I would have to spend the day in glasses. I had been wearing them all morning, so it wasn't a total catastrophe. We were all skipping our normal beauty routine, and they knew by now that my eyes weren't blue. Last night, as I exited the bathroom and headed back to the living room, I had passed Mira who stopped in front of me.

"Oh, Allison, your eyes are brown!" she'd said. Then, staring at me a split second longer than usual, Mira had added, "They're beautiful." The comment had made me feel sheepish. I found it hard to believe she really thought my eyes were beautiful, but that is what she'd said.

Now, this morning, the automatic action of pulling down my lower lid, the shiny wet light blue disc perched upon my extended index finger, was not going to happen. On a typical day, I never considered my routine, I just did it. Today, everything was different, and I would just have to cope.

Within minutes of finishing the coffee, Ruth Ann announced that the road was still blocked. I looked down at the crumbs from the pastries and thought about our next meal. Together, we devised a plan to catch our lunch. It was odd that Eve's pantry was so bare; it held only two dusty old cans of peaches, another of peas, and a dozen jars of raspberry jam, also quite dusty. I saw a few boxes of pasta, and a container of flour that was full of little bugs. We weren't going anywhere anytime soon, so why not see if we could catch a fish? Would there be any in the flooded road?

We looked at the road again. Even though Ruth Ann had given us the road's status, we all had to march out to see for ourselves. Yes, the road was blocked and flooded. There we stood, staring at the water rushing around us like we were on an island. The water was well over twelve inches deep and churning over and through the guardrail. The line where the water met the asphalt had extended far to our side and well over the banks on the opposite side.

"If we could get across," Joesie said, "we could probably walk to some kind of a gas station or a store. I think I remember seeing one last night. It's just past that curve up ahead."

"The water's moving too fast," Roxie said. "Look."

Ruth Ann, looking at Roxie, said, "I bet the Hoosick River overflowed—if we're where I think we are. I grew up nearby."

"DeeDee's a good swimmer," Mira said with an irreverent tip of her head.

"Ha!" Deidre said. "Not that good but glad you're using my nickname."

"Just kidding anyway," Mira said. "Nobody's swimming across that."

"Fish," I said, "this water has to have fish in it. Look! Right there." I pointed to the deeper part churning just beyond us. The dark shadow of a decent-sized fish, probably about four pounds, shuddered through the guardrail and disappeared. "See? There... Did you see that? What a good-looking fish! Probably some trout. Maybe we can catch one or two."

"Who's *we*?" Joesie asked.

"Okay, *me*," I said. "I know how to fish. Jess, my former husband, taught me years ago, even though I didn't go very often with him. I was always staying home with the kids. I'm not sure they will bite in this crazy water, but we could try."

"Well, have at it," Roxie said. "Fresh fish would be great for lunch."

"Okay, let me think about this," I said. I wasn't about to stand in the moving water. That would be stupid. I could lose my footing and easily hit the railing, or worse, be sailing downstream before anyone could do anything about it. "I'll go see if there's anything in that old shed that we can use."

"We'll come with you," they chimed in. Despite their lack of interest in fishing, they were all curious to see what would happen.

"I know a bit about fishing, also," Ruth Ann said. "We used to go out as kids, although Boston Harbor was pretty polluted at that time. I hear it's been cleaned up a bit."

As the shed was around back, it was dry enough to get to. The old wooden doors refused to open, but we could see that they were unlocked. We tugged and pulled. Finally, Ruth Ann kicked them. "There," she said as her foot connected near the bottom of one of the doors and the wood made a splintering sound. I pushed, and the metal hinges creaked open. A few strands of a spider's web blocked our entrance, but Ruth Ann moved them aside with a swipe of her hand.

"Over there," I said eyeing some poles, buckets, and a net leaning against the far wall by the back window. Very little light was coming through the smudged glass. I looked at Ruth Ann and said, "Nobody's cleaned in here for a long time. Eve must have let this place go. Maybe her husband is ill."

"What about Jimmy John?" Mira asked. "The caretaker."

"Who, your 'special' friend?" Deidre placed her hand on her heart. "It's late morning and he hasn't shown up yet."

Mira responded, "Of course he will."

"He better," Deidre said.

"Do you think they would care if we use this stuff?" I continued.

"I can't imagine they would. Didn't Eve say to make ourselves at home, that we could use what we needed?"

"Exactly. We'll have to add something to our 'bill,'" Ruth Ann answered.

"Yes, I agree," I said as I grabbed two fishing poles and handed Ruth Ann a bucket and net. "We can use these other buckets for flushing later. With six women we'll need them all."

"Oh, here are some pairs of Wellies." I said, pulling them on and handing pairs to Mira and Ruth Ann. Miraculously, they were our sizes. As we made our way back to the flooded road area Mira noticed dozens of worms around us, where the water had receded.

"We won't need to dig," Mira said. "Look at the worms. They're everywhere." Sure enough, there were some on the road and a few in the mud alongside of it. Ruth Ann and I scooped up some of the worms, which quickly made Roxie, Deidre, and Joesie decide to head back to the safety of The Inn.

"Have fun with those wet wiggly worms," Roxie called out. "Sorry—not my Palm Beach style. I prefer eating my fish at The Breakers."

"Let us know when you catch one," Joesie yelled.

"I'll send Mira and Ruth Ann," I replied. When we arrived at the edge of the "river," Mira squinted into the depths of the water.

"I saw two more," she said.

"Good," I said. "Hmmm. I should have thought this through before we left the shed. We didn't bring anything to dig up bait."

∽

The Inn

Well, though it was technically just a shed, it was a part of me. Each time someone went in there, I made sure they heard me. Just because The Inn at Raspberry Hill was closed didn't mean I should be forgotten. Creak! Jimmy John, when he had the time, used to go fishing. Charles did as well. They often served fresh trout to guests. Very popular. Lately Jimmy John's been too busy with the upkeep to have much leisure time. I was impressed with the ladies' willingness to fish for their lunch. I was beginning to like having guests again.

⁓

Allison

The three of us walked out of the shed, ready to fish. "Cross your fingers there'll be something in the larder to go with the fish we'll catch," I said.

"Do you really think we can cast these lines?" Ruth Ann asked Mira. "The reels look pretty old and rusty." She examined one of the poles and fiddled with the lever to see if it would catch to lock the line. Both lines still had hooks attached to the ends. One still had a delicately tied fly.

"You might have a point," I nodded. "But let's see what they can do." I grabbed a worm. When it curled and wiggled, Mira screamed. For some reason, the same pitch erupted from me and I dropped the creature. All three of us chuckled.

Mira apologized. "Sorry. It's just so gross."

"I'm trying not to think about it," I announced. "Okay, here goes. Take two."

I lifted the thing again with my index finger and thumb and, narrowing my eyes, poked the sharp point of the hook through its body. Glossy red guts oozed out and onto my fingers. My stomach lurched. I had only baited a few hooks, preferring to let Jess, my husband, do the slimy work, and that had been years ago. Yet, here I had established myself as some kind of an expert, and this fishing expedition had a different feel to it. We could survive without food for the day, but this adventure was turning into more than just a bunch of women who were stranded. Inhaling deeply, I took another loop of the worm's body and pushed the section through the hook. Then, looking up, I noticed that Ruth Ann was already preparing to cast, a fat worm dangling securely from her line.

"How did you get that done so quickly?" I called out.

"Experience," she said. "I remembered more than I thought."

Maybe I didn't really want to remember fishing. Maybe I had never even liked it. In marriage counseling, the therapist had told Jess and I to try a little harder to maintain some hobbies together. Neither of us could muster the motivation, though.

It took three awkward tries, but my line finally landed in the water right where I had last seen the trout. Now, of course, not a single fish appeared. When I yanked on my line to make the worm look more enticing, it didn't budge. "Damn," I said, then winced. I glanced up to check their reactions, but neither woman seemed concerned by my choice of words. "I'm caught up on the guardrail."

"Me too," Ruth Ann said, walking along the edge of the water to see if she could loosen her line. I walked the other way. We had the sense to put some distance between us. She chose the southern part of the area, and I the northern. It didn't matter. The force of the river had tangled the lines as if we had tied them to the guardrail.

"I think we're going to have to cut them. Even if a fish bites, we won't be able to pull it in."

Ruth Ann said, "You're right. Might as well give it up. I don't have a knife though, do you?"

"Nope."

"I'll go get one," Mira volunteered.

"Nah." Ruth Ann yanked hard and the line snapped, blowing in the wind as she reeled it back in.

"Maybe we could use the net instead," Mira said, reaching for the long-handled tool.

"That kind of net is just for lifting fish out of the water, but it might work," Ruth Ann added.

"The handle isn't all that long." I pulled hard, breaking my own line.

"Maybe we can extend it with something." Ruth Ann lowered her rod to the ground, examining the net.

"It's not going to work without some really strong fasteners and supports," I said.

"Yeah, you're right," Mira agreed. "Let's just stand here and see if a fish swims by close to the edge."

"Oh, now you're on to something," I said. "Mira, can you stand upstream a bit? If you see one, call out, okay? Then we'll be ready by the time it gets to us."

"I'll stand in the water, if you're nearby to hold on to me," Ruth Ann offered.

"That could work," I said, feeling hopeful. "Let's try it."

Mira stood about twenty yards upstream. Ruth Ann stepped into the water a few feet from me, and I moved as close to the edge of the water as I could. "How am I supposed to hold onto you without getting in the water myself?" I asked.

"Just keep an eye on me," Ruth Ann said. "If I lose my footing, I'll need to grab onto something."

"How about one of the poles?"

"Great," she said. I stood with a pole extended from my waist, as if I were fishing for Ruth Ann. I wasn't at all sure I could save my friend from drowning by holding a pole out to her. Maybe this wasn't such a great idea.

It was then that Mira screamed, "One's coming your way!"

Ruth Ann and I scanned the churning water. "There!" I said pointing to a dark shape that I imagined must be the fish.

"Where?" Ruth Ann said. "I can't see anything with the glare."

"There!" I said again, pointing just in front of her feet. I wasn't entirely sure I could even see it anymore. The water was moving too fast.

What should have been a road was a fast-moving river. I braced myself on what was now a shore and tossed the doctored fishing line into the ongoing current. Hopeful that Mira and I could catch something for lunch that was halfway edible, I turned to prayer. It was not the first time. Ever since it became clear to me that my marriage was on the rocks, I had turned to a higher power for comfort and a therapist for guidance.

Now seemed to be a good time to enlist the former.

I edged further from Mira. I had come to the writing conference anticipating some *me* time—what a joke! Not that there wasn't an element of adventure with this group of women, but I was concerned that this trip might turn into a disaster: that we would squabble, or worse.

Pushing those negative thoughts out of my head, I turned to the mission at hand. Staring at the churning water just seemed to amplify my swirling thoughts. *Had I made a mistake in divorcing*

Jess? Were the kids going to be okay? How much negativity had they internalized? The divorce had been a major topic of conversation in my extended family as I had been the first to go through one, with lots of running commentary, most of it unsolicited. I had struggled with the concept of divorce as my strict Catholic teachings had emphasized the sanctity of marriage. I remembered gazing at Jess the day we married and thinking, *this will be forever.* A black hawk had hovered over the ceremony; some had even joked about it being an omen. I had laughed it off at the time. But the joke was on me—or rather, on *us.* After an initial honeymoon period, Jess had become more verbally abusive. At first, I had tried to ignore the recriminations, the offhand jabs. Thinking that parenthood would cure all, I chose to push his comments aside and focus on my children. A mistake. Even after he consented to therapy, the insults just became more veiled and he surreptitiously chose to denigrate me when the kids and others were not around. A clever ploy. Finally, after extensive counseling, we decided it was best to separate. The kids were surprisingly accepting as at least we had agreed to an amicable settlement.

It still gnawed at me that Jess could be so accommodating where his children were concerned, but where I was concerned— that was another story. On a positive note, all of this had been fodder for my writing. In many ways the experience would test my ability to move on and adjust to a solo life.

My "sister" writers had been so supportive and non-judgmental when we had first met and formed a closed writing group. Although they were at varying stages of their lives and their experiences did not mirror mine, they got me. There was an unspoken bond that generated a sense of security. It was just what I needed right now.

I decided Ruth Ann looked stable enough, so I rethreaded the line with a new hook and baited it with a fat, squirmy worm. I felt an immediate pull on the fishing line when the worm hit the water. It was the tug I needed to reorient myself. No more tugging at heartstrings. *Yay for us! Just stick to the task, waiting for a bite on the line.* My compatriots were counting on us. When it became clear the tug was a false alarm, I sighed.

I saw Ruth Ann swipe with the net. "Ah, shoot! I see it now," she said. "There it goes." The tip of a tail barely broke the surface of the water, well downstream.

"This is going to be harder than we thought," Mira called out, still patiently on lookout.

"Maybe," Ruth Ann said.

"Don't be discouraged," I said just for her ears. "We can switch places, if you want."

"No, I can still do this for a while," Ruth Ann said.

We waited for what seemed like a half-hour, and the sun bore down, hot on our heads. "I'm going to have to get in the shade soon," I said.

"Oh, of course," Ruth Ann said, looking at me. "Are you okay?"

I opened my mouth to say that I was fine when Mira screamed, "Another *fiiiiishhh!*" as she pointed, jumping up and down.

"Ok, let's do this," I said.

"There, Ruth Ann," I said, throwing the pole to the grassy area on the bank and stepping carefully into the moving water with her. My finger followed the fish as it moved towards us, and Ruth Ann's eyes locked on it. She lowered the net slowly so she wouldn't spook it, and neither of us said another word. As the dark shape came toward us, it suddenly shifted and began swimming away from us, into the deeper water. Ruth Ann lunged. She must have been on the edge of the ditch as the water was suddenly near the top of her Wellies, much deeper than where I was standing before. I grabbed the tail of her shirt as she swung the net down and up. Pulling hard, she dragged the net to the surface. The fish was flipping and twisting, but he was in the net.

"*Woohoo!* We did it!" I screamed, throwing my free arm into the air.

Mira ran along the water's edge. "Fantastic! Yes!"

Ruth Ann and I sloshed out of the water and scrutinized our catch. "A trout. Maybe four pounds."

"Yeah, it's a small one. But, hey, it's something," Ruth Ann said.

"I'm not discounting it. It's just that the filets will be kinda small," I said, already imagining dividing the flesh between the six of us. Still, I didn't want to stand in the water to try to catch another one. We might spend an hour and get nothing.

"Let's go show them what we got," I said.

"We can open that can of peas, and have the peaches for dessert," Mira said. "A real lunch."

"Yep. A real lunch," I said. "Good job, ladies."

I picked up the pole I had thrown aside, and Ruth Ann took the other. She strung the fish through its gills with some of the line and then we walked back to The Inn. Our boots sloshed and squirted water. We took them off in unison and were thankfully now just in our shoes. My shoes were most likely ruined. Yet, once again, I didn't care.

"I'll filet it," I offered. "All we need now is a knife, a fry pan, and the woodstove or grill."

"Be my guest," Ruth Ann replied. "I never really liked cleaning the fish. I'll do the grill."

"I'll help," Mira said, and I high fived her. Then Ruth Ann reached over to do the same.

The Inn

Yes, I know. Yesterday, I was quite excited to welcome guests after such a long time of being without them. From such unexpected disuse, my portals were squeaking like a dissonant symphony of rusted instruments. My strong shoulders holding the bones of my beams, hewn from nearby trees, were weary from indifference. But that was yesterday. Was this but a small taste—mind you, a nibble—of what I'd have to endure with new owners?

This unexpected group was oddly comprised of head-strong women. So damned unpredictable! They acted nothing like my former guests who languished in the comfort of my welcoming arms in the protection of quiet rooms. Not these new arrivals. I could smell trouble like the odor of their unwashed bodies and heard the tones of their bitching about getting out. They seemed so ungrateful, without the manners befitting me, overseen by such a courtly lord and elegant lady.

Heaven forbid these guests would become my new owners! They have already taken untold liberties on the property, tromping around exploring hidden treasures, sacred places, and gathering the fruits of my earth and water. What next?

Gracious me! There could be real trouble brewing. The two nosey busybodies, the ones called Joesie and Roxie, are flitting about like a couple of frisky mares in a freshly mown pasture. Worse yet, they've been scheming. Ever so clearly, I heard the word "snoop." Not young enough to be called whippersnappers, they could be conjuring up childish pranks. I watched when, with a knowing glance, they high-fived one another and backed away from the group without a word of explanation.

With my luck, these rabble-rousers will be the new owners of my domain. Might they replace my glorious solitude and beauty with a theme park? Maybe they'd make me into the ticket center with lines of impatient and noisy tourists—or worse, tear me down! Woe is me! My grumpiness is getting the best of me. I couldn't sleep a wink last night with all the wanderings.

And where might Hazel be? No doubt wandering or sleeping instead of monitoring these heathens. Hazel must particularly watch out for the one with the camera slung around her neck. Selfies and unexpected photo shoots were not welcome these days. They walked along with a spring to their steps. Happily, for me, the door squeaked when Roxie opened it. I love the way guests get nervous when they hear my sounds. Joesie had put her finger to her lips, as though they believed they were not alone. What now? I better listen and watch carefully. Don't want to miss a thing.

It was inevitable that they noticed and moved toward my remaining unexplored doors. T-R-O-U-B-L-E! I felt it deep inside my electrical connections that will be nibbled on by our mice if we don't get reconnected soon. There was so much mystery in this building. I thought some of the women understood how great I am. That Roxie woman has an eye for beauty, but I didn't like it when she touched me without permission. I could have retaliated. Sometimes, I do. Maybe a hallucination is in order… or a mirage. I have to think that one through.

∽17∾

SNOOPS

After leaving the others to their fishing escapades, we made our way up The Inn's main staircase to explore. Reaching the second floor without any mishap, my eyes followed Roxie's finger pointing first to the right, then to the left. With a more determined pull by Roxie on the camera strap, I snapped a picture of Eve and Charles' carved bedroom door. We wanted to be discreet but also wanted pictures of the unique carvings.

"Maybe Deidre couldn't deal with the uncertainty and turned back; she'll be fine on her own," I said.

"Maybe she'll find something to do," Roxie answered. "We need some life in this silent movie." I wished that Roxie's voice could have been more of a whisper. "Don't be such a worry wart. What are you afraid of, Joesie?"

"Nothing. I'm a military brat. Anyhow, what's the worst that could happen? Haven't seen anything dangerous yet. Let's hope it stays that way, Roxie."

I turned the knob of the next closed door and pushed it open. A grey form came scampering out and ran across Roxie's right foot. My hand instinctively covered Roxie's mouth, stifling her scream. Poor Roxie—she'd been the obstacle course for a runaway mouse! "*Blech*!" I breathed, wiping Roxie's spittle on my now-grungy clothes.

"Yikes!" she said. "Look at the hair on my arms. Not so funny, Joesie. What if it'd been you or better yet, Mira?" Soon we both shook with stifled laughter.

Once in the room, we closed the door and were captivated by what we saw. It was the latest surprise and had us turning around and around like two spinning tops. First, we focused on a window seat crowded with porcelain dolls and stuffed animals. I pointed to the cat sitting in the middle of the pile. "It looks like my cat, Mabel," I whispered. "I'll call this one Pickwick, Pickie for short." With that, the cat hissed and jumped off the seat, coppery eyes ablaze. "Obviously pissed off and *not stuffed*. Guess it didn't like the name."

"My nose and eyes are full of dust the damned cat raised up," Roxie said. "One more unexpected scare and you'll have to give me mouth-to-mouth resuscitation."

"That's a negative, Roxie. Devotion only goes so far."

"I'll try to get the darker side of your humor," Roxie blurted as she managed a nervous giggle. "I'm petrified of cats—and mice. In fact, animals and other critters are not my passion."

"I often wonder if animals can read our thoughts and pick up on our feelings. And babies. Don't you wonder what babies would think if they knew what they were eating—mashed peas, or worse? Then their parents scare them with warnings about all kinds of stuff. Be careful of this or that. Why else would cats scare some people but make others feel cuddly and happy?" Roxie didn't bother to respond. As if to apologize for his rude behavior, Pickie ran over, purring and rubbing against Roxie's legs, then retreated into the shadows.

Roxie, shaking off her cat phobia, focused on a cherry-wood cradle on the far wall that was full of lacy, dainty pillows as well as more dolls in lace dresses, scads of Steiff animals, Madame Alexander and Barbie dolls, and assorted rag dolls and antiquities. Among the stuffed animals was a small tiger cat. It spontaneously meowed.

"I pray that animal doesn't decide to jump out, too," Roxie pleaded, looking up toward heaven, hands clasped in a prayer-like pose. She moved from object to object. She stopped and hovered

in front of an oval, gilded frame above the crib. It held a portrait
of a chubby-cheeked baby with curly hair and a high lace collar
framing her face.

"Isn't she gorgeous?"

"Roxie, you might think you'd never seen a beautiful child
before."

"I can't help it if I regret never having had a child, especially a
daughter to have dressed to the nines. Wonder who this beauty is?"
Roxie answered her own musing. "Maybe it's Baby Broadhurst."

"Who?"

"You remember, the small grave Mira saw on her promenade
last night."

I nodded. "Thanks for the reminder. Guess that info didn't
make it to my brain's diminishing storage disk."

"Never seen so many damn doors in one place," Roxie said.
"This is better than *Let's Make A Deal*. I perish to think what might
await us behind so many portals."

"No, save that one for last," I blurted and retreated a few steps
as Roxie reached for the middle door. "I don't know why, but I
feel like it's a door to be saved. You know, the icing on the cake.
Let's start with this one and see what we find."

"Okay, what's the difference? We hope to try them all eventually. So, here's to a prize behind Door Number One."

"Oh, look! Maybe this room was for a governess—or a nanny."
Roxie couldn't resist fingering the coverlet on the bed and curtains.
"Dimity Swiss," she concluded.

"I haven't the slightest idea what 'Dimity Swiss' is. Never heard
it formally named before, Roxie. You're a treasure trove of information—our own guide to antiquities."

Roxie responded with a proud pounding of her amply
endowed bosom as she moved past a chest of drawers and a table
with a washing bowl on an oak stand. "Wow, I bet there were a
lot of stories washed clean in this old ceramic pitcher."

We backed out of the room and opened Door Number Two. It
was a large closet. Adding to our perplexing discoveries, we found
an abundant array of books, toys, baby clothes, blankets, and

sheets for the crib. Roxie fingered a couple of dresses and seemed stunned by their texture.

"There's more stuff here than any child would ever need," was my feeling.

"Eve mentioned that she never had any children," Roxie mused.

"Yeah, conspicuous, dust-collecting items. Strange for me to be in a closet. Takes me back to my childhood, hiding from thunderstorms. Oh well, add mine to our collection of oddities. Someone must have left the door open during a storm. Looks like they were expecting more children," I added.

"Let's move on—just reminds me of what Ben and I never had." Roxie's look was far-away.

"That's another thing we have in common. We're both childless."

"Don't see anything remarkable here to text home about, even if we could. Not even a good story yet."

Skipping over the next door, we jumped back when opening another door. It turned out to be a tall wooden bookcase that had started to fall on us: another closet. Together, we shoved it back in and moved onto yet another room, wondering what was behind Door Number Three.

"Will you look at this? Military! Right up your alley, Joesie! A sword collection. We could have a picture with a couple of these, huh?"

"Yeah! Here, pose with this one, Roxie. I'll snap. You can tell Ben you found a secret weapon. Wouldn't my dad have had a good old time with this stuff? Bet he could've identified all the British ribbons and badges. Look at the woolen uniform! Can you imagine these itchy pants rubbing your thighs? Wonder how many moths have lived off the threads of these old British uniforms— and all these piles of letters and newspapers wrapped with string and ribbons?"

"But look what else is here," Roxie gulped. "Photos! Piles of pictures in and out of frames. So many of them with people in costumes. Seems as though this was once a real party place. We came here at the wrong time. Wish we could have been here back in the days when there were parties. Look at all these pictures."

"I can almost *feel* the material of the costumes they're wearing."

"You are such a Sarah Heartburn, Joesie. Definitely, you belong in another era. It's like you came out of one of the pictures."

"Yeah, especially the one with the cowgirl get-up. Boots and all," I said, strutting with my feet apart and thumbs under my armpits.

"Joesie, what are you up to?"

"This snooping is such fun," Joesie said with a giggle. "Got to get one picture to remind us of this alternative universe to show the rest. And look at all these handkerchiefs. So many colors, and they're all embroidered. Linen, cotton, lace. I'll be damned. Here's one with an *R*, and another with a *J*. Would you believe, scattered right on top of this table are four more—*RA, D,* and *M,* and even an *A*? Do you believe in coincidences?"

"I plead the Fifth for now, Joesie."

"What'll we do if someone comes up and finds us? Think up a good excuse, please."

"Like what? 'Oh, excuse me, but we heard a dripping sound and decided to investigate upstairs?' Come on, we still have one more door to open. This may be fascinating, but this room gives me the creeps. It's like a mausoleum. But for whom?" Roxie interrupted herself as she walked back into the hallway and immediately turned the handle on the door we had saved for last.

"This is going to be good; I can just feel it." We locked pinkie fingers for good luck. I barely caught myself from a likely fall. I grabbed the small penlight attached to my camera case and turned it on. It flickered as I took a bunch of pictures.

"I don't have a strong enough beam. Another technological invention about to fail," I reported to Roxie, who was close behind me. A steep set of stairs going down faced us, in an odd configuration I couldn't make out. "Here, take a look for yourself. But remember, when this is out, so is our snooping in the dark. None of us brought survival gear. We don't even know if there are matches if the candles downstairs burn out."

We agreed we were facing a steep, narrow staircase. Carefully sidestepping down the angled stairs, we encountered numerous steps, a landing after each set. We held onto the cold stone walls to steady ourselves on treads that begged for smaller feet. The stairs stopped abruptly.

"My God, what have we done? Where the hell are we? Will we ever get out of here?" I fretted.

"Listen, Joe," Roxie said, "the larger question is, if we're out of this godforsaken place, will we ever make it back home?"

"Watch it! Don't pile into me," I pleaded.

"Another damn door! Joesie, help me have a quick look with the flashlight—whatever we can see," Roxie said, groping from behind me with her long arms and height advantage.

"Thanks. I think I can see angels carved on this—halo and wings on something. Somebody must have had an angel fetish. What is that sound, that fluttering?" I asked.

"Must be birds outside. Or bats? Or the carved angels?" Roxie asked.

"Don't be ridiculous, you can't hear birds from down here and bats wouldn't be down here either." We kept going as the ground slowly inclined then leveled off and we were greeted by some more strange carvings.

"Angels," we said in unison.

"Look at all these doors. Was there a fire sale on doors from heaven? Girlfriend! I never saw such ugly angel-like creatures," I said, grunting while helping Roxie push the heavy, oddly carved door. It opened just enough for us to fit through. We almost fell into the back of a sofa facing a glowing, inviting fireplace. Looking into what appeared to be a kitchen, we could see a large white cat sitting smack in the center of a square, wooden table set.

"I've had my fill of critters, Joesie. You go first."

"Okay but let me snap a photo or two. I hope there's battery left. Please, trusty camera, give me a few more shots. Guess it depends on whether the flash is necessary. Times like this I wish I were more of a techie."

"Help, help, help!" called a familiar pathetic voice. A figure seemed to grow out of the front of the sofa, like a whale coming up out of the sea. We pointed at each other until one of us coughed up something coherent.

"It's okay, Hazel," Roxie calmly said. "Don't be afraid. It's just us, Roxie and Joesie. Remember? We're part of the unexpected crew you let in during the storm yesterday. Sorry for the intrusion, we got—um—lost. We don't mean to interrupt your day."

Hazel gave a nod of recognition and seemed relieved.

"Merlin, Merlin, Merlin!" Though his haunches were raised, and his thick white fur coat stood straight up, the feline leapt from the table and obediently sauntered over to his mistress.

"My baby, baby, baby." Hazel picked him up, sat back down, and set her furry friend in her lap. His body looked like a white coverlet. He was purring. Then Hazel cooed into his neck. "Please sit down and join me and Merlin. Relax, ladies. With a name like Merlin, how bad can he be?"

"With a name like Merlin, can he use his magic to get us out of here?" I asked. *We're delighted to have a visit and chat with you, Hazel.*

"Thank you, that would be lovely. Merlin is a pure Persian Longhair, at least that's what we British call them. They're known for their round, expressive faces and beautiful long fur as well as their affection toward their owners. Right, Merlin? They need to be groomed often to stay as beautiful as my Merlin. I brush him at least once a day and he loves it. Enough about Merlin."

"Perhaps you can tell us a little more about The Inn," Roxie said quite spontaneously.

Hazel rose from the sofa and placed Merlin in the cradle next to her seat. She walked to the other side of the room saying, "Tea, tea, tea." She set the teapot on the woodstove insert. Her plump body jiggled as she walked back from the kitchen. She daintily placed the tray with cups and saucers, a sugar bowl, lemons, and a pitcher of milk, on the low table that faced us.

"That milk smells rancid," I whispered.

"I'll take mine with lemon," Roxie said.

Once seated, Hazel absentmindedly swiped at a few wisps of hair that had escaped from the bun at the nape of her neck as she placed Merlin back in her lap. The silence was deafening. I couldn't stand it. "I would love to take a picture of you and this wonderful display of tea," I said to fill it.

Hazel smoothed her hair as Merlin jumped out of her lap. "Me, me, me. Pretty, pretty, pretty. I'm happy to tell you about The Inn. Just what is it you want to know? Wouldn't you first like a cup of tea? I specialize in tea. Tea, tea, tea. Why do you two look so surprised? We'll have a short chinwag before I have to start cooking for tonight's dinner. I expect Jimmy John will bring over some fresh venison soon."

Roxie and I looked at one another. "Dinner?" Roxie asked.

"Don't look so astounded. Well, you see, it's been our tradition to…"

She was interrupted by a succession of events: the door opened as though the fierce winds from the previous night had begun again, and a familiar mouse—or a close relative—ran out through it, as did Merlin, right on its tail.

"Good thing Mira isn't here. She would have squished him in a heartbeat," I mused.

"Sir Lance! Stop! Stop! Stop!"

"Who ever heard of naming a mouse?" Roxie whispered.

"I have. In children's books," I said. We glanced at each other. "We don't want to be rude but—"

"Bye! Bye! Bye!" Roxie shouted as we ran out the door, close behind Merlin and Lancelot.

We stopped to catch our breath behind a large apple tree. "Whew, this place and its residents are really wacko," I said.

"This place is really weird, weird, weird," I said. "How come Hazel stops repeating herself whenever she's holding Merlin? And what was she about to say before she was interrupted, Roxie?"

We both shrugged.

The Inn

Whew! Quick thinking on my part, sending out the mouse. Ditzy Hazel! She had diarrhea of the mouth again. No telling what she could have revealed. The poor thing could barely remember her own name to boot, but when she speaks, you never knew what might come out, often in triplicate. Our lovely Hazel is so devoted to this place. And she and Eve and Charles doted on Jimmy John. Jimmy John still has a way with Hazel. He has been talking about putting her away in a rest or assisted-living home, but I don't think he would really do it. Let's see what the travelers do after lunch.

～18～

MYSTERIOUS
PATHS

God bless Ruth Ann, who had found coffee this morning to feed our caffeine habit. I didn't care how it tasted or that it lacked half-and-half. Manna from heaven is what it was. Maybe our breath didn't smell bad. Maybe our underarms weren't screaming for deodorant. Maybe our hair didn't need washing. Maybe we just had to make the best of this puzzling but interesting situation. Maybe later, we could check the cars to see if we had left anything in them we could use. Phooey. Of course, we hadn't! All of that stuff was safely ensconced at the Abenaki Lodge. I heard Roxie wonder aloud if anyone had sent out a search party for us.

We all sat in the living room, sipping our coffee, nibbling on our meager fish lunch. Allison pondered how well six men would get along in our situation. Then the comments flew around the room. Ruth Ann chimed in, "Women are so much stronger than men. We've been multi-tasking all our lives."

"Yeah," I added. "You never see a man in the fields with a baby on his back."

Allison broke in, "You'd think they invented multi-tasking."

Joesie piped in, "All men would do in this situation is shoot themselves in the foot. Sometimes I wonder…."

Deidre interrupted. "I know my husband is bright, but he has tunnel vision like most men."

"My obstetrician tried to kick Avrom out of the delivery room when I was in labor with our son. He was white as a sheet and looked like he would faint any minute," I giggled. "Avrom made it by staying at the head of the delivery table."

"I agree," Allison echoed. "My ex-husband couldn't stand the fact that I was not perfectly healthy. He thought it was my fault or something. Between morning sickness and this cold and that flu, he had a point. It seemed I was always under the weather. Mine were just everyday ailments. That's life."

"I don't know why you're talking about men—you won't believe what we just saw," blurted Roxie.

"Can it be summarized in twenty-five words or less?" Deidre croaked.

"Oh, Deidre, don't be so snarky," I admonished.

"Anyway, Joesie and I went upstairs and snooped around. We found made-up bedrooms…"

"So?" Deidre said. "That's what you should find at an inn. What's so unbelievable about that?"

"Let me finish," Roxie said. "A nursery, a stairway, a cat, *and* a pet mouse!"

"Stairs?" Ruth Ann asked. "Where to?"

"Hazel and Merlin's cottage," Joesie interjected.

"Merlin who?" Allison asked.

"Not a *who*. A *what*. Remember? Hazel's white cat? She picked up the damn cat and she suddenly stopped repeating herself," Roxie explained.

"Magical Merlin?" I asked sarcastically. "And a mouse, too? I hope there aren't any more mice."

"Me too. This mouse was a pet. Hazel called him Sir Lance," Joesie explained.

"This is getting creepier. I'm leaving as soon as possible," Deidre responded.

"I see this as an adventure," Allison said. "We won't be here forever. Think of the stories we can write."

"First we have to get out of here," Deidre mused.

"Oh, just think of this as a time out," Ruth Ann said. There was a pause.

Joesie looked thoughtful. "Okay, okay, okay" she said, grinning. "I can go with a time out."

"Are we experiencing an alternate universe? Is this a sign of changes to come? It's hard to tell these days," I said.

Deidre piped in, "Oh Mira, speaking of menopause, my family thought they were living with a creature from another world when I went through 'the change.' My moods are still crazy."

"I know I'm not in menopause because I'm too young," I said. "Damn, I still get my period. I told my gynecologist that I think I will go to my grave wearing a tampon. He said it was possible."

"Well," Roxie added, "instead of getting hots I get warms. Marriage is hard enough without raging hormones."

"Yes, well," I continued, "I was working part-time when my husband decided he needed a new car and a bigger boat. I reminded him calmly that he promised me a new kitchen. Needless to say, we got the car and the boat. How could I complain? I was raised to be a good girl. My mother had violent mood swings. I never knew whether I was going to be hit or hugged. I guess that feeling of obedience carries over today."

"There she goes again—off topic." Joesie said, under her breath.

"One of my lasting memories was when we docked our boat, *The Adventurer*, in Norfolk, Virginia. I was standing on the bow, when I suddenly saw a brand-new Hatteras fishing boat aiming for the slip beside us. The captain seemed somewhat inexperienced, and his wife looked terrified. He ordered his two children to sit down and shut up, then yelled for his wife to grab the forward starboard line first. She hesitated as she knew that starboard meant the right side. The good Lord was with her. Her aim was on point and the dockhand tied the line to the cleat. Then he yelled, 'Okay, okay, now the stern line. Come on, come on, dammit! Get that stern line before we hit that big old yacht beside us.' Why do we always have to deal with their toys?" I asked, smiling.

Ruth Ann turned to Allison and, in an audible whisper, said, "I can't believe Mira's story," Allison shrugged.

"The point of this tale is?" Deidre asked.

⌒∽⌒

It was early afternoon. The sun was trying to creep out between the low-hanging clouds.

"We have to get out of here," I said. "Even if we just take a walk, at least we'll be doing something. Let's find that cemetery I found last night. We'll have to go out the back door. Higher ground. And maybe we'll find Jimmy John. Jeez, he was *so* hot! I'm sure he can help us."

"I hope there are some old gravestones. I love to take rubbings of the names and dates," said Ruth Ann.

"Great! I'll bring my camera. Remind me to show you my photo collections of cemeteries, especially old ones," Joesie added. "Who in the world is Jimmy John? And what's *The Adventurer* got to do with him? Was he a different fantasy?"

Deidre followed with, "Holy cow, Mira. He has to help us get out of here."

"Sorry, girls. He's the caretaker. I'll fill you in along the way," I said.

"Okay, let's go find Jimmy John. Do you think we'll find the cemetery? Is it kind of creepy?" Ruth Ann asked. "I like to wander through cemeteries reading all the headstones. Each one tells a story."

"Maybe not so much in the daytime," I answered. We gulped down the remainder of our lunch. Our shoes were still damp from the day before and the fishing mission. We stuffed our feet into them anyway, wiggled our toes, stood up, and stretched.

"Okay, troops, off we go!" I exclaimed.

"Oh, my gosh, look at Joesie," Deidre exclaimed. We all turned around to watch our friend carefully putting fresh lipstick on her lips and positioning her veiled hat on her head.

"Well, I do declare," Allison said in her best southern accent, "Here comes Miss Joesie, ready for afternoon tea."

Giggling, we walked out the door into the dreary day, the sun behind the clouds. "I hope it's not going to rain again," Joesie said.

We had not noticed the enormous trees surrounding the house, their leaves still dripping. Squirrels and chipmunks scampered over the wet leaf-covered ground. Birds sang. We paused to enjoy this play of nature, starring birds and wildlife that we city girls rarely got to enjoy. The birds ignored us, busy devouring the worms that had been washed up from their underground hiding places.

"Look at the worms." Allison noted. "There's enough bait if we need to go fishing again."

"God forbid," Deidre whined.

Joesie stopped to pick up small rocks.

"How incredible. Even here I think of the old Jewish custom," I said as she handed some to me.

"What custom?" Ruth Ann asked.

"You put them on the grave to let people know someone's been there," Mira answered. "I've put them on my grandmother's grave."

"Why?" Ruth Ann countered. "Isn't that a bit strange?"

"Not really. It's a sign of respect. I used to see my mother place stones on graves," Joesie said. "Jewish tradition. I was the product of a mixed marriage. Despite my father being Christian, I followed my mother's Jewish tradition by placing the stones on graves. I remember going to the edge of our back porch and seeing a trail. Let's see if it's there."

I turned to see my five compadres ambling behind me. Allison looked as if she would rather stay inside, but as usual she was not complaining. I had to stifle a giggle at Joesie's headgear, a hat with a veil hanging over her face. She called it her sunscreen.

A stab of fear nagged at my brain. *Maybe we shouldn't do this.* But the trail was where I remembered it, and I stepped off the porch onto the rocky path. The others stayed in line behind me like a colony of ants. We seemed to walk for so long, I had the feeling we shouldn't have gone this way. In the daylight, it was clear there were multiple paths. The trail we chose was uneven and full of holes made by gophers and moles. Thick vines grew around and above us. Ruth Ann asked if anyone knew the difference between poison ivy or poison sumac, and plain weeds. Deidre said she did.

You would have thought Joesie's headgear would limit her vision. She was the one who spotted the bushes ahead of us, laden with raspberries. I would have left them, having tasted them last night, but one after another, we stuffed our mouths with sweetness. Deidre suggested we continue exploring to see if we could find the cemetery.

"I'm not going. Darling Mira, were you dreaming last night?" Roxie asked.

"Maybe," I said, doubtfully. "But I think it's just over that hill." I wanted to go on. Deidre and Ruth Ann decided to go with me. Roxie, Allison, and Joesie turned back, linking arms, singing, and skipping toward The Inn.

I watched as a bird flew over the rise. I imagined that this creature would look down and see a young man tending the graves of his family, carefully straightening the gravestones, and weeding the plots. Maybe Jimmy John would even say a prayer when he was finished. Maybe he wondered if he would ever see me again. It was then that I knew I couldn't stop, even if I had to go alone. I was on a mission.

Ruth Ann, Deidre, and I started walking again. We laughed at our shoes that were caked with mud. Most of us weren't used to this terrain and just after she stepped over a fallen tree, Deidre landed on her backside. I gasped and held my breath. This usually well-dressed woman was sitting in a pool of gooey brown mud. Good thing she had put on leggings and the t-shirt she'd bought for her daughter at the Destiny Life Institute. It wouldn't have been a good look had she stayed in her wrap dress. She started to giggle. It was contagious. The three of us laughed until we were teary. Ruth Ann and I helped our friend up. We all sat on the trunk of the fallen tree. Deidre picked up leaves to wipe off the mud. Ever sensible, Ruth Ann suggested we stop to enjoy the scenery. Deidre agreed. "It'll give my clothes a chance to dry. Dear Lord, whatever am I going to wear?"

"It's just over the next rise. I know it is. I'll go up there and look, okay? But you guys have to promise to wait for me. I'll be back soon. I'll just go up a little to see if I can find the cemetery. I'll be back."

Ruth Ann volunteered to go with me. I looked both ways and found an opening between two waist-high bushes. We made ourselves as small as we could and walked sideways through the opening, trying to stay as dry as possible. There was a bench of some sort that looked as though it had been made from a fallen tree. When we got closer, we saw a beautiful clear lake and a small cabin overlooking the water on the other side. A rowboat bobbed in the water.

"See, that must be where he lives. I couldn't see it in the dark."

I stepped over the rise and started down into the clearing. My jeans were covered with small sticky burrs. As I bent to pick them off, I heard a loud voice. "Hello! I see you've brought a friend this time."

I found my tongue and introduced Ruth Ann to Jimmy John. In seconds, I might have well been invisible. Their eyes locked and the electricity was palpable. Ruth Ann looked into Jimmy John's eyes and said, "We were looking for the old cemetery, if it exists."

His eyes fixed on hers. He said, "Yes, there's a cemetery here on the grounds. Are you interested in such things?"

"Well, yes, I'm fascinated with old graves. They tell amazing stories if you listen," Ruth Ann replied. They were my sentiments, too. I was happy my friend had spoken them.

"It's just behind my cabin. C'mon." We followed Jimmy John around behind the cabin that was built of hand-hewn logs and had large windows and a roof with asphalt shingles. At last, about a hundred yards ahead of us, we saw the cemetery. There were a number of old graves. I was afraid to ask about the two newer mounds. *Oh my God!* I'd thought I'd been hallucinating last night. Now it was clear. I asked about baby Louisa Broadhurst. Jimmy John had mentioned she was Hazel's daughter.

Ruth Ann closed her eyes as if to say a prayer and Jimmy John couldn't seem to stop staring at her. To give them privacy, I told them I would walk around and meet them in front of the house in a bit. As I approached the front of the cabin, Deidre walked out from behind the trees, into the clearing.

"You've been gone a while," Deidre said breathlessly. "I'm so glad I found you. Where's Ruth Ann?"

"She's with Jimmy John back by the graves. Let's just wait here. They don't need a chaperone," I said reluctantly.

Deidre looked puzzled and then laughed out loud. "What a story this'll make!"

❦19❦

Raspberries

Joesie led Roxie and me back through the woods. Mira, Ruth Ann, and Deidre stayed behind in the clearing. My energy lagged as I dropped back a bit, even though I was already bringing up the rear. Most likely, I figured, Roxie was tired too. She was just ahead of me, and I had slowed my pace to match hers. The path narrowed in places, and the leafy underbrush was thick. The long soaking rain had made the foliage an intense green. The moist dirt gave off a pleasant earthy odor. Someone had planned these paths by laying steppingstones where mud tended to form.

"I'm thinking about a nap right about now," Roxie said to me, looking down at the path as the three of us walked single file.

"Sounds good to me," I muttered, just for her ears.

"Well, we might as well keep heading back," Joesie called out. She stood in yet another clearing ahead of us and announced, "I'm not sure how I could have gotten so turned around, but who cares about the cemetery. But I'm glad I gave Mira my rocks."

"I don't care, either," I said. "I was fighting the current when we were fishing this morning and I'm tuckered out. All I want to do is go back and take a rest. This survival thing is exhausting."

"This whole thing is getting to be a real B-I-T-C-H!" Joesie said, stamping her feet.

"You're right, Joesie. This is wearing on me too!"

"One night was an adventure but now I wanna go home," I said, echoing Joesie's tone.

Roxie tried to rally the troops with, "Hey, girls, suck it up. We can keep going a little more, right?"

"I'm going to have to pee," I said. At least I was well hydrated.

"You know what that means, don't you?" Roxie giggled.

"Yeah, I know," I said. "Please keep an eye out for bears, won't you?"

Roxie announced, "Alert the media! Allison's got to pee! But seriously, Allison, you can't wait?"

"No. I thought I could. There's no way."

We stopped and scanned the area. "You could go up there, behind that tree," Joesie said. "You got a tissue?"

"I do," Roxie said, and she rummaged in the front pocket of her tailored pants and pulled out a perfectly folded rectangle of tissues.

"Thanks," I said. "I'm going to litter with this though. There's no way that I'm taking that tissue back with me."

"Oh, it's okay," Joesie said. "This is one of those times when it's acceptable to litter. Besides that, the tissue will disintegrate in a few weeks."

"Go ahead, we won't watch," Roxie said.

"Don't forget to check for poison ivy," Joesie said.

"I didn't think much about those things until now, as I'm dropping my pants to my ankles. Something about the vulnerability—I'll be careful. *Leaves of three, let them be.* Does anyone know how to identify poison oak or poison sumac other than that?"

"Oh, come on, now. All you have to do is hover above the ground. Just don't let your naked ass touch anything but that tissue," Roxie said.

"Good advice for life, maybe," Joesie said.

"All-righty then," I said. "Here goes."

I trudged up the slight incline. Mud and wet leaves clung to my shoes. My ankle twisted slightly as I stepped into a little hole. I caught myself. Josie and Roxie exploded with chastisements to be careful. I made my way to the opposite side of a tree so that I would have some privacy and unfastened the top button of my jeans, slid the zipper down, pulled my jeans and panties down to my ankles in one motion, then quickly dropped to a squat. The cool summer air brushed my sensitive skin, and my nakedness distracted me. If a bear came up behind me, I wouldn't even see the darn thing. The women below talked quietly in tones that were designed to keep me calm. I didn't get the sense that they were watching for any bears coming up behind me.

"Watch for bears!" I shouted down to them to scare any bears in the area. Damn. Anything could sneak up on my bare ass, like snakes or spiders. I had to finish quickly. How could I escape with my pants down around my ankles?

I felt shaky and preoccupied, and my bladder cramped and refused to release the built-up urine. I closed my eyes, then I panicked and opened them and looked behind me. *Maybe I should have my back to the tree's trunk,* I thought. I shifted my feet bit by bit, still in a crouch, when I felt it. Something furry tickled my bare skin.

"Aaaaahhhh! Crap, what was that?" I tried to jump up, but with my pants holding my feet together like handcuffs, I fell over into the wet leaves. I heard laughter, and then someone called out to ask me what was going on.

"I'm fine," I said as I righted myself. So much for not letting anything touch my skin but the tissue. I looked down where I had been and saw a thick black-and-green striped caterpillar with furry spikes.

"It was just a caterpillar," I called. The damn thing was still reaching up in the air as if to see if it could latch on to me. I moved uphill a bit and squatted again, still with my back to the tree so I could keep an eye on the interloper. The scent of urine, sharp and pungent, reached my nose at about the same time as the stream trickled down towards the bug. It lurched and flipped itself, and I almost screamed again. I finished, swiped once with Roxie's tissue, and yanked my pants back on.

Running down the little hill back to the path, I could see Joesie and Roxie staring off to the side of path. Joesie screamed. "They're raspberries!" She pointed at something a few yards away.

We couldn't get enough of the scrumptious berries here on the grounds of The Inn.

"Come on! You've got to see this." Roxie yelled.

Bushes of plump red raspberries lined both sides of the path. Numerous untended trails cut spaces between the bushes, even though the branches had overgrown most of the space. Still, we could walk in between rows and rows of raspberries if we were careful.

"What a find, Joesie. This should improve the mood around here," Roxie said.

"Oh my God, they're delicious." Roxie said, popping one into her mouth.

I pulled one from the stem. Tiny star-shaped leaves surrounded the base of each berry. The berry was so ripe that my fingers crushed it, releasing bright red juice that dripped to the ground. My mouth salivated at the sight. Sweetness and a hint of tartness hit my tongue at the same time, and I chewed the seeds lightly and swallowed it only a split second before I had another one in my mouth.

"This is why they call this place Raspberry Hill," Joesie said.

"Amen to that!" I said. "Just in time. I needed something to give me some energy, and here we are."

We held back the sharp brambles for each other and gorged until we were satisfied.

"Just delicious," Roxie said. "Let's fill my shirt with berries and take them back to The Inn to eat later."

"You're not worried about staining your shirt?" I asked. "That's a switch."

"What do you mean *later*? I don't know about you, but I'm leaving this place *asap*." Joesie said.

Finally, we reached The Inn. As we mounted the back steps of the porch, we were greeted by Merlin, who lingered by the open garbage can. The cover must have blown off in the storm. Though the small fish had yielded only two filets about the size of my hands, Deidre had found a can of slightly rancid shortening, with little left, towards the back of the pantry. Still, I figured the flavor of the fish would be stronger, and there was just enough to grease the fry pan to keep the fish from sticking. I had used it all, scraping the can. Deidre found salt and pepper too. With the peas and the can of peaches for dessert, we had made a pretty decent lunch, although a slim one. It certainly would not hold us until dinner. My stomach growled. Burning more calories with this hike didn't make sense to me. I walked slower, saving energy. I needed Eve's couch and her bathroom, too. My bladder was starting to fill again. It was only a matter of time before I was really uncomfortable. If we got back in time, we might be able to catch another fish for dinner. It was just as possible that we would remain hungry until we could leave tomorrow.

After filling our bellies with raspberries, we regrouped and plopped into our same seats. My stomach let out a small burp, and the hint of the trout reminded me of lunch. We could smell the fish remnants, from the open door to the porch, beginning to rot in the open garbage can.

"I wonder how my husband would feel about this place?" Roxie asked. "I wonder where that lid is? Joesie, want to go look for it?"

"Okay. On my way," Joesie snickered.

"Husband? I'm just glad I don't have one anymore," I said.

"What happened?" Joesie asked. Then she quickly added, "Maybe I shouldn't have asked."

"Oh, no. It's okay. It's been a while. I'm over it." I paused, took a breath, then continued. "I always tell people that we didn't grow apart. It's just that we were never really together in the first place."

"Oh, I know couples like that," Roxie said.

"Yeah, we didn't get into a brawl—no black and blue marks, just a bruised ego. But we sure weren't super happy together either. In retrospect, he was verbally abusive. We weren't anything, really. The kids were our life, and beyond that, well, I don't know what we were."

"Did you love him?"

"Yes. Yeah, I did. Still do, I guess. I just couldn't live with him. Anytime I was sick, I decided that I could take better care of myself without him. We're too different. I think we just got married too young. He was the principal at the school where I landed my first teaching job right out of college."

Joesie turned around and said, "Yeah, I think a lot of young marriages have trouble." I hadn't realized she was listening; it was a nice confirmation. She knew my whole story already. I had told her last year when we had had lunch together one day after class. There was no judgment. If anything, these women celebrated life's challenges for the material they could offer to our writing.

"You know," I said to them, "Jess never really knew me. I suppose I didn't know the real him either. I wanted to. It's just that he didn't want to share his deepest feelings."

"Do men know how to do that?"

"I wonder, after so many years, if Ben and I really know each other," Roxie mused.

I thought about how Jess had only known me with blue eyes. I had hidden the fact that I had blue contact lenses. I had avoided sleeping at his place, or having him stay at mine, for months. He had figured I was old-fashioned. When I finally spent the night for the first time, I had waited until the bedroom was dark to take them out. I had planned to wake early to put them back in before he could notice. Yet, he was up before me, making coffee and pancakes. I had tried to sneak into the bathroom. He came into the bedroom before I did. My brown eyes startled him, but he politely recovered. Now, I wondered if maybe I had made a mistake in deceiving him. Such a small deception—but wasn't every bit of makeup the same, though? Still...."

Roxie glanced at me, "Are you okay?"

"Sure," I said. "Just thinking of a new reason why things didn't work. It's surprising after all these years to see something else that was problematic."

"Well, at least you keep recognizing that it wasn't meant to be," Joesie said. "I have a friend who is constantly fussing over her divorce. She's not sure she should have gone through with it."

"You know, I think a lot of people who divorce have moments like those," I replied. "I know that I am better off now, but there are times when I wonder—you know, divorce isn't ever really final. Unless the person dies, you hope there might have been *some* kind of a chance."

"I guess you're talking about marriages that aren't horribly abusive," Joesie said.

"Heck, even then," I insisted. "I would bet people in hellish marriages still find themselves daydreaming even after the judge stamps the documents. If only we had done *this*, or if only I had done *that*.

⁓

As we gathered at The Inn, Roxie said, "Look at this. My fingers, lips, and clothes are stained, but I couldn't care less. Can you imagine that? Me, of all people."

My eyes adjusted. "I'm still a little woozy. Was it the raspberries?"

"Strange, I feel woozy, too," Joesie said.

"Think it was the raspberries? They tasted so good going down, but I feel a little weird, too." Roxie agreed.

Our full bellies murmured in agreement. Were we all caught in the moment?

"When we get back to our normal lives, raspberry stains will be a faint memory," Roxie said.

This was just a temporary change. I was going to have no trouble getting back to clean clothes and a refrigerator full of food. Forget about my blue lenses.

⁓

∽ 20 ∽

INN THE LIBRARY

After safely making it back, we regrouped. The sunroom/parlor had become our adopted all-purpose and planning room. "I'd do anything to distance myself from that stinking fish smell," I remarked. "Must be coming from the garbage. How I wish the three of you fisherwomen could wash your hands with lovely lavender soap. I'm still smelling fish."

Everyone stared at me in disbelief. Oops, I knew that negative comment out of my mouth would be a bad omen, considering all the efforts Allison, Mira, and Ruth Ann had made to capture and prepare lunch. I was once again compelled to explain yet another of my issues. I always seem to be uncomfortably inserting a foot into my open mouth and then offering a balancing apology.

"Joesie, I thought it was great. Considering we don't have too many choices for filling our guts, what's your problem?" Roxie scolded gently but deservedly.

"I loved the raspberries," I said. "All of you, please excuse my inconsiderate blurting out. This is what makes me appear as an ungrateful wicked witch. Sorry, I know that I should think first. Explanation forthcoming. As a kid, whenever my father took an infrequent leave, we'd head for our family cottage beside the Allegheny River in Western New York. It's west of here off old

Route 17. Fish was our staple food from the river—enduring and unpleasant aromas from the past."

"That sounds like fun," Allison said. "So, what's so bad about that?" She sounded so logical.

"Well, as usual for me," I said, "some history is in order as to why I passed on eating the gift from the swollen river. I didn't mean to be rude. I have a strong aversion. I cannot stomach the smell or taste of cooked fish. I only like the actual fishing itself. Now I love to go fly-fishing and catch-and-release. I still prefer living off the veggies grown by the farmer and his wife, who are living on and maintaining our riverside house in Western New York. The farmer still grows the food, and his wife spends days canning the fruits of their labor. I consider them my adopted family. How lucky Mother and I are to have the retreat we call Riverview, the perfect setting for writing with or without my husband! Maybe we all could go up there sometime. Open invitation."

"Got it, Joesie," Ruth Ann said. "Understood and apology accepted. I need some down time. I'm going to find a place to read."

"I'm going to find a quiet corner in the living room, to write," added Deidre. "I have a sudden inspiration to at least take some notes on what we've been through so far."

"I need some rest. Those fish were fighters," Allison said.

"Understandable, Allison. You look exhausted," comforted Mira. "I'm beginning to doubt my own eyes. Now, in in the light of day, I'm going back to the cemetery. See you all later back here at headquarters."

"Wait, Mira. What's your fascination with cemeteries?" Deidre asked. "It would be your third trip —are you really looking for Jimmy John?" Mira blushed in response.

"Don't be so snarky, Deidre," Roxie said. "It is about Jimmy John."

"Who's being snarky now?" Mira asked.

"So, what do you say we divide and conquer," our Mother Superior Roxie suggested. "I want to peruse the dining room. Think we can be unobtrusive and still be nosey? I'm revved from braving the upstairs and finding Hazel's cottage. Hope there's more to come."

"Well, I for one am dying to find the library," I continued, still wearing my veiled hat. "I can't get away from being a librarian. I'm always curious to see what people collect besides books in their libraries. Maybe I can get some ideas for the next story time. I often dress up and visit schools or libraries to read a story in character."

"How did you start all this? I mean—let's talk later and go look around while everyone is busy and it's still light." Roxie had cut it short and sweet. "How do you even know there's a library?"

"I don't," I emphasized. I continued, heeding Roxie's always-direct messages, "I can't imagine there isn't one—just betting on it. Anyhow, you're right, Roxie. Let's go. I've got to see more of this fascinating house firsthand in daylight."

Roxie and I exited what had turned into our common room. We tiptoed through the first floor like recalcitrant children. She gave me a thumbs up and a mischievous grin as we parted, and she turned toward the dining room we had seen when Eve first greeted us last night. It seemed like so many days ago, even though it had only been one. This time, the luscious deep mahogany wood struck me. It seemed to go around and up wherever my eyes wandered. Before heading to the library, I stood at the bottom of the grand staircase, wide at the bottom then narrowing in a spiral towards the second floor. It looked like the spiral even went up to a third floor. I was not brave enough to go there so I stayed on the ground floor.

For a passing moment, I didn't want the water covering the driveway to recede. Imagine that thought coming from me! It was another memory of the past: a frightening flood with possible adverse consequences. I thought how this was the most delightfully intimate interaction I'd had with any group of women, despite our years together at writing workshops. I needed to allow myself to have fun and enjoy the spontaneous moments of sharing. That would be a change and welcome escape for me. We were having such girlie fun with nothing from the outside world intruding on us—yet.

In the hallway in front of me, there were more doors like the ones I'd seen upstairs. I was trying to decide which door to pick. Would I win with a fabulous gift or lose with a *zonk*? This was better than a game show. Deciding to try the closest, Door Number One, for convenience's sake, I of course found it locked. Thinking that maybe there was a key behind the registration desk, I headed there and noticed a note on top of the guest book which read, in bright violet calligraphy, and dated today:

Hope you're having a good day at The Inn

Trying not to be distracted by the note, I continued on my quest to find the key. Sure enough, I found it conveniently labeled *Bibliothèque*. Success! I went back to the door, turned the key in the lock, and entered a paneled room lined with bookshelves. There were so many exciting collections to peruse, I hardly knew where to begin. The available light was filtering through the clouds of dust I had awakened. I scanned from left to right. Yellowed photographs, certificates, rocks, and clocks were the most obvious, then I was startled to see a cradle with a baby blanket.

It was similar, if not exactly the same, as the tattered magazine photo I had carried with me for so many years. The photo, and the small square of pink blanket I had knitted, still rested in an ordinary plastic sandwich bag in my purse. That small keepsake kept my recurring dream of motherhood alive. I had *so* wanted an antique cradle—and here it was. I took a deep breath. Was I hallucinating? Perhaps everyone had the same cradle design in bygone centuries? I began stroking the pink blanket lying neatly in the cradle. I couldn't get over the similarity.

Through tears falling gently and scattering helter-skelter, I once again rehearsed the Poor-Pitiful-Pearl saga that rested within. Would I—*could* I—ever let it go? The past certainly dictated my future. Making love with a graduate student when I was a sopho-more at a girls' college had resulted in pregnancy. I knew so little then. Maybe I still do.

Oh, Lord, so complicated. I had wondered if the more priv-ileged girls in the other rooms would judge me. At first, I hadn't used any protection. At other times, I used foam. Naïve, and a fool, besides. Well, it didn't work. I went home for the short break between the end of spring semester and summer session and told Mom and Dad I'd be living off-campus in a boarding house, without revealing why. Although they had met Josh, I dared not reveal he was paying for both of our expenses. They would have said I was a "kept" woman. That's how it was back then. Josh supported us from his earnings of working two jobs and managed to get his credits to graduate early. Lies, lies, lies. Except I did live in the boarding house, in a separate wing by myself so I wouldn't "contaminate the morals" of innocent girls. New England mores prevailed. The baby grew inside me. Soon the nausea ceased. I eventually had to stop working at the college library.

Why do I keep hearing the faint sound of "Rock-a-Bye Baby"? Maybe to distract me from thinking of the premature delivery at the boarding house. I swore I had heard the baby cry, but the sounds ceased under my sobs. Then there was nothing. It was a horrible night. I never got to hold her alive. Even now, I can't even fully face the loss Josh and I had to endure.

I hadn't even realized I was holding the life-size baby doll that had been peacefully snuggled under the pink blanket. She cried, saying, "Mama," as I lifted her up on my shoulder. I put my lips to her cold hard porcelain face, and the baby's cries ceased. Somehow, that eased my pain, and I began to explore again. I hadn't even looked at the books on the many shelves. Instead, I opened the drawer of the desk and found photos tied in pink ribbon. I placed the baby doll on my shoulder and searched through the pictures.

Next, I headed to a pedestal that held a large book. I thought it might be a dictionary but no, it was a huge family bible with genealogy entries drawn in beautiful calligraphy in the front pages. The records must have gone back centuries. What a treasure trove for those with patience to delve into their descendants! Some of the ink was too faded, making it difficult to decipher the names. If there had been more time and better light, I might have found actual royalty. Instead, I focused on the most recent that included the marriage of Eve and Charles; he was from Scotland, she, from England. I imagined for a quick moment what my family bible might have looked like if there were recorded information in it. Although my father was such a sorry Anglophile, he revealed little of his lineage. His knowledge of his genealogy died with him. I hoped to trace the lineage one day.

I looked at a picture of a young couple next. It must have been Eve and Charles. So young, so charming. The picture had been on a dusty wooden box on top of the desk, so I looked inside and found an assortment of ladies' handkerchiefs. They were decorated with cross-stitch and chain-stitch embroidery, tatting and delicate lace, and each had been monogrammed. Some appeared so fragile that I was reluctant to touch them with my bare hands. Wait. There were two initials. Wasn't there only one before when I found them upstairs? They looked like the *same* handkerchiefs. *How did they get here?* Who had added the second initial? I had no answers. I had to remember to mention this to my sisters, as it was truly strange.

I moved on. Without upsetting too many layers, I unearthed a beautiful gold and silver brooch with pearls. Still, my mind kept returning to the yellowed photo of the newlyweds, which reminded me that *I* had been a newlywed—twice. Josh and I had eloped after I recovered from the birth. Then we had a religious ceremony for my family. I did eventually learn to love him. He still felt responsible for the fact that I could never again conceive.

I could never accept that our baby died, even though I could still clearly see the baby that was wrapped up and brought to me. Had she really been a live baby, or was it wishful thinking? Years later, I read a couple of stories about babies being switched at birth. Over the years, I have fantasized that she is alive somewhere, living a good life. Why couldn't I accept my baby's death? Did I hear a baby crying? Oh, those piercing cries, still calling me after all these years…

If the couple in the photographs were not of the young Eve and Charles, then surely at least they were related to them. Why else would these now-faded mementos have been saved? I turned over a frame that had toppled onto the floor. It held a military service certificate of someone who had served in a Scottish infantry regiment, the Seaforth Highlanders. My father would have loved telling me what he knew about the Scottish military. In time, I might yearn for his unforgettable personality and fixations.

Next, I turned to a large collection of old first-edition books. "Old" was the operative word. I seemed to be groping around without purpose, being Nosey Joesie. The nosey won out before I ungraciously tripped over the edges of a faded antique Persian rug. I stopped myself and the doll from falling over but landed hard against a shelf on the bookcase. *Oh darn! What would Nancy Drew do next, Joesie?* Suddenly, part of the bookcase slowly creaked open, revealing a passageway. I heard a soft thud. Looking down at my feet, I picked up a small flashlight. I shined the light into the darkness, wondering the distance I would have to go. I carefully leaned forward as I peered inside. It sloped on a downward angle. Allowing curiosity to be a stronger force than my fear, but still afraid that the door would close behind me, I pushed the desk chair over to block the bookcase segment from closing. Bravery was definitely at war with the yellow streak running down my tingling spinal column.

In every place we had ever lived, the closet door in my bedroom had to be checked before bedtime. I always asked my mother to help so my father wouldn't call me a "sissy" yet another time. At night, Mom would leave the door of the closet open to scare away any evil spirit that might wish to hide and pop out when I least expected. With so many moves, I had little time to gain security or comfort while alone in any of my new rooms. Suddenly I remembered the only words of Stephen King that I had memorized, "Monsters are real, and ghosts are real too. They live inside us, and sometimes, they win."

Taking my first steps forward, the two opposing forces fought to take control. I was really feeling uneasy and didn't want to be there with my "baby." The spooky monsters who followed me from scary childhood closets were picking up momentum. I could feel myself shaking, damned scared of being alone in an unsecured, hidden hallway. *What if the blasted door closed? Everyone might leave without me. I'd never be found and would die and turn into an unrecognizable skeleton, only to be identified by my DNA years later.* Until then, I'd be unidentifiable. No dental records left.

I guess I spent too much time watching episodes of those CSI DNA-solve-in-an-hour programs. Plus, I never seemed to find out what happened in those episodes that continued the next week.

I was about to turn back because it was almost too dark to venture forward. If Roxie were here with me, perhaps I'd be braver. I instinctively patted the "baby," more for my comfort, obviously.

"Go ahead, girl," I said to instill an ounce of courage. The flashlight dimmed. I was able to find my way back into the library, mostly by feel. There was some light coming through the hinged panel held open by the desk chair, which helped. Not again. Another door I hadn't noticed before.

I bravely opened the door. I was suddenly looking outside at a nearby cottage. A semblance of logic set in as I closed the door behind me. *Must be another side of Hazel's cottage?* At least I'd be outside and not locked in a dark, hidden hallway. I smiled at a gnarled apple tree, its fruit waiting to ripen. I bet kids loved climbing it when they were little. It reminded me of climbing trees when I was a kid. Good hiding places.

I returned to the library and closed the secret door by pulling out the chair. I kissed the baby's cheek, reluctantly laid her back in the cradle, and pulled the pink blanket up over her. I left the library, locking the door behind me.

There was one more door in the hallway not yet opened. *Voila!* It opened to a mirrored ballroom. A fluffy red boa was hanging over the ballet barre gracing one wall. A silver tiara with "2000" molded onto it was on the floor. Next to it was an invitation with "Happy New Year" written on it. Had there been costumes to go with the tiara and boa? Must have been some party. I love costumes and dress-up clothing. I have my own enormous closetful of costumes. There are some items I haven't worn yet; I couldn't resist buying them "just in case."

Fondly, I thought of the times I dressed up in character when I had groups of children for story time. I would surprise the eager minds as often as I liked, dressing in fantasy costumes. We would "travel by book" anywhere into the vast recesses of children's imaginations, including my own.

Looking at my watch, I knew I'd better hustle back to report what I'd found to the group: hidden doors, hankies, photos, and an antique cradle. I wondered what Roxie had found in the dining room. I placed the library key back on the empty hook behind the reception desk.

~21~

ROXIE'S TREASURE HUNT

We settled back at The Inn. I released the berries from my shirt onto the kitchen table.

"Ta-da!" Allison exclaimed.

"Is that the latest Armani trend?" Deidre asked, pointing at my stained white shirt.

"Now I have to wash the damn thing," I griped as I walked across the floor and pulled on a robe. "Girls, this isn't going to be pretty, but I'm taking my shirt off. I don't care—so it looks like blood." A moment later I added, "We had so much fun."

After that, we were ready for some downtime. Not surprisingly, after all our delays, Ruth Ann, Deidre, and Mira had beaten us back to The Inn.

"Listen guys," Allison said to us. "I am so pooped from hiking and peeing in the woods, I need to take a nap. Mira, how 'bout you? Are you okay?"

"I feel great." Mira replied. "No nap for me. In fact, I'm up for another walk." Mira started pacing then headed to the door.

"You know she didn't sleep last night. What's she on?" Deidre whispered to Joesie.

"Damned if I know, but I think Allison does," she replied.

"I *do* know," Allison replied softly. "She is acting a bit hyper. She is so much better when she's on her meds. She left them back at the Abenaki Lodge."

As I walked by the living room ten minutes later, I could see Allison curled up in her chair, blanket tucked under her chin and snoring softly. Deidre, in true fashion, was sitting in a large Queen Anne chair, papers surrounding her as her creative juices flowed into the new novel she was writing. *That's our Deidre.* Across from her, Ruth Ann was ensconced on the sofa, reading. I mouthed "hi" to her as I paused.

"I wish I could indulge myself and lie on that chaise in the corner and read," I said. But I needed to see that dining room. "Enjoy yourselves. We all deserve a break after that hike to nowhere." Looking out the window, I saw Mira walking away with a determined stride, I assumed back towards her cemetery. "Good luck to you," I whispered, as I wondered why she was so obsessed with it.

Joesie and I left the common room and continued on our way. We chatted by the staircase before she headed to the library. I entered the dining room—a treasure! The furnishings, though in need of polishing, could only be deemed magnificent. From the many years of working in real estate, I, Roxie Ross, had become somewhat of an expert in period furniture. So many of my high-end clients sold their houses completely furnished, and I had to be fully aware of their value. I came to love browsing and acquiring more knowledge in the furniture stores and antiques shops in Palm Beach. Most of the owners now knew me by name and welcomed me, whether I was looking or bringing new clients to them.

Against the side wall of the room was an old, dusty Hooker buffet—burnished gold with rounded cabinets on either end, one with a double door in the middle. All of them had tarnished round knobs. Gingerly, I opened an end cabinet. Inside was a stash of wine—for dinner perhaps?—and cloudy Staffordshire decanters housed in now-dull sterling holders. They were similar to the expensive ones I'd considered purchasing as a gift for one of my clients only a few months ago. I'd fallen in love with one in a shop in the antique district in West Palm Beach.

The other end cabinet held a variety of barware, shakers, jiggers, and corkscrews. When I opened the middle cabinet doors, I was not surprised to see the collection of Staffordshire cut crystal, wine, water, and champagne goblets. I was taken aback to see a half-full glass of red wine sitting there. I sniffed it cautiously and was surprised that the bouquet was still fresh and of a high grade, likely a pinot noir. The hair on my arms stood up. *My Lord, what's going on around here?* Shivering at the strangeness, I moved on cautiously.

Directly across from the buffet was a Chippendale breakfront, a companion to the dining room table and chairs, which were also in need of a good polishing. It had wide glass doors through which I could see The Inn's china. Upon investigation, it turned out to be a pattern by Rosenthal, called "Queen's Bouquet." The flowers matched the cardinal color of the raspberries I had carried in my shirt. The long drawer beneath the china held blackened Reed & Barton Sterling flatware. When cleaned and polished, I was sure it would have been a graceful addition to any table. The doors below the drawer opened to yet another set of crystal that I recognized at once as Waterford's crisscross Lismore pattern, which I myself owned. My word, this dining room was exquisite! I envisioned guests in formal dinner attire enjoying the atmosphere along with the finest china and crystal available, to say nothing of the meals, which must have been presented in style. Wouldn't it be wonderful to find a hidden guest book revealing the names of those who sat at the table over the years? If only these walls could talk!

I turned and saw Ben in the mirror above the buffet, deep in conversation with a young woman clothed in a royal blue satin gown, her face turned away.

"Ben?" I blinked, reaching out. "Why am I seeing Ben?" *Am I hallucinating?* I turned and looked for the glass of wine. There it was, with only a few drops left. *What on earth?* As quickly as Ben and the woman had appeared, they were gone. I must have eaten too many raspberries.

Taking a deep breath, I held onto a chair for support. I had to gather my wits. How would I tell the others what I had seen? Would they believe me?

~22~

ALLISON'S AFTERNOON AT THE INN

Allison	Tuesday 2:00 PM

The warm air of the house clung to me, making my damp clothes feel even stickier, but my need to nap propelled me forward. I considered the chair in which Roxie, or someone else, had slept last night. It was cushy, apart from the rest of the furniture, and next to a window. I lifted the sash to its most-open position. The slightest of breezes teased the curtains while I pulled a small ottoman over for my feet. As I sank into the chair, I examined the needlepoint design on the top of the small rectangular footstool. Although old and musty, it was a beautiful testament to someone's painstaking work. A bouquet of raspberries, flowers, and leaves sat on a dark gray background. In its earliest days, the colors would have been bright, the background, black. I wondered if it had been Eve who sat in this chair by this window, patiently moving a needle through the canvas. I considered my filthy socks hanging outside on the railing but decided that my bare feet weren't too dirty. What was an ottoman for, anyway? This one had seen its share of life at The Inn.

I stretched my legs out, folded my arms across my chest, and closed my eyes. I thought of my children. Most likely, they weren't concerned about me. For all they knew, I was safely involved in the conference. I wouldn't hear from them until I got back. They might try to call me at some point, but their dad would tell them not to bother me. One of the benefits of divorce was that I got regular breaks from parenting, something I had rarely gotten when we lived together.

Sleep came faster than usual. Oddly, I went immediately into a dream full of brilliant splashes of color. I was in a garden with lush, thick leaves that twisted and turned in corkscrew shapes. Then I saw a number of tropical plants and trees: bougainvillea, hibiscus, banana, orange, and pineapple in a brilliant splash of colors. I knew they didn't grow here, and I marveled at how they could coexist right alongside the rows of blackberry, blueberry, and raspberry bushes that filled the rest of the space.

Then the scene shifted. I was in a house full of books, knick-knacks, and old furniture. The hues matched the garden colors I had seen. The carpet had many shades of green: mint, vibrant neon green, and dark hunter green. The colors displayed were fuchsia, pink, yellow, orange, and red on the walls and covering the furniture. The colors danced, as if alive. The effect was disturbingly beautiful, and I wondered what this place was. *Where exactly am I?* Just as I thought this question, a disembodied arm pointed me to the next room. I simply went there with no qualms. I saw two women standing at a closet, pulling and tossing gowns around the room. Gold, maroon, deep purple, indigo, celadon, and again, a bright fuchsia. As I got closer, the two turned and I recognized Deidre and Ruth Ann. They smiled. It came to me that this might not be a dream at all.

My body shook, and my shoulders twitched alternately against the back of the chair as a rush of sweat woke me. Directly in my line of sight, across the room, Deidre's eyes stared back at mine. The fact that she was looking at me felt strange, and yet somehow familiar and comfortable, as if we were sharing words without speaking. The thought made no sense.

"You okay?" She tipped her head, and her forehead creased.

"Uh, yeah," I said, sitting up. "I'm fine. I was just dreaming. That's all…"

"Me too!" she said.

"Strangely enough," I ventured. "You were in my dream."

"Really?" Deidre stared at me, curiously.

"Yeah, you and Ruth Ann."

Deidre got up and crossed the room in quick strides. "I've got to tell you something," she explained in a whisper. "Both of *you* were in my dream also, and there was a whole lot of color—intense color!"

"Me too," I whispered back. "I've never dreamt like that before."

"I don't think I have, either."

"Look, Ruth Ann's waking up," I said.

The two of us made our way slowly over to the chair where Ruth Ann was sitting up, rubbing her eyes.

"Colors," she said as soon as she saw us. "Incredible colors."

"Did you see us, too?" Deidre asked in a high voice. Ruth Ann just nodded.

"This is weird," I said, my own voice two octaves higher than normal. "I've never had a shared dream before and a trio to boot!"

"Neither have I," Ruth Ann exclaimed.

"Me either," Deidre said. "Maybe we all ate too many raspberries."

Deidre

After our attempt to shake off our mutual dream, the group of us eventually gathered again. "You know, we should try to salvage some writing time," I said.

"What did you have in mind?" asked Allison, who seemed to perk up at the suggestion.

"We don't have our laptops or paper," Mira observed. She had come back from her walk without revealing what she had encountered.

"Ah, do not be dismayed, dear ladies. I have supplies." Joesie began to pull lined paper and assorted colored pens out of her purse. I began to think she was like Mary Poppins, extracting items from her magical bag.

"Leave it to Joesie. Do you have an escape hatch as well in your bags of tricks?" teased Roxie.

"Don't I wish she did," I sighed. "Anyone know whose notebook this is?" I asked, waving a piece of someone's enterprise.

"Just some random drawings I was working on," Allison replied, grabbing the notebook from me before the contents could be exposed.

"Random?" Ruth Ann asked. "I can recognize pictures that will catch children's imaginations. Why won't you share them?"

"Well, up until this point, I didn't think they were worth looking at. I doodle for my kids. However, I never thought about incorporating them into my stories. I figured publishers were more interested in using their own illustrators. I've thought of using a pen name for the illustrations though. What do you think?"

"I think you should be proud of your work—and embrace it," stated Roxie.

"It proves you are multitalented," I said.

"Thanks," Allison said, letting out a deep sigh that made the group snicker. "This shared dream is ripe for sketching. And the swirl of colors we saw! You did see a swirl of colors, didn't you?"

We nodded in confirmation. For a moment I panicked, thinking I had lost my mind because of the strangeness of our mutual dream.

"Ruth Ann, tell us about what you're working on and maybe we can come up with a writing exercise."

Before Ruth Ann could answer me, Roxie interrupted. "Ladies, I have to tell you this first. I can't be stranded here too much longer. When I was in the dining room, I thought I saw Ben with a young woman reflected in a mirror. I couldn't handle that. I'm not even sure if it was real."

"This is going to be my next writing project," Joesie blurted out. "With all the weird things happening around here, I can't believe all we've experienced."

"Good idea," Mira piped in, simultaneously jumping up.

"When we go to Boston later this summer, maybe we should go to Salem and visit the witch museum," Mira continued. "Another adventure. Who sees this as an adventure?"

"I don't," I said.

"I think it's a great idea," Joesie said. "Maybe we'll be inspired to write our Abigail Adams project. I heard there was a reenactor who plays Abigail Adams. Maybe she could give us a retrospective opinion, Mira."

"Oh, Salem is a hop, skip and a jump from Boston," Ruth Ann said.

"I've had enough creepy for now," Deidre responded. "I don't even like it at Halloween."

"Could be a new twist on history," Mira said. Then, with a smile, "Things are getting a little crazy around here. Crazy, crazy, crazy!"

"Relax, relax," Allison said. "I'm not going to say it three times like Hazel." She rose, gave Mira a hug and whispered in her ear. The result was instantaneous. Mira flopped back in her chair and said, "Okay, I'm game." There were sideways glances from the others and a sigh, this time from Roxie.

"Well, since I write about mysteries, we could try to imagine six women stuck in a haunted house," Ruth Ann continued, answering the question Allison had asked her before everyone had started talking.

"Oh, please," Roxie said, "Too cliché."

We all looked nervously away from one another. "The walls must have ears. Let's think of another topic or angle," I suggested. There was a risk of getting too close. A word could be misinterpreted and then a relationship fractured. I knew from experience.

When talking to Amy about her initial cancer diagnosis, I had wrestled with the right words. After one misstep, I was reluctant to make further suggestions about her lifestyle. "Don't you..." I had tried to say, but she had cut me off.

"Oh, I already have cancer. You think this cigarette is another nail in my coffin? I'm going to indulge myself now. Who knows what tomorrow will bring? Besides, they have cures for this type now," she had stated emphatically.

This was the carryover behavior from our college years. Then, we'd been invincible, immortal. Maturing should have changed that attitude. "What the hell?" had always been her mantra. I was the one who was timid. She had grabbed life by the throat. I was always the one prepared with the lozenge.

As difficult as it was for me to see her retreat into bad habits such as sneaking a cigarette or scoffing at meditation, I'd had to back off. That's what I was doing now with Roxie. Had I made a mistake in the past with Amy? Was I repeating it?

"What about 'friends and their secrets' as a writing prompt?" Roxie interjected. "Why don't we list the qualities of a good friend and include their secrets, then write a paragraph or two about that experience?"

I folded my hands in my lap and stared down at my fingernails, ostensibly examining my manicure. The tension was thick. Would we share our secrets?

"We're getting off course. Let me tell you what I do when I'm stuck with my writing. Maybe this will help." The words tumbled out of Mira as she recapped her research and struggles to create identifiable protagonists. "So, I take a walk and use my surroundings to help develop the plot."

"She probably looks for cemeteries, too," Roxie added in an undertone.

"There's hope, Mira, for our Abigail Adams project," Joesie said.

Who would have thought Mira would come to the rescue? But she did! We settled into a lively discussion of how to bring a main character into focus.

∽

∼23∼

FRIENDS

The afternoon was upon us and I really wanted to go home. Not that I had anything to go home to. I was getting tired of this place. I vowed to invest in one small cat when I got home. I'd buy it a cedar-scented bed, a Hello Kitty food and water dish combo, perhaps a matching litter box. I was done with living alone. Every night when I'd come back from work, my new baby girl kitty—and she would be a girl—would greet me. I would name her Adramja, an acronym of the beginning letters of all our names, or "A.J." for short.

Now that I was one of the "sisters," I couldn't live alone. What would I say I was doing if one of them called me? Having a cat would round out my life and keep me company. When they called, I could be playing with my kitten, feeding her, brushing her, or coming in from her vet appointment. The conversation material was endless. Though I'd been feeling like I'd known these gals all my life, details of their lives were emerging. Maybe I didn't actually know them at all. What I did know was that they had lives, real lives that were exciting and interesting, compared with mine. Every aspect of their family lives fascinated me since I didn't yet have children. Thank goodness I had my preschool students.

I dreamed about being a published author. Deidre was going on tour soon and Roxie had her glamorous career. Joesie was her own person, not afraid to be different. Allison was a great artist and writer. Mira had her own vibe and was creative. Like me, she loved cemeteries. Still, we were more alike than different, all loving the turn of a word, the power of a phrase. Deidre had said it best when she used "dorm room" to describe our place at The Inn at Raspberry Hill. Can a bunch of dissimilar women connect in a meaningful way? Maybe.

"Ruth Ann," Allison said to me, "I am so glad you're here with us. I feel like you're my little sister." It made me smile and I wanted to hug her. I felt such a solidarity with them, especially Roxie, our Mother Superior. We were like sorority sisters, somehow each of us a cross between a favorite cousin and a wise best friend. Having had neither, plus my own sister being the twit she is, I thought for a while that I was done with friends, at least female friends. In my experience, most women were catty. It always felt like high school all over again when a bunch of women got together. It was snipe about this one, put down that one, complain about another. It didn't feel that way with us. We talked childhood, love, feelings, anything and everything, without judgment. These ladies made me feel complete, special. No matter what subject I raised, I didn't have to worry about being criticized.

Yet, despite the kinship and the declarations that we'd always remain friends, would they bother with me when we were finally back to civilization? After all, I was the newest member of the group. I fantasized that my "sisters" would call me for a lunch date or a movie when I got home. Perhaps we'd all get together and take in a show. Then my insecurities told me that no one would call. I dared to hope at least Roxie would keep in touch. *Don't go there, Ruth Ann. Your sister may have scarred you, but you are still a really good woman with a lot to offer.* Boldly, I decided that after we'd all been home a month or so, I would suggest an activity for those of us who lived in Florida. I'd never done anything like that in my life.

While deep in thought, I'd been wandering around The Inn and suddenly came upon a large library. Seeing the floor-to-ceiling bookshelves and soft, inviting window seats, I realized that perhaps

I could look for a book to pass the time. Only Joesie was in the room. I guess she didn't notice me. After so much conversation in our dorm room, I welcomed the silence and assumed she did too, but I boldly asked if there was anything good to read. I was getting hungry. My stomach rumbled. The small offerings from lunch had been lovely. I wanted something more substantial. There was nothing to eat here. I had distracted myself with a copy of *To Kill a Mockingbird*. The beauty of the lines would have to sustain me. Joesie selected a book, and revealed it was a first edition.

Eventually, I joined Deidre and Allison in the parlor. I sat down on a furry rug by the fireplace. It was lit and lightly flaming. Weird—it wasn't lit before. Who would light a fire during the daytime in August? Maybe Hazel. *Cozy, though.* It took away the dampness that had settled in since the storm. I positioned myself on my side to read and I guess I dozed off. My first recollection upon waking was a stream of colors.

Our shared dreams were incredible. I didn't understand why or how we were sharing dreams. This was getting more and more weird.

"I feel like I'm losing my mind," I said. "You?" I asked Deidre.

"Forget about it," she answered. "We should get a snack." She didn't have to ask twice. I still was starving and was longing to spend more time with my new-found sisters. I prayed they felt the same, but I definitely wasn't eating any more raspberries.

"Let's explore the larder that Eve told us about," Deidre suggested.

"I hope we find something," Allison said. "I'm hungry too."

"Maybe it will take our mind off of getting out of here and those weird dreams. I hope Jimmy John is making some progress," Deidre said.

"I think I hear a chain saw. I knew Jimmy John would come to the rescue." I started to imagine how he would look. *My hero!*

"Come on girls, to the larder," Deidre said.

"You two go ahead. I'll wait here for you," Allison said.

"I'm coming. Even peanut butter and jelly sounds good," Ruth Ann lamented.

~24~

EXPLORING

I had a case of the "grumps." My magic meds were in the special pocket in my luggage at the Abenaki Lodge. Not that I had taken them lately. I had been feeling really good, so I decided this was a perfect time to put them away. I'd fooled my brain for four weeks into thinking I was just like everyone else, but I wasn't. I was restless and knew I needed sleep; however, I wasn't tired. My nose told me, in no uncertain terms, that I needed a shower and some deodorant. My legs and underarms needed shaving and my hair, a good shampoo and blow dry would be a gift. As if this wasn't bad enough, I had been so afraid no one would believe my cemetery story of the night before.

"We thought you'd had a dream," Allison had said, hiding her grin with her lovely hands. "But then we found it, thank goodness."

"I had an amazing dream," giggled Deidre. "It seemed so real! Maybe yours was realistic, too. This place seems a little mystical, doesn't it?" I thought Deidre was blushing as she spoke, but I must have been mistaken. Miss Dee was always in control. *This Inn is driving us crazy*! Then Allison, Deidre, and Ruth Ann compared dream notes and, lo and behold, their dreams were so similar, it was weird. I shuddered. This place was otherworldly.

When I returned from my walk, I noticed Joesie and Roxie had taken off, deciding to explore The Inn. Joesie had said there had to be a library someplace and she was determined to find it. The two of them were the most fascinated with this place. They both loved antiques and went about "oohing" and "aahing." All the lamps had curlicues and tassels on the shades. The portraits on the walls were of unsmiling old people. Some of the men were in uniform. *Veddy British*! There were some interesting things, I would admit. I loved the wall hangings. Wouldn't it be something if Jimmy John's mother had made those?

Dust stuck to my fingers when I touched a lamp. Fairy dust perhaps? I wondered what everyone's children would do with their inherited treasures. *Maybe one of my unpublished manuscripts will be a hit play or a best seller? Maybe, I should make the best of the situation.* Anyway, the only one interested in my story was Ruth Ann. She was like a butterfly, struggling to emerge from the chrysalis. I thought her quiet demeanor and air of mystery hid a flaming interior ready to escape. All she needed was a reason—Jimmy John perhaps. If it couldn't be me, let it be my friend.

After our meager fish lunch, I had been desperate to get out. It certainly wasn't dry outside, but I knew I'd find the high ground. No one was interested in my grumps. While everyone was resting, I announced I was going for a walk.

"Say hi to Jimmy John and ask him where he was and why he didn't clear the road this morning," Deidre snickered. I could feel my muscles twitch in response to her comment.

Two words were in my mouth. I smiled instead, stuffing my dirty feet into my muddy shoes.

I turned and said, "Hey, I'm sure that Jimmy John will be our way out of here. I'll bet he could get our cars out to the main road, too." Just the thought lifted my spirits. I skipped off the porch onto the soggy ground.

Outside, the birds were busy feasting on the worms that had escaped the muddy water. Their songs filled the air. The dark clouds had moved on, leaving the sky pale bluish gray with white fluffy clouds. I decided I'd walk the same trail as I had before. In the light of the clearing storm, I felt temporarily disoriented. A pile of fallen leaves scattered in the breeze. A small furry thing that was neither a squirrel nor a rat scooted into the brush beside me. A chipmunk, perhaps. I giggled and hoped such a cute thing wouldn't be any predator's dinner. I hoped it wasn't a relative of the mouse from the Lodge.

I found the trail and breathed a sigh of relief. Everyone else was relaxing. I wondered why I couldn't be like other people. *Why am I so freaking nice? That's what everyone thinks, isn't it? Nice, calm Mira. Well, nice is boring. I want to be glamorous! Sexy! Alluring! Yes! Humph—fat chance! Speaking of fat, I think my pants are a bit loose even when they're damp. No meds lately. Anyway, that must be it. It couldn't be the lack of food at The Inn, right? Hah!*

Speaking of hunger, I was sure "my boys" were eating fine. I had prepared enough homemade meals for them for a month. Avrom doesn't cook. He'd die without me. At least I've taught Elijah the basics.

I stopped to pick fresh berries off a bush, letting the juices stir my taste buds and fool my stomach into thinking they would be more filling than they were. The path led over a hill to a fork that I didn't remember. I followed the one on the left. I thought about taking the road less travelled. I wondered if the poet Robert Frost had ever been to The Inn at Raspberry Hill. I sang, "I found my thrill... on Raspberry Hill." My steps went in time with my song. When I finished my rendition of *Raspberry*, "Blueberry Hill," I started "This Land Is Your Land." Singing brightened my mood and made me forget about being hungry and odiferous. My English teacher, Ms. Sanders, would be proud. "Odiferous, o–d–i–f..."

The tree lying across the path in front of me looked as if it had been there for a while, but I didn't remember seeing it last time. Small shoots grew out of the fallen trunk. It was Mother Nature at work to resupply herself. I tried stepping over it but couldn't quite stretch my leg far enough to reach the ground on the other side, so I ended up straddling the trunk. This was no sapling. I was too stubborn to go around the other way. So, I boosted myself up on my tiptoes, and was finally able to throw one leg over the trunk. Instead of jumping down, I paused. The sun was breaking through the clouds, warming my face. This place at this time gave me a welcome feeling of peace.

"I'll just sit here and relax for a while," I said to myself. My watch said I'd been gone less than an hour. I thought surely it had been longer. I leaned forward, put my head on my folded arms and fell asleep.

Seemingly all at once, I was standing on the ledge of the balcony on the third floor of the Fontainebleau Hotel. I could see the pool below me, the blue water rippling with the breeze. I climbed onto the railing, held out my arms and heard the voices shouting, "Jump! Jump! You can fly! You can be—"

"Good God, is that you, Mira? What the hell are you doing out here? I heard you screaming. What happened? Look at your mouth. Did you eat those raspberries? Some folks think there's something strange in those buggers."

I stepped down from my perch on the log and nearly knocked him over, throwing my arms around his neck. "Oh, Jimmy John, I fell asleep and had the worst dream. I'm so happy to see you."

"Where are your friends?" he asked. I swore his voice quivered with disappointment.

I quickly moved away. "They're back at The Inn. Nobody else wanted to come." *Of course, it's Ruth Ann he wants. Not an older woman like me. I had the bitter taste of bile in my mouth.*

"Well, come on then, we'll have some tea, and you can see my place. I left the kettle on low. I was trying to clear the road, but the current was still too strong, so I was heading back to my cabin when I heard you."

The path narrowed, making it necessary for us to walk single file. I had a good view of Jimmy John's body from behind. He had one beautiful derriere. His front wasn't bad either. *What if he and I.... No one had to know and.... Stop it Mira! Yeah, I know, we want him for Ruth Ann. It had better be quick, though. We've got to get out of here!*

"We're almost there, Mira. Look, you can see the rise above the lake." I stopped at the top of the hill, trying to catch my breath. The scene before me was like a *National Geographic* photograph. There was a large lake, surrounded on three sides by woods. The fourth side, one that I had missed on my last adventure, looked like a carpet of flowers surrounded by neat rows of what must be fruits and vegetables. I hadn't recognized its beauty before.

The inside of Jimmy John's cabin was cool and comfortable, furnished in what looked like hand-hewn furniture with colorful cushions. The kettle whistled on the old woodstove. We sat at a small hardwood table on benches that were surprisingly comfortable and sipped our tea. "So, have you seen Eve and Charles lately?" I asked. His ruddy face paled as I continued. "We did meet Hazel. She seems a bit confused."

"I'm afraid she does get confused sometimes, but she has lived here for years and keeps the house up as best she can."

"One of the girls spoke to Eve through their bedroom door. We saw her briefly the night we arrived, although we were all so tired, it seemed more like a dream. Haven't seen Charles, though. Maybe he's not feeling well."

He gave me an "are you kidding me?" look, then changed the subject. "Come see my garden, Mira. Perhaps you can take some summer squash back to The Inn with you. It looked ripe this morning."

We walked on what looked like a slate slab pathway that led up a hill to the garden. There was broccoli, three varieties of squash, and butter beans. At the end of one row, small tree branches were fashioned into a stake to support a large tomato plant. "Oh, those tomatoes look delicious." I bent over, took one off the vine and wiped it on my shirt.

"Take a bite," Jimmy John called from the other side of the row. "They're better than apples." He watched as I bit into the flesh of the ripe fruit. I blushed as the pink juice dribbled down my chin onto my shirt. "Nothing like a ripe tomato right off the vine," he said laughing. "If you're still here, I'll bring you some vegetables later."

I accepted the cold water from the ladle he held out to rinse my hands and face.

Jimmy John suggested I start back to The Inn. "I'm afraid it's too hot to go to the cemetery. Perhaps next time…and you could bring your friend."

"Next time? We have to get out of here. Can't you help us, Jimmy John?" I pleaded.

"I hate to disappoint you, Mira, but with a storm like the one we had, no one is getting out any time soon. It could be another day or more. I'm working on it. It takes a while to clear all the fallen trees just to get the tractor safely through the mud, down to the road. Even some bridges went out."

"My friends were expecting you earlier."

"Ruth Ann?" he asked, giving me an eager look that I ignored. I didn't bother to update him on Ruth Ann's interest or intentions.

"Some of them are really getting antsy."

∽

～25～

LARDER

After our afternoon break, I woke up hungry, craving my daily piece of chocolate. The dreams that Allison, Ruth Ann, and I had supposedly shared left me with an uneasy feeling. Part of me was counting the minutes until we could escape this "fun house." The other part of me wanted to embrace the adventure. I never did spooky well.

Despite Ruth Ann's valiant effort to brew coffee on the gas grill she had found on the rickety back porch, it had only provided me with a temporary caffeine fix. I could feel that sensation I get when a headache is going to erupt. Since my Excedrin was back at the Abenaki Lodge, and I highly doubted Eve would stock such an item in her bathroom, food was essential. The lunch that the other women had made was not filling, although I gave them an "A" for effort. I wasn't sure if or when dinner would be on the horizon. The day seemed to be unfolding in the most unusual manner.

Ever since Mira had described her mysterious cemetery, her behavior had become increasingly bizarre. First of all, she kept interjecting Jimmy John into every conversation. She hadn't slept last night, wouldn't take a nap today, and walked in circles, muttering about raspberries and names on headstones. Some old-fashioned names such as Louisa were among them. Horror films are not my genre. I hear the musical score from the movie *Psycho* and my stomach turns and I feel a chill. Speaking of stomach turning, that was just what was happening. Scrounging around the larder and finding something edible might prove to be a challenge. I had faith that Roxie and Allison, the cooks among us, could whip up something if only there were something in the larder.

Coming out of my reverie, daydreaming of Mocha cake, I had relayed my cravings to the group. They had appeared out of nowhere, much like the ones I encountered when I was pregnant with my children. I remembered asking my husband to pick up coffee ice cream at a local Howard Johnson's on his way back home from a business trip. It was one of the few HoJos left.

"So back then, I asked him to go to HoJos," I'd explained.

"What's a *hojo*?" Ruth Ann asked, when I'd brought up the topic of food.

"It was the moniker for the Howard Johnson restaurant and motel chain. They were everywhere back in the day, usually right off the highway. Now, back to my cravings story," I continued.

"It's on Route 101," I had pleaded with my husband, Paul. "Just off the service road by the airport. It is one of the few still open—please!"

"But it's one in the morning! I just got off the delayed leg from Dallas. I am beat." He'd sounded like one of our children whining.

This was before the ever-accessible cell phone. So, my husband had properly found a pay phone to assure me he had safely landed. In those days we seemed to touch base constantly. Our conversations these days seemed to be briefer and briefer. Perhaps our verbal shorthand was a sign of a certain level of comfort, perhaps something else. Whatever the circumstances, satisfying cravings was a priority for me during my pregnancies.

I wouldn't have risked being so demanding the second time around. Firstborns do get perks that their younger siblings become acutely aware of. But, truth be told, subsequent children get away with murder. I recalled my younger child complaining about how few photo albums there were of his preschool years.

"Where's me on *my* first day of school?" my son, Greg, had whined.

"Oh honey, I have them—they're in a box," I'd apologetically countered.

Faren, my ever-loving minx of a daughter, had stuck her tongue out behind his back. It was all I could do to stifle my laughter. There was no defense; no explanation would suffice. A *mea culpa* would have fallen on deaf ears. It was only years later, when the situation was reversed between Faren and Greg, and curfew was more lax, that retribution seemed to be achieved. "Greg can stay out later than I can. Not fair! Just because he's a boy."

Now that the roles had switched, I honestly got some perverse pleasure out of pointing this out. Realizing my mind had wandered enough—it was the hunger pangs I was feeling, perhaps—I turned my attention back to the task at hand, scrounging around the larder. I swallowed my normally squeamish tendencies, pushing aside the rug and lifting the larder door that Eve had mentioned yesterday. I descended into a cool, deep space. Surprisingly, the small, grated window down below provided ample light to peruse the contents.

The shelves looked like they were from back in time in a grocer's museum. Canning supplies lined ledges that were sagging from the weight of crockery. The old English-style lettering on them was faded and somewhat indecipherable. The crazed canisters had seen better days; they were more suited for a flea market venue or decorating the interior of a quirky restaurant. I was almost afraid to touch them for fear they would crumble in my hands. Jars and jars of preserves lined the lower shelves. English biscuits in boxes that had been chewed on the edges informed me that the mice might eat better than Eve and her husband. On what did they subsist?

I felt slightly guilty raiding their larder and made a mental note that we should all pitch in enough to leave them adequate funds to buy food. Always the list maker, I surveyed what essentials they might need. Not only was I fascinated with the assortment and names of the products on the shelves. I wondered how Eve would have acquired them. Had she brought them from England? Had she traveled frequently to distant shores to touch base with her heritage? Despite story lines swirling in my head to sustain me—that and being famished—I was becoming increasingly light-headed. It was all I could do to control my mounting frustration. *I-want-to-go-home!*

In the rear of the room was a narrow, diminutive door. I was too curious not to open it. Its creaking provided evidence that it was not often used. I was immediately reminded of the fruit cellar in the basement of my childhood home. I became aware that my mind kept wandering back to my past. Was this seesaw action indicative of early onset Alzheimer's, excessive fatigue, or just plain old hunger?

With just the benefit of the dim light from the larder, I used the cool, rough texture of the stone walls to guide my way. The large white freezer with its prominent stainless-steel handle caught my eye. I hesitated, wondering if I should call for reinforcements or brave opening it myself. *Oh, what the hell? Stop being a wuss.*

Still, the morbid thought occurred to me that a body might be stuffed in there. Writer's runaway imagination or license was my only explanation as I gingerly pried open the top, peeking with one eye shut. Realizing the power had been off, I was also tempted to hold my nose. But, to my surprise a whoosh of cold air emanated from the depths of the freezer.

I stepped back, astonished that Eve had packed this full of dry ice. I knew this because of the gassy odor, and how my fingertip stung when I tentatively touched it. I slammed the lid shut, not interested in pursuing the contents of the freezer. Who would have delivered these items to this odd couple? Jimmy John? My imagination went wild as I stooped down to exit the small door. No lunch meat in there, I concluded. It was everything I could do not to gag at the thought of its contents. Mira's mysterious Jimmy John's hunted vittles, perhaps? I grabbed the preserves and biscuits, heading back to the group, eager to reveal my findings. I temporarily forgot we had previously stuffed ourselves with fresh raspberries.

Impatient to tell everyone, I tripped over the doorsill of the larder. I hugged the precious stash so as not to drop anything, thereby incurring the wrath of my fellow writers. I folded over my body as if to protect a newborn. Successfully, I righted myself, only to relax my grip on my hoard. Arms full, I tried to maneuver everything within my embrace. No such luck. One jar slipped from under the crook of my elbow. I don't know which they responded to, the sound of glass breaking or my yelling at the top of my lungs.

Roxie, Allison, and Ruth Ann ran to my rescue. I stared down at the oozing red raspberry concoction gracing the floor and announced, "Tea and crumpets are served." The peals of laughter brought Mira and Joesie.

I was laughing so hard from the absurd nature of our circumstances that it was all I could do to control the rest of my bundle. I slid down the side of the kitchen cabinet, holding onto the rest of my find, tears streaming down my face. I was half laughing, half crying, and landed with my legs spread wide apart.

The preserves now appeared to have exploded from my lower anatomy.

❧

~26~

EBB AND FLOW

We stood in the anteroom watching the rich, reddish-purple juice of the raspberries spread out on the floor like paint on an artist's palette. I was amazed and fascinated by its changing shape. Finally, Deidre grabbed an embroidered dish towel to wipe up the berries. They left a faint stain on the floor. Maybe when it dried it wouldn't be noticeable. The cleanup done, we retreated back to the living room to our chosen seats.

"You know, the way the juice spread, and its color, reminded me of my period," I snickered. Murmurs of agreement surrounded me.

Ruth Ann looked around shyly, saying, "You're so right, Roxie. My gosh, I haven't thought about my first period for a long time, and this just brought it up to the forefront. When I was young, I couldn't fathom the mystery of those blue boxes at the grocery store." Ruth Ann went on to recount how every Thursday was grocery-shopping day. The entire family was loaded into the car for their weekly shopping excursion together, as her father always drove.

"My dad," she continued, "would often drop us off at the store, while he went to the local watering hole to grab a beer. As soon as we got to the section holding those mysterious boxes, I'd inevitably ask my mom, 'What's in the blue box?' And just as inevitably, she'd answer something like, 'Oh, we'll talk about it at home.' Of course, the question was never answered. To this day, I wonder if my mother was embarrassed, secretive, or just being arbitrary."

She told us about her rather bossy, arrogant older sister who had made fun of her for not knowing that the pads were to keep clothes free of blood during her "monthly." Her sister demeaned her intelligence constantly, by indicating she didn't have any. We were all horrified.

"That must have been so hard on you," Joesie lamented, "to have your own sister mistreat you." We nodded in harmony.

"That's why we don't speak often," Ruth Ann continued. "There comes a point where you can't—no, *won't*—tolerate negativity. I reached mine, and though I do miss her at times, it remains a strained relationship."

"Keep going," Allison urged. "What else happened?"

It was as though a dike had burst open. Ruth Ann poured her heart out as she recounted seeing her mom put the blue box in the linen closet for her sister and realizing one day that box would be for her. Like most of us, she wanted to be "developed" and have her period, too.

"I began to feel my body changing, and my hormones must have been raging. I remember going on a trip to the amusement park, an annual event for the Notre Dame School. Since I took piano lessons there, I was included on the trip. My friend Claudette saved me from having to be embarrassed in my pink seersucker blouse. She gave me a more "hip" Red Sox t-shirt, and we matched in our jeans and white Converse sneakers. At almost eleven years of age, I was chagrined that I still got nauseous from long car rides. At the end of the bus ride, a hot dog and Coke made me feel better, but I still had a strange, crampy feeling."

"Oh no, tell me you didn't start your period on a field trip," Roxie whispered.

"Ruth Ann," Allison piped up. "With the straight hips you described, it doesn't sound as though you were developed enough to have your period."

"Yes, I was ready," Ruth Ann replied. "I did have breasts, micro-ones—much smaller than 'my girls' now, and I had shaved under my arms too."

"I was a skinny kid also when my period came," Deidre ventured. "How about the rest of you?" The women filled in the details of what their figures were like and the ages when their periods arrived.

Ruth Ann went on. "Although I had this crampy feeling, Claudette convinced me to go on the biggest roller coaster in the park. At the end of the ride, I was nauseous again—dizzy—and thought I'd faint if I didn't pee. I went into the restroom where I discovered, of all things, blood in my underpants. At that precise moment, I finally understood what my sister had meant. I cleaned up as best I could and wadded toilet paper in my panties to contain the flow."

Allison and Joesie groaned.

"Claudette kept asking me if I was okay, and when I finally admitted to her what had happened, she got a pad out of the machine for me, and even though it was not a self-sticking one, I was able to keep it in place until I got to the stash back home. From then on the 'blue box' was a monthly constant in my life."

We had all wanted to grow up fast and the "menstrual" milestone was on our minds. Allison began her first-period tale by telling us how her tomboy-self had loved playing football with the boys.

"I can relate to that," I interjected. "My mother was convinced something was wrong with me. I preferred any kind of ball game with the boys to playing with dolls. Honestly, can you believe that? She'd yell at me all the time, 'Why can't you be like the girls next door, Deana and Terry? They're so quiet. All I hear is your voice yelling with the boys. It's not very ladylike.' I would mumble under my breath, 'Who cares?'"

"Well," Allison said, "I had to give up most sports when my nipples started hurting after being bumped by the boys. Why couldn't they have invented a chest protector for girls like us? I eventually gave up football for good and scrutinized my underwear daily for even the tiniest hint of color. My mother kept telling me to be patient. I didn't want to be. Living in a woman's body certainly is a different experience. I got used to my boobs being confined in a bra, feeling somewhat alien, but could not fathom why I had not gotten my ever-elusive period. One afternoon, after finishing my homework, I went into the bathroom, only to discover a red streak in my panties. I found my kit, given to the girls in my class two years before, and 'fixed' myself up. I wondered if that was what wearing a diaper felt like."

We were fascinated by her analogy of the bulkiness of her pad being the same softness as a baby's diaper but still uncomfortable. Was it possible she remembered all that? I did. "What a lucky girl! You got to wear a stick-on, not like the elastic and metal belts we wore," I interjected, waving Mira into the room.

"Oh, you're back, Mira. Join the discussion," Allison offered.

"You must have been so proud and happy to tell your mother 'it' had come at last," Joesie said.

"Yeah," answered Allison. "She looked as though she had been stricken and was only concerned about the cramps making me uncomfortable. Oh, my God. Within a few months I knew about the pain big time. I'd lie in bed with a hot water bottle on my lower pelvis wondering what the hell I had been in such a hurry for. Leaks on sheets and pants, smelly, awful pads to change, and pain to boot—bloody mess between my legs," Allison continued to the nods of understanding from the group.

"Thanks, all of you, for your understanding. At least we know why some people call it 'the curse,'" Allison said.

"God, I'm *glad* I'm through menopause," I added. Everyone laughed as they looked at me.

"Does anyone know a good Dr. Boob? If we ever get out of here, I want a 34C, at least, now that I'm divorced."

"Can we forget this topic?" Deidre remarked just as a shadow darkened the doorway. "Joesie? Is someone listening to us?" she asked.

"Maybe it was Eve?" Joesie responded. "Let's keep it down, girls."

"Blood, blood, blood," Hazel sang, as she placed a silver tea service on the sideboard. We froze and watched her silently leave the room.

"She pops in when you least expect it," Deidre said under her breath.

"Isn't that the tea service you described from the dining room?" asked Ruth Ann.

"I think so. You can hardly tell, it's so shiny now," I said.

"Did you see what I saw? How did she make that tea?" Mira asked.

"I'm not touching that tea or those scones," Deidre sneered.

Joesie added, "Don't look at me. How did she boil the water?"

"Oh, come on girls. Grow up. Mira and I will try them. Right?" I said as Mira bit into the scone.

"Mmm, count me in," Mira said with her mouth full. Sipping her tea, she continued with the same subject. "Ladies, I have to tell you something. I was quite different in my younger days. I was insecure. I gained confidence after working and marriage, which bolstered me, too. You, my new sisters, have made me feel as if I 'belong' to this group. But… It was the Fourth of July. I was sitting on the toilet and saw blood on my underpants. Thinking I was bleeding to death, I screamed for my mother. Are there any among us who hadn't felt that moment of panic—impending death—from seeing blood for the first time?" As it was clear that she was thinking to herself while asking that question, no one responded. We waited quietly for Mira to continue.

"When my mother saw the situation, she slapped me on both cheeks, laughing when I cried. She declared me a woman. Why do mothers do that? What a crock! A twelve-year-old woman? I was still a kid and wanted to stay one. And that god-awful sanitary belt with the hooks, from back in my mother's day, which she insisted I use. Yikes, I can still feel myself shifting in my seat to feel more comfortable. I hated that thing, and I hated it hurting, too. Why did I give in? Not long after, I found more modern pads and eventually tampons."

"I never had a sanitary belt. I don't even know what they looked like," Ruth Ann said. "They had 'stick ons' by the time I first got mine."

"Lucky you, Ruthie," Deidre said. "We had to suffer."

Didn't we all? It was so easy to sympathize with Mira and to understand how it felt thinking that everyone would know we were wearing a pad or could see it beneath our clothes. Going through puberty was difficult and having to handle all that while having our period made us even more vulnerable.

"You know," Mira continued, "my mother really wasn't too forthcoming with facts about puberty, periods, babies, or even sex in general. Thank heavens for my best friend Penny and her baby-doctor father. Penny's parents didn't want her to learn the facts of life on the streets. I also benefitted from her new-found knowledge. It certainly helped to know the facts of life before my first time."

I was looking directly at Deidre when I said, "Thank God for friends." Deidre avoided my gaze and shifted in her seat. *What was that all about?*

"I guess each of us has stories to tell about our friends, filling in the gaps of our 'street' facts, or adding to the limited things our mothers told us."

"Well girls, I have to tell you I never thought I'd be sitting in a group, talking about my period. To be truthful, I couldn't fathom dredging up that 'period' in my life, which was so uncomfortable. The very idea of it is too painful. I thought I'd buried those feelings. Listening to all of you has vividly brought them back. In fact, I could vomit right now," Deidre said.

"Why don't you go outside, then," Joesie snapped.

Allison blanched, saying, "Take it easy, Joesie."

Deidre rolled her eyes. At first, she was tense and holding her breath, but then she began to relax and breathe easier as her story unfolded.

"It was on a Saturday when I was about twelve. I was enjoying one of my guiltiest pleasures, reading the latest edition of my favorite comic book, *Millie the Model,* when my mother walked into my room, dropped a pamphlet on my bed and said, 'Read this. Then you can ask me questions if you have any.' She said it all extremely fast, turned on her heel, left my room, and shut the door behind her. I was confused as to why she had left so quickly as she usually lingered, plumping pillows that didn't need fixing, and fluffing my pink bedspread."

"Maybe she was embarrassed or afraid to stay and talk with you?" Joesie asked in a softer tone.

"To be honest, I didn't know what was going on. Then I looked at the title of the pamphlet, *What Every Young Woman Should Know*, and saw all of the diagrams and explanations of how one becomes a woman. It was so cursory and said nothing about menses or pregnancy. Like Mira, I got that information from my friends. Frankly, I was thoroughly annoyed by mother remaining mute. She had no advice about cramps, or my feelings about my period, to the point of avoidance. It wasn't until years later I realized the great attributes of birth control pills. I bless the day they were invented." Heads around the room nodded in agreement.

"Deidre, I can certainly empathize with you and with Mira," Joesie piped up. "Being an army brat, I really never had the time to cultivate true friendships. This writing group is the closest I've come to it. Except for two forever pen pals, my dearest friend was—*is*—my diary/journal. I talk to it, and it always listens. You can imagine what it was like to live with a staunch, militaristic father who wanted a son, and had me instead. Thus, the name Joesie. And to make matters worse, instead of being a tomboy, I was all frills and lace, much to his chagrin." Any of us who had a family member in the military sympathized with Joesie.

Deidre looked bored and muttered under her breath, "Aww."

"We were in Washington, DC, where he had been called to the Pentagon," Joesie continued. "That was move number 274. We never really counted moves. My mother called each move '274' so we wouldn't feel too bad about it. It was much easier that way. On this particular day, my father barked out his orders as he usually did, telling us his/our plans for the day. 'Joe. Be ready at eleven hundred hours. Assemble at the front door with your mother. Wear your sneakers, and I don't want to hear any sissy complaints about too much walking or feet hurting. I could be doing a number of things today, but I acquiesced to your mother, and we are going to the National Zoo for a family outing.' So, I put on my ratty old sneakers, covering up some of their defects with my pretty frilly white socks. I wore my white peasant blouse, and even my white shorts, defying what they might have chosen for me instead."

When Joesie mentioned her mother was a stickler about not wearing white after Labor Day, the room shook with laughter. All of us, it seemed, had mothers like hers. God forbid we stand out, a sight for sore eyes in white. Lordy, what would people think? We might just become outcasts. There was no room for individuality back then. Just follow the pack, and all will be well.

"Wow! Is that based on religion, too? Oh, yeah, it's the 'Fashionista's Bible,'" Deidre said.

"Just like on the day Kennedy was assassinated, the Challenger Disaster, or even 9/11," Joesie continued, "the day is etched in my mind. If I ever forget either of those days, I know I'll be in deep, deep trouble. I had a horrendous stomachache, but I knew if I complained, the trip to the zoo would be abandoned. I went to the bathroom one more time and ended up screaming for help. No doubt, with the windows open, the whole neighborhood could hear me.

'*Eek*! *Yuck!* Mother help me, I'm bleeding to death! It's all over me and still running down my legs. Come quickly before I die!' Mother, upon entering the bathroom with her skeleton key proclaimed, 'Oh my God! You're wearing white. Well, young lady, you deserve to get your friend today and miss the zoo trip. And why are you so upset? You should know from me and all of your friends that this is just the natural way of things, and we women all go through menstruation so we can have children one day.'"

"Surely, every twelve-year-old girl is beyond thrilled to hear that," Allison interjected. "What a difference it is for girls today. No big deal for my daughter."

"My dad couldn't have been happier that he didn't have to go to the zoo," Joesie explained sadly. "He soon disappeared for the day. I was 'on the rag' until my mother went to the pharmacy to get me that confounded belt with the metal clips. The plastic clips in later years weren't much better. From that day on, I wasn't sure I would want to have any children. I also wasn't sure if I would know how to be a parent a child would love."

"We all had our doubts. You would have been a great mother," Allison said and patted Joesie's knee.

"Despite my mother giving me the book *The Facts of Life for Teenagers*, I really didn't learn about all the aspects of sex until much later on. I learned to use tampons late, also. When I was in college, my dorm mates coached me and a couple of friends while we struggled behind stall doors in the bathroom with our own 'mini missiles,'" Joesie explained.

"Every twenty-eight days without fail, except when I was pregnant, my 'friend' appeared," Mira said. "Why do they call it 'friend?' Ain't nothing friendly about it. There were months I wished menstruation on some of the males I met, and still do. I'd really love to see them suffer as we do. I'm glad Avrom's not here to voice his opinion." Again, smirks of agreement from all of us.

"Is that 'Little Miss Goody Two-shoes' speaking?" Deidre asked, as she paced the room impatiently.

"I'm sitting here listening to all of you," I interrupted, "and I, Roxie, could take a piece from each of your stories to make mine come alive. I recall so vividly the day I got the 'curse,' a much more appropriate name for it. I was also twelve, in junior high school, wanting to be more grown up and to wear a bra because I had big boobs instead of those little molehills. On one particular day I was wearing that horrific blue gym suit—you know, the one with baggy shorts, elastic waist, and short sleeves? It was so unattractive and not at all appealing to the boys, but it was comfortable for riding my bike to and from school." There were murmurs of assent, and for a few moments we all reminisced about our gym suits.

"Enough, already. Aren't we done yet with this 'bloody' talk?" Joesie exclaimed.

"No, Joesie, Roxie hasn't finished yet," Ruth Ann said.

"Late in the day," I went on, "I thought I'd burst if I didn't make it to the bathroom. I got a hall pass and went to the restroom, where I discovered blood in my pants. Great, just great.

Now I needed to figure out how to ride home, balancing my books and the lemon meringue pie I'd made in home economics, all the while praying that I wouldn't have blood dripping down my legs. It must have looked like a scene out of a comedy.

When I got home, I handed the pie to my mother and ran past her to my bathroom, where all of my period needs were waiting under my sink. I put on that ridiculously painful belt with the clips, as I would every month after that, and went to tell my mother what had happened. As one might predict, knowing my mother, she proclaimed me a woman and slapped my face— 'Tradition,' she said. She kept saying 'it's tradition, an age-old Jewish tradition.' For God's sake, does it say in the Torah all women must be slapped when they get their period? I'm sure not, but if I'd have asked that of my mother, she'd have given me far more than a slap."

"Naturally, I got slapped too. My mother said it was to assure good behavior, though I don't know if it was religiously oriented. What the hell did she think I'd do at age twelve?" Mira wondered aloud.

"Your mother slapped you, too?" Ruth Ann asked. "Why?"

"Superstition said it would knock sense into the young woman, to not embarrass herself or her family by becoming pregnant," Mira said.

"Another superstition was that the slap would ward off the evil eye," I said. "Tradition! Like I would chance having to tell my mother I was pregnant?"

"At age twelve, I just didn't like the sting of the slap," Mira added.

The ebb and flow of our tales came to an end as the afternoon waned. Period, curse, friend, whatever we named it, it was a monthly constant in our lives. We were linked together as women, accepting our religious differences and customs, as well as furthering our bonds as writers. To think it had all started with spilled raspberries!

∾

～27～

EVE'S DESCENT

How would I convince everyone to go into the library with me? After laughing and sharing adventures of blood and youth, the library would seem rather dull and elicit few laughs. But I really didn't want to go back there alone, so I crafted a summary of my last visit that was both factual and also a little fanciful. I told them about seeing a trick panel and a maze of doors and passages. In truth, I needed their moral support. Then, as though a message from my grumbling belly, I smelled the distinct aroma of roast beef.

Mira asked, "Do you smell something cooking?" Then, turning her head while wrinkling her nose, Deidre tried to pick up the scent. "It's certainly not perfume. Maybe it's an illusion."

"Are you all nuts?" Ruth Ann cried. "We must be losing it. Phantom smells, perhaps?"

"Not I," Allison exclaimed. "I don't smell a thing."

"Do you think it's coming from Hazel's or Jimmy John's cottage?" Mira pondered. "I wonder if he's a good cook?"

"Anyway, ladies, if you don't mind waiting a second, I have to run to the front desk to get the key to unlock the *bibliothèque*," I said. No one asked how I knew where the key was or uttered a sound as they waited for me. But before I could do anything with the key, the door opened.

I was busted: caught red-handed, the warmth of embarrassment creeping from my neck to my forehead. Standing like a queen inside the library doorway was Eve. Her regal attire was a deeper shade of red than my flushed cheeks. She was clad in a smashing, perfectly fitting, long-sleeved, velvet gown with a jeweled necklace. Her jewelry, presumably rhinestones and not *real* diamonds, was set off by a large ruby-like stone hanging from the sparkling strands that must have numbered at least four. Silver Cinderella slippers peeked out from under the bottom of the gown that I surmised had been fashioned especially for her.

All five of my "sisters" assembled behind me. We stood at attention as though my late father was due for an inspection tour of all the troops on base.

"I alone am guilty of exploring this room and discovering, quite by accident, the maze of passages," I explained to Eve, blushing as I hung my head in guilt. "However, the darkness combined with the yellow streak down my back prevented me from going very far. Please forgive me for my zealous curiosity. Not very becoming of an uninvited intruder to whom you've been so generous. And I'm unquestionably responsible for dragging my friends along as seeming accomplices. My parents would not have approved of such behavior. I assure you they raised me to have better manners and not be a snoop—certainly at this age." I knew I was babbling, but at that point couldn't stop myself.

"Knowing you all were out fishing, raspberry picking, and wandering afar, we just knew you were having such fun discovering Raspberry Hill and its environs. Then Charles and I could hear the rummaging around from upstairs, even with our old ears. But that comes from years of hearing curious guests. All your exploring is so natural and a compliment to this unusual house that we have created and loved. We can't imagine being anywhere else, especially an old-age home. Don't think for a moment that we were upset with you… Joesie, right?" Eve gestured gracefully as she spoke in her soft, unmistakable accent and smiled charmingly at us.

I wondered how Eve remembered my name. Was that a good or bad omen?

"Joesie. Did I have that right?" she repeated. "My mind is not so sharp as it once was, my dear. You're the prettiest 'Joe' I've ever met."

"Thank you… And for remembering my name."

She nodded and continued. "Well, Charles, Hazel, and I have decided to have a celebration."

There were other open but unusually silent mouths besides mine after she said that. Mira was the first to burst forth with a comment. "What kind of celebration have you planned? And for whom?"

"Well, for all you cheerful and lovely surprise guests, of course! Charles and I have grand plans for dinner in the special dining room tonight. Hazel has been cooking for hours. And I think we should all dress up in costumes. How do they say it now? 'Just say yes?' We hope you don't mind our directing the evening's festivities."

"Mind? Hardly. We're overwhelmed," Roxie said, speaking for us all, but with a perplexed look on her face.

"How can she cook without power?"

"You know that Hazel. She has her ways."

"I knew I smelled roast beef," Joesie added.

"We've been starving, and they can cook around here?" Deidre whispered to Allison.

"I can smell the aromas coming from somewhere. You mustn't go to such trouble for unexpected guests who aren't able to leave yet. But Eve, help me, please. I'm a few thoughts behind. Costumes? We have only the clothes on our backs. I can't imagine what we could fashion from your terry cloth robes and white sheets except Halloween attire."

"But surely, Joesie, you've found our costume closet?"

"No!" Joesie said. "All I remember is an empty ballroom with only a feathery boa hanging over the ballet barre and a 'Happy New Year' tiara from the year 2000 on the floor. There was a closet, but I think it was empty."

"Well, my dear librarian, just open the closet door over there then," Eve said.

Allison leaned into Roxie and said, "How the hell does she know Joesie's a librarian?"

"I d-don't know. Do you think she's been listening to all our conversations? Charles, too?" Roxie whispered. "OMG!"

Surely, she must have known the closet was virtually empty. But, as Eve had directed me, I obediently walked over and opened the door. I was aghast. I even checked to make sure it was the same door I had opened a few hours ago. It contained not only the feathery boa and tiara but was filled with a multitude of hangers bulging with an array of colors and textures: silks, suedes, velvets, sequins, beadings, hats and belts, gloves, swords, skirts, dresses, pants, and shirts—too innumerable to absorb.

"Eve, how did I miss these costumes and accessories? And I didn't even drink any of the Scotch Mira passed around last night."

"*Elementary*, my dear, to quote my favorite, Mr. Conan Doyle. Hazel brought the clothes out of storage. We had some good laughs, reminiscing about the years of fun we'd had, dressing up for so many parties. We continued to add more garments and trinkets to the collection over time. We have been a favorite resource for the local amateur thespian group as well."

She held her ruby pendant as she continued, "These foolish family treasures have been in storage far too long. After we're gone, the local thespians can comb through the boxes. Let them haggle over them." I was staring and consumed with my earlier erroneous assumption. Eve was wearing an incredibly beautiful necklace of actual diamonds surrounding the real ruby pendant. *They must be real. Look at how they sparkle!*

Roxie nodded in agreement as if I had spoken.

"I've seen enough jewels in Palm Beach to recognize the difference." We wondered why these items weren't in a safe deposit box. "Won't their heirs be lucky some day?" Roxie commented aloud to no one in particular.

Eve continued, "And the costumes haven't been used since our last New Year's Eve party. Hmm, I can't remember how long ago that was. Anyhow, enough of all this falderal. Would you ladies mind terribly much sorting through the costumes and making some decisions on your evening's attire? I hope you will be as excited as we are to share our food and a bit of theatrics. Any objections?"

We shook our heads to the negative, with unexpected awe in our eyes. We snapped out of our military stance realizing we could now happily explore whatever we wished to wear to dinner. Fabric and accessories began flying out of cartons and into hands. It was like Filene's Basement when they used to open for their annual wedding dress sale called "The Run of the Brides."

Eve broke through the clamor to give her parting instructions. "I'll see you back here promptly at half past six, in full regalia, of course. We'll go down the stairs, past the larder, then into the lower dining room. Oh, it'll be such jolly fun, with wonderful bits and bobs to taste."

"Is this all a dream about to become a nightmare?" I wondered aloud.

Everyone except me continued pawing through the closet and found dresses that fit them perfectly. Fixed on a western theme, I was certain I'd never find what I wanted, and lamented out loud, "You know, even American Indians traveled abroad as part of troupes entertaining eager European audiences. I remember reading that one chief married a wealthy European lady after they fell in love following one of his shows."

"Always the librarian, full of tidbits," Allison said.

I became like an omniscient observer. Their collective excitement, amazement, and comments began to unfold like a scene from a drama as I listened to their shared musings.

Roxie

I was almost speechless. The costumes were hanging in an organized row and begging to be worn. They reminded me of a detour amidst a promising modeling career. While in college, I had been chosen for a collegiate fashion shoot, the result of which led me to be picked by Ralph Lauren for his college collection. In turn, I had offers from *Seventeen* magazine, Lord & Taylor, and the biggest prize, Chanel, to model its fall collections. Juggling my class schedule and runway shows was not easy, but I loved it. After I met Ben, modeling came to an abrupt halt as I became immersed in real estate with him.

Mira

The heap of autumn colors caught my eye. I had an image filling my head of lovely things soaring above us, catching the breeze of the summer night, slipping through the door and into the closet. And one was mine—only mine. I lifted the mélange of leafy cloth draped on a hanger. I saw there were two pieces, a skirt, and a blouse. It looked as if the fall leaves from the trees outside of Raspberry Hill had found their way into the finesse of the seamstress' hands that put them together.

Allison

It seemed odd that something that had been hanging in storage for at least a few years could look so fresh and new. I couldn't believe these were the same colors from my dream. How ironic! Fibers usually show some wear and soften with time, but these could have come from a window display of a contemporary department store, except for the style.

Roxie

Eve has such an eye for period costumes. Oh, the feeling of them! The touch was so pleasing. Wouldn't I have loved to own this collection.

Ruth Ann

Maybe there's still some hot water on the woodstove? It would be nice to have a warm clean-up.

I volunteered for the mission, returning with some washcloths and two buckets of water; one was for a respectable wash, the other to rinse out some of the grime.

Roxie also came to our rescue. She rushed out and returned with a travel-size atomizer of Coco perfume from her purse and toilet tissue from the loo. Visiting each of us, she carefully sprayed puffs in all the right places to help mask any lingering unpleasant scents. "Like eating onions, Joesie. If we all smell the same, what the hell!"

Mira

I couldn't help but smile. Look at these vintage costumes! If we hold them up and twirl, we'll look like princesses. Deidre found clips and bobby pins in one of the boxes. All of our gowns fit so perfectly that we didn't need to enhance or stuff our chests with wads of toilet tissue as some women do. We transformed ourselves from accidental waifs to glorious aristocrats—almost. I knew I had to dress first and be the greeter, hoping not to end up like a crazy costume monster, and get blamed if our outfits failed. Maybe that's because I've always been uncomfortable picking out dresses for special occasions. For Avrom, I had to be careful to dress conservatively, going against my natural instinct. Not that I didn't look good in dressy clothes, but I hated the trying-on and looking at the too-lumpy hips and too-round behind. But this dress called out to me, "I'm yours, Mira, I'm yours."

Ruth Ann

"C'mon, Mira. What are you on, girl? My dress doesn't talk."

Josie

Pulling myself from my mental screenplay, I shook my head in wonder. *How did I do that? Take a deep breath, Joesie.*

When my faithful Timex glow-in-the-dark watch read six fifteen, I looked out the door and up the stairs towards Eve's residence. It remained off limits, which only enhanced my curiosity.

Promptly at half past six I opened the door again. Eve was standing at the top of the landing, looking stately. The train of her dress cascaded down over the stairs, looking light and airy as if she could float, if so inclined. I could hear two loud voices.

"Charles!" Lady Eve called. "Don't forget your ascot and matching cummerbund."

I assumed, due to the volume of Eve's voice, that Charles was hard of hearing. A shimmering tiara sat atop her silvery mane.

"What color would be appropriate, lovey?" I heard Charles inquire.

"The one that matches my dress, of course. This is like a holiday. And certainly, you can wear the ribbons and brass you tell everyone is your royal crest-of-the-whatever that makes you a knight or something. No one will suspect the truth—mere trinkets that the Scottish Regiment returned to your family when Uncle Percy perished in World War I. Here, now, let me help you pin them on. Don't forget to brush your hair. I shall meet you in the dining room anon with our guests," she gushed.

"Righty-ho, my dear. Now be on your way."

I quickly returned through the library to the ballroom. It was an incredible sight. Allison and Ruth Ann were about to wear the colors described by Allison in her dream. First, Allison slid her jeans down her legs and removed them, leaving her socks on. Then she lifted her black t-shirt over her head, stepping into the yellowed crinoline and then the dress. Bosoms and bustles were being rearranged into the right places with perfectly fitting waistlines and hem-lengths. How incredibly unbelievable! Tiny pin tucks gathered at Allison's waist, and a line of fine lace ran along the sweetheart neckline. The indigo-colored fabric of the dress moved and flowed as Allison twirled around gracefully.

"I wonder if it's taffeta?" Allison sighed happily, "But it seems far more fluid. I think it has to be silk. It shines with a soft luster. I love the way it goes all the way to the floor."

"And the tight bodice and full undergarments hold the skirt out. You don't think my sweetheart neckline reveals too much? After all, Charles will be there," Ruth Ann, who'd dressed quickly next, fretted.

"Not at all," she replied. "The Celtic Renaissance style is utterly becoming and conservative. I love the way it laces up the back with the cream-colored ribbon. Here, let me help tighten it for you. And don't worry about Charles looking at your chest. He must be a perfect gentleman with those aging eyes. There won't be any lecherous males to contend with except maybe Jimmy John. Does he count?" Allison looked a bit mischievous as she said this.

Ruth Ann's waistline was perfectly pinched with the princess-style lines, which fell down to a full skirt of vivid green velvet, flowing gently to the floor. The bodice was taffeta with a muted pattern.

"I know flip flops had been my trademark, at least in the summer," Allison said aloud. "But even I feel they are inappropriate for this occasion. Oh, what are we girls to do?"

"I just reached into the closet, under the skirt of this dress that I'm trying to pour into, and *voila*! Luck be ours again," Mira said. I was stunned at what lay beneath her dress. Five pairs of shoes, one set to match each of the dresses, awaited our smelly feet. I had already declared that I would only wear boots.

"You don't think they'll fit us, do you? Now that would be too coincidental," Allison stated.

Roxie, the indomitable one, touched the pair that matched her satiny silver creation, crying out, "My big feet will never fit into them." And like a stepsister in Cinderella, Roxie pressed on. We shared a hearty giggle as Roxie's right foot slipped into the shiny size nine. Her face paled and her dark eyes widened with disbelief as she softly managed, "What's going on here? I guess I'm Cinderella after all!"

"Well, now that Deidre, Ruth Ann, and I have had a laugh at your expense, you can slip into the dress to match the shoes," Mira suggested. "Joesie and Allison, stop staring. Time's a-wastin'!"

"What are the odds that this is a custom piece for someone with my exact measurements?" Allison wondered as she held her arms out to highlight the perfect fit. She looked at herself in the full-length mirror on the inside of the closet door. I marveled at her eyes, their rich chocolate hue complimented her skin and hair.

As if reading my mind, Allison said, "I used to call my eyes 'bovine brown,' or the color of dirt. Thank you, Joesie. Suddenly the blue contacts I've been wearing for years seem garish in comparison." I turned away from Allison with a smile, opened the library door, acknowledged Eve, and curtsied. She greeted us warmly.

"You look perfect!" Eve said as she glided soundlessly into the room. "Let us go two-by-two. We will journey down the stairs in pairs, leaving this 'Raspberry Hill Ark' that saved you from the near-biblical storm." She was holding a velvety pouch that held tiaras, and she presented them to us with a flourish. Now, everyone was crowned. "You shall all be my ladies-in-waiting. After all, you *are* waiting to go back to your own worlds. I'll be back shortly for the next two."

"I'm partial to the gold-lamé gown with embroidered velvet flowers along the hem of the skirt. It reminds me of one I saw in the 1920s costume exhibit at the Met," Deidre said, positively glowing.

"I've always longed to wear Chanel," Roxie said. "Ben had told me many times that he would buy me one if I found a dress I really loved. Until now, I have been disappointed. Come on, Deidre."

"You can't be telling me that Eve has real couture gowns?" Mira asked incredulously. "Deidre, you and I will go next," Roxie continued. "I can't wait. I couldn't help but recognize my dress, in the style of my favorites, Chanel and Charles Frederick Worth."

"See for yourself. It's gorgeous, isn't it? Look at the workmanship. I can't imagine what something like this must cost," Deidre said, looking knowingly at Roxie.

"Well, don't just stand there. Put them on! You've got the shoes, Roxie. Now put on the expensive dress," Mira said, exasperated that they weren't ready yet.

"Can you ladies even believe how each costume enhances our best features—like instant makeovers?" Deidre asked, putting the dress over Roxie's arm. She went into the closet and emerged quickly in a silver satin gown trimmed in Alençon lace with crystal thread and beading.

"Come on, Roxie, you'll be fashionably late again. Shake a leg. Adjust the bodice already—I'm hungry!" Mira was tapping her foot, clearly impatient.

"This takes me to some other world. The glittering threads enhanced the silver in my hair. How could anyone not be pleased to be in my shoes? The only thing missing is Ben being able to share my thrill of being in a Chanel," Roxie said, still focused on her amazing luck to be in such a dress.

"You look sensational. Your husband should appreciate what you're worth. I'm utterly amazed mine fits. I love the dropped waist, wide skirt, and burnished gold color. The gown makes me feel like a courtier. It hides my muffin top," Deidre said, smiling hesitantly.

"Give us a whirl, Deidre, so I can see the embroidery." Mira had finally stopped pestering Roxie to hurry. "I'm trying to imagine who the previous proud owner of such a glorious gown was," she said as she stroked the velvet flowers. "One would think that given the stifling heat of the summer's day, I'd be hot in this, but strangely, I'm not." Deidre was still fixated on how the dress had instantly lifted her looks to another level.

This time, Eve opened the door without knocking. After all, it was her house. As she placed tiaras on Roxie's and Deidre's heads, she exclaimed, "How wonderfully fun this all is! Now, one of you on my right, and the other on my left. Take an arm and we are on our way. See you two soon," she said to us, the last pair.

Before leaving with Eve and Roxie, Deidre paused, turned back for one last glance, and whispered, "I'm spooked, but the food smells terrific. Let's go."

Thoughts flashed through my brain's more sensible side—will we ever leave, or have we entered an alternate universe? Will we need the Marines and helicopters to rescue us? After all, there was a surprise dinner awaiting us somewhere below. How trusting had we become?

The last costume hanging was mine, whether I liked it or not, I guessed. All I wanted was a western old-time cowgirl look, from any century. The last to be amazed, I discovered a fuchsia brocade jacket with black, looped frog closures. The shoulders were well padded. The sleeves narrowed down to the wrists. The black skirt, sculpted shorter in the front and dipped down in back, was a perfect complement. A black felt lady's Stetson was attached by the drawstring over the only satin hanger. Next to it hung a studded-leather double holster with two realistic toy six-shooters.

"Don't worry, Mira. My father took me target shooting and I can hit the bull's-eye," I quipped as I strapped on the holster.

A beautiful, sparkling, studded pin was attached to the front of the jacket. I smiled at the faux rubies and rhinestones, which twinkled like the real thing. I could be the madam in any saloon. I so wished I could have found the perfect boots, too. Why not? They would complete the outfit. I didn't even want a Worth or Gucci or any other designer anything. The western look is my gig.

"Let's see if the magic is real!" I exclaimed as I rummaged through the closet. No one had ever seen me speechless, but I sure was as I picked up a pair of gold cowgirl boots.

"Joesie, you've found a costume right out of a western novel. You look *right purdy*," Mira exclaimed with an exaggerated accent.

"Why, a mighty big thank you, Mira. We're the last girls still standing. Let me help you with your buttons in the back when you're ready." I watched, aghast, as Mira ripped off her clothes. I buttoned the back of her bodice.

"Look at me. I look absolutely gorgeous. And I didn't even need to spend a dime," Mira exclaimed as she twirled around.

Finally, Eve returned for Mira and me and put my tiara around the brim of my hat.

"I'll be the first cowgirl to wear a tiara. A tiara and a Stetson on a *really* bad hair day. Imagine wearing both."

I had turned an unexpected corner and made an emotional detour. I was on the other side of fear—well past "what if we had drowned?" No longer obsessing about when we would get back to the Abenaki Lodge, let alone home, I was even enjoying our newfound adventure. The telephone wasn't ringing, the television wasn't blasting. Although The Inn certainly wasn't a luxurious spa, we were exchanging emotional massages with one another, plus the promise of a gourmet dinner ahead rather than fish and raspberries. From what might have been death and destruction, we had, by chance or divine intervention, stumbled upon another world.

⁓

The Inn

Things were peaceful here at The Inn at Raspberry Hill. Though I could use some repairs, Jimmy John did his best with the upkeep. I kept a close eye on my little family, making sure never to scare the guests. After all, I was their livelihood. Now, I'm to be sold. That cannot happen.

Since going on the market, The Inn at Raspberry Hill has been dormant. Realtors brought a few people through, but no offers had come. Jimmy John wanted to own me, but he did not have the capital. He had the most to lose if someone else bought me.

The cabin on the grounds was his home, the only home he had ever had for himself. Growing up in the main house, he had wanted to find his own place when he returned from college. His aunt, Hazel, had moved to a small cottage on the grounds. Eve and Charles encouraged him to stay on as the caretaker and chef, as Eve, Charles, and Hazel needed that extra assistance.

Jimmy John had agreed to stay, mostly for Aunt Hazel's sake. He felt both the pull to go out on his own and an obligation to stay. After all, Eve and Charles had put him through college, where he had learned his culinary skills. He longed to test his favorite dishes at a gourmet restaurant. However, there was enough to do here at The Inn to keep him interested. He had learned so much at college, but Eve and Hazel had taught him, too. He knew all the family recipes and delighted guests with scrumptious blue-berry buckle, a full English breakfast, including orange juice, eggs, bangers, and whatever else the guests requested as a full country breakfast.

Each night, Jimmy John would leave a basket of goodies at the door for any guests who were checking in or returning late, along with the breakfast menu for the following morning. He loved to pass the time talking with the guests. There was so much to learn about the world. Guests would share details about their hometowns, places they'd been, and places they were going. Jimmy John, having been born in the south, only remembered two places in his life: Massachusetts, where he was raised, and Florida, where he went to college at Johnson & Wales to become a chef. In his mind's eye, his life was pretty narrow. He longed to explore the world, perhaps with someone special. To be an innkeeper like Eve and Charles was an even bigger dream.

Since childhood, Jimmy John mostly hung around with Eve and Charles and Aunt Hazel. He learned that doing for others was the life of innkeepers. Watching the two hovering around their guests, fixing this, cleaning that, preparing fabulous breakfasts, and always making sure they were happy and comfortable, felt like old times. With the help of Aunt Hazel and the young Jimmy John, the four were a team, a family that made others comfortable, and set an example for innkeeping.

Hazel was the one who picked up the slack. She cleaned endlessly, dusting, sweeping, and filling in for whatever role was needed. Though getting on in years she still loved to help. She no longer had a "job" at The Inn; she had a life-long contract allowing her to age in place. Whatever happened to The Inn, Hazel, her cat Merlin, and mouse Sir Lancelot, would be able to live out their lives here. So, for that, the older woman continued to putter around, keeping the place as presentable as possible.

Charles, always the gentleman, did the chores assigned by Eve. Not that he was a pushover. Eve was the love of his life and he did whatever he could to please her. One of his favorite things to do for her, besides the regular upkeep of The Inn, was to find small things to please her. He might leave a select dark chocolate morsel on her pillow or polish some silverware.

On Sunday evenings, Charles would take Eve's car keys from the key box by the door and clean her car, inside and out. Eve "would catch him in the act," so to speak, and insist she could clean the car herself. But the chivalrous Charles would chuckle, wiping down the leather seats, vacuuming the carpets, washing the windows inside and out. At least quarterly, he would hand wax the exterior. He was so proud of that shine, and who could blame him? When Eve looked at him with the same love in her eyes as on their wedding day, he gladly toiled for her.

Not that Eve was a slouch herself. She loved to entertain and had a wide array of costumes. She kept Charles in pressed clothes, home-cooked food, and provided all the love and affection a good wife could give. When the couple became empty nesters, since Jimmy John had moved to his own house, they came together as one.

While many couples their age slept in separate bedrooms, Charles and Eve enjoyed their four-poster bed on the second floor of The Inn. Neither ever considered having a bedroom of their own. In fact, they looked forward to their special time together. Whether I was full of guests or empty, Charles and Eve made it a point never to go to bed angry. It was a ritual. Charles would say, "Eve, have you had a good day today?" And Eve would answer, "I am blessed with another good day. Good night, Charles." And, of course, Charles would answer, "Good night, my Eve. Pleasant dreams." Then they would kiss goodnight.

So, with the furniture covered, no guests to arrive, and only Jimmy John to do the upkeep, I was in a bit of disrepair. How I longed for the old days when life here bustled. But sell me to strangers? No! Perish the thought!

∼28∼

BANQUET

What a sight we were! All decked out in our "period" costumes, plus our own Ms. Joesie in cowboy boots, right out of the old television show *The Wild Wild West*. I couldn't help but ask myself why we were snaking our way into the basement of this old inn.

Despite our glamorous costumes, I worried I was in a bad slasher movie where the climax had yet to come. The cautious person that I am, I should have been at least a bit more nervous, but wasn't. I felt beautiful. The smell of the food spread through the halls like a gentle breeze, tickling my hungry tummy. I didn't question how the food was being cooked. I entered the room like a virgin to the slaughter.

Sitting down at the table, I adjusted the bodice of my gown, pulling the bust up a bit more on my chest in case Jimmy John came in. I didn't want to reveal too much. I sat near the end of the long banquet table, feeling as special as a prom queen but still a bit exposed. A preschool teacher like me doesn't get many opportunities to wear a ball gown. I was not used to my bosom, as my mother would say, on display like this. The green gown clung in all the right places; the lines were form-fitting but not tight.

Joesie had laced up the back. My chest puffed out like a pigeon. I was proud as a peacock.

My skin was as white as the linen napkin in my lap. I felt like a princess in my Celtic gown. I had never dressed this way before, like a porcelain doll that might break at any moment. Try as I may, I could not make the dress less revealing. I loved the flowing sleeves, finally deciding to concentrate on the company around me instead of how exposed I felt.

The table was set for ten, with four chairs on each long side and one at each end. There were the six of us plus Eve, Charles, and Hazel. I assumed Jimmy John would eventually appear. Charles sat at the helm, looking suave and debonair in his medal bedecked dinner jacket and ascot, with Eve to his left on the long side of the table. Next to her sat the sparkling duo, Deidre and Mira. Joesie, Allison, Roxie, and I sat across from them. The seat at the end of the table next to me was empty. I fantasized that it was reserved for Jimmy John but to my disappointment, I did not see him. In my mind's eye, Jimmy John would enter the room, fully able to see my exposed bosom. I would be mortified yet somehow stimulated. Feeling like an old maid had not completely destroyed my natural desire.

Yes, if he did arrive for dinner, I would have the opportunity to get to know him. I continued to hope that the empty seat near me was saved for him. Who else would it be for, anyway? Not easy to get to The Inn with trees down. Maybe he was out working on the storm damage or perhaps he had something else to fix. Finally, I worked up the courage to ask, "Is Jimmy John joining us?"

"Oh no, dearie. He's trying to clear the road. Don't worry yourself. We'll save him a plate," Eve replied.

After the teasing I took this afternoon, I vowed not to be interested in this man, but I was disappointed he wouldn't be joining us. Yet, despite my self-protests, the memory of his clear green eyes and our brief conversation kept intruding. Though I didn't want to admit it, I was smitten.

"Oh," Roxie exclaimed, looking from one of us to the other. This is the china pattern I saw upstairs. Who polished the silver?" It sat so elegantly on the crisp ivory damask tablecloth. Hazel, with a starched apron covering her navy-blue dress, mumbled as she served. I glanced around the table and noticed pre-set glasses of water and champagne.

"This place is becoming more and more bizarre," Allison remarked. "What next?"

"Look at this feast. Bizarre or not, I'm eating," Mira declared.

Charles sat at the head of the table, offering the toast. "To our lovely lady travelers. May you find your way home and take a bit of Raspberry Hill hospitality with you wherever you may go. For tonight, let's raise our glasses to new and old friendships." With a smile as big as Santa Claus himself, he held his glass high in the air but did not drink. His hands were pale, almost translucent, and displayed a slight tremor. As he made the toast, the lit sconces on the walls dimmed, leaving the candelabras on the table to lend us their intimate lighting.

"Joesie, you're pale as a ghost," Mira exclaimed. "What's wrong?"

"I am out of here if the candles go out," Joesie replied, pointing at the candelabra on the table. As she spoke, the sconces flickered back on, brightening the dim room again.

I raised my glass and clinked it lightly against Joesie's, Allison's, and Roxie's, but couldn't reach the rest so we raised our glasses in unison. I sipped the champagne cautiously, as I am not much of a drinker. I have to say it tasted heavenly.

The banquet table, laden with china and silver, appeared picture-perfect. The prepared feast before us looked like something out of a medieval romance. I stared at the food, salivating. Normally not a big eater, being stranded had a way of whetting my appetite. Some of us had smelled the dinner cooking, which turned out to be English roast beef, whole boiled potatoes, a luscious brown gravy, the brightest green beans I had ever seen, and my favorite, Yorkshire pudding. Like a popover, the Yorkshire pudding was delicate, light, and delicious. It was served first, as Hazel explained the tradition. She set one in front of each of us, uttering, "Tradition, tradition, tradition... eat, eat, eat... pudding, pudding, pudding."

"Why does that woman say everything three times?" I whispered across to Roxie, who laughed a nervous little laugh.

She nodded in understanding and asked, "Where are the raspberries?"

Deidre signaled across the table and said in a low tone, "I'm just as glad. I swear I felt weird after eating them. You?"

"Beats me," I answered. "I'm not questioning anything. Eat, eat, eat."

"Where did all this food come from?" Joesie asked, looking at Eve for answers. "She certainly didn't cook all of this on the woodstove."

"What the hell is going on here?" Allison whispered. "Who knows? Who cares? Let's eat!" I said, reassured that the earlier smells were from the cooking of this incredible feast.

Eve just smiled and raised her glass with a simple, "Enjoy!"

I noticed even more vegetables: carrots, Brussel sprouts, and peas. Charles took the lead and sliced the side of beef with a large, ornate carving knife, laying each slice on a silver platter that Hazel passed around to all of us. The sides were served family-style. The steam coming up from the food filled the room with aromas that again called to my empty tummy.

"Where were you hiding all this food?" Roxie asked.

"Yeah, and who cooked it and on what and with what?" Deidre whispered loudly enough for all to hear.

Taking no notice, Charles smiled and said, "My apologies to you. My lady and I are less accustomed to guests than we once were. Hopefully, this feast will make up for our inhospitality."

"These dresses are lovely," Allison said, changing the subject, her glittering brown eyes focused on Lady Eve. "When were they last worn?"

"Long ago, dearie," Eve said, fingering her jeweled necklace.

Hazel milled around, serving food, and pouring water into our glasses with odd efficiency. I would have guessed that Hazel was on the verge of succumbing to dementia, but tonight, she did herself proud. She kept repeating, "Water anyone? Water anyone? Water anyone?" She served us, nodding, and smiling at our hosts. Hazel was last to fill her plate. She sat down next to Mira, laboriously cutting her meal into tiny chunks. She adjusted her false teeth and ate.

"You have a long journey ahead. Eat up and be ready. Otherwise, I'll have to make a scramble out of the leftovers—bubble and squeak for tomorrow!" Eve exclaimed in her lilting accent.

"My favorite, dear," Charles added, gazing at Eve with the look of a man deeply in love. His gaze inspired me to believe that romance still existed. My hope was that if Charles still loved Eve, maybe I would find someone to love—maybe Jimmy John.

"Enough about us, dearies. What about you?" Eve interjected. "Charles, don't you want to hear about our ladies' travels?" Without giving Charles a chance to respond, Eve continued. "What brings you all here?"

"Well, we were at a writers' conference in Washburn, New York and decided to visit the bookstore at Destiny Life Institute in Rhinebeck. We were on our way back to the Abenaki Lodge when the storm hit. We almost went off the road. The thunder, lightning…" Mira exclaimed.

"And we came to a 'bridge out' sign," I added, "and almost got washed away."

Eve and Charles, raptly listening, exchanged glances. Then Charles spoke. "You know, you're not in New York anymore."

"Then where in the world are we?" Deidre asked.

"This is Western Massachusetts, better known as the Berkshires," Eve explained.

"I knew this place looked familiar," I mentioned. "Wasn't it the Hoosic River that overflowed in the storm?"

"Indeed," Charles confirmed.

"Oh, we're in paradise without electricity," Joesie added, her expression flat.

"You're right, Joesie," I stated, "the Berkshires are considered a little slice of paradise. Many people from New York and even Canada have vacation homes here. You can swim and shop in the summer. There's a lively arts community here as well. Summer stock theatre brings in many famous actors and there are museums to visit. Hiking up Mount Greylock is also popular. In the winter, skiing and other winter sports bring in many vacationers. My mother lives just south of here, where I grew up. But I agree about the electricity. Hope it comes back on soon."

"You should know, Ruth Ann. You grew up here, right?" Allison asked.

"There'll be plenty of writing material after this detour," Roxie muttered.

We continued exchanging pleasantries as we ate, drank, and chatted. At the end of the meal, I needed to use the bathroom. My constant need for the bathroom was a family joke. I swear Eve was clairvoyant and read my mind as I do with my young students, except I wasn't wiggling in my seat or showing other signs.

"Darling, not to worry. The loo is just up the stairs to the right," Eve gushed, and I swear she winked at me.

It was as if she'd read my mind. "I need to go but I've lost my bearings."

I pushed back my chair, carefully lifted the full skirt of my gown, and tried to tiptoe out of the room. I still managed to step on the hem, lose my balance, and nearly landed in Roxie's lap. I apologized, held the gown even higher, and made my way upstairs to the bathroom. The glow from a hurricane lantern flickered and provided just enough light for me to finish my business, which wasn't easy with yards of material to manage. *This must be how a bride feels when her bladder has the audacity to need emptying.* I bumped into Jimmy John in the hall of the main floor.

"Here, let me take your arm, miss," he said. "I've been waiting for you." I felt my face flush.

I tried to recover some dignity and out of the depths of my being, I heard myself speak, "You can call me Ruth Ann."

"Well, Lady Ruth Ann, I see you found the costumes. You look beautiful in that gown, a lot different from when I saw you earlier on the trail. Let me adjust your tiara." He leaned over, looking directly in my eyes, and straightened it. I blushed, thinking he was going to try to kiss me.

"What's the occasion?" Jimmy John asked.

"Hazel made us an elegant dinner. It was delicious," I answered. "What a wonderful time it must have been in Eve and Charles's heyday."

"To be sure," Jimmy John answered, looking downcast.

I wondered why.

The Inn

I willed my old door to open with less difficulty than usual as the two lovebirds headed through it and toward Jimmy John's cabin. The others would settle in for the night, with thoughts of tomorrow. I was saddened that they would leave, and I would again be without guests. With my shutters closed, I descended into a quiet but watchful mood.

Perhaps these guests were not so bad.

⌒

❧29❧

MYSTIC HAND

The food was so rich, I was getting sick to my stomach. I couldn't figure out where it had come from since there had been no sign of the daffy Hazel all day. Where had she been when we needed lunch? Joesie and Roxie mentioned that they had seen Hazel but didn't say anything about her preparing any food.

Allison sat across from me, arranging, then rearranging her silverware. We glanced at each other and simultaneously pushed our chairs back. I faced Joesie and mouthed the words, "Where's Ruth Ann?" What if she'd disappeared into that main hallway, from which we had descended? Mira must have read my mind.

"Are there other ways to get upstairs? I wonder what's happened to Ruth Ann?" she quietly asked Eve.

"Now, dearies. Don't be concerned. I'm sure Jimmy John found her," Eve answered.

Mira's face flushed. "What is he doing with her?"

Roxie interjected, "Why didn't he join us for dinner?"

"Well, well. I'm sure he's been busy trying to figure out how to clear the road while it's still daylight," Charles said. "He has a lot on his mind. Besides, he's not used to eating with such distinguished guests. Let's not trifle over small details. Hazel, please serve the trifle." He giggled at his own joke.

"This has been lovely but…" I pushed back my chair, stood, raced up the candlelit stairway as quickly as I could, then promptly threw up in the bathroom. I splashed my face with what little water we had preserved from the well.

"Breathe, breathe, breathe…" Now I sounded like Hazel. I wanted to get out of here. The novelty had worn off.

"You okay? Deep breaths," Allison said. She had followed me upstairs into the bathroom and gently took my arm as I started to feel better. She and I made our way back to our common area. Adjacent to the parlor, across from our home base, we saw a table set up in the middle of the room. And there was a Ouija board on it! Only five seats had been placed around the table. The drapes were drawn, and candles were flickering. It was both ominous and inviting at the same time. Eventually, the others trailed in, speechless when they saw the setup. Though I couldn't wait to rip my gown off, we stayed in costume. What had once been a distraction had now become thoroughly spine-chilling. Our dilemma of being unable to escape had been minimized, only temporarily, by the banquet—the extraordinary interlude had been just that.

"What in the hell is going on here? And where is Ruth Ann?" Roxie broke the shocked silence and asked what we were all wondering.

Mira started pacing and mimicking Hazel, mumbling, "Jimmy John, Jimmy John, Jimmy John." I didn't know whether to laugh or cry. Fantasy and reality seemed to be morphing into one. I felt unhinged and wondered if the others felt the same way. Although I was feeling more comfortable with them, I still didn't want to show that I might be vulnerable.

Mira and Allison sat at the Ouija board table. Roxie, Joesie, and I gathered around them. I wrapped my arms around myself and shivered. It was all so surreal.

"I don't want to know about the future. Get away from that evil thing," Roxie said. Mira laughed at Roxie's reticence and placed her hand on the planchette alongside Allison's. The room took on the atmosphere of a séance and a warm glow overcame the room like an aura. Then the questions began.

"Are we ever going to get out of here?" asked the group in unison. I held my breath as the mystic hand pulled to the *YES* at the top left corner.

"What a relief," Joesie stated. "If you believe in such things. What do we want to ask it next?"

"Ask if Ruth Ann is okay," I said. The two obliged and the answer again pointed to *YES*.

"Deidre, what should we ask now?" Mira queried. I turned to Roxie who said, "Fine. Let's see how smart it is. Who's missing from the group?" The planchette quivered a bit and moved to the alphabet, landing on the letter *B*.

"Ben?" she questioned but the mystic hand moved to the *A*.

"Look, it's still moving," Roxie exclaimed as a second *B* came into view. Finally, it stopped on the *Y.*

"Baby!" Allison exclaimed. "That makes no sense."

"Well," I spoke up, "it's got to mean Ruth Ann. She's the baby of the group."

"Could be," said Joesie. "Or someone else's baby?" She looked close to tears.

"Maybe Baby Broadhurst?" Mira asked. The planchette dragged their hands toward the upper right-hand corner, then retracted and returned two more times.

"I guess it's not Baby Broadhurst? Ouija just said, *NO, NO, NO!*"

"Stop, Deidre. I for one am tired of this silly game. I have enough to handle with my own brood," Allison said as she rose, but her fingertips still touched the planchette.

"I agree," Mira said. Deidre sat down and took Mira's place.

"Wait," Allison exclaimed. "I can't take my fingers off the planchette. It vibrates when I try to leave. How ridiculous is that?"

"Here, let me try," Roxie said, pushing Allison off her seat, forcing her hands away from the board. Allison shook both of her hands as if in pain and said, "I can still feel the vibration. I think it's mad at me. Roxie, I thought you said it was a toy?"

"Yeah, I did. But what the hell? I needed some answers."

Roxie placed her fingertips lightly on the planchette. She gave me a look, then asked her question.

"What's Ben doing right now?" The planchette wiggled and began to move with force. I read the letters as they spelled out, *DO NOT GO THERE.* Roxie gasped and said, "I knew it! Even Ouija knows. Ben is having an affair!"

"Why would you say that Roxie?" Mira asked. No one spoke but I shifted my weight from foot-to-foot whispering, "Just breathe. Breathe Deidre, just breathe." Then Ouija, without any question being asked, began to move, and spelled out, *HELLO DEIDRE. DID YOU FORGET YOUR OLD FRIEND?* I tried not to have a heart attack.

"Come on guys," I said, "you're moving that thing. There is no way that it knows my name. And what old friend?" I was shaking as I spoke. The planchette began moving again, spelling out *AMYAMYAMY.*

"What kind of word is that?" I quipped. "Oh! It's *Amy*, my friend Amy. She's talking to me from the grave."

"What the hell? Three times? Who invited Hazel to the table?" Joesie asked.

Mira immediately stood up and said, "I've had enough of this scary stuff. How does Ouija know so much about all of us? If Amy is trying to contact you, then you keep sitting here." Tears were welling up in my eyes.

"Amy, I'd never forget you," I said. "You were my best friend. Talk to me." But no matter what I did or asked, Ouija wouldn't respond. Then, our hands shot straight to *GOODBYE* at the lower center of the board.

Guilt. It is a strange beast. I think of it as a fiend because it roars to consciousness when I least expect it. It can grab me by the throat. A stealth creature. I got choked up; a lump formed in my throat. I shook my head as if to throw it off me and to dismiss negative thoughts. Sometimes it worked. Others, not so much.

The occult is not my thing, but I had participated in this bizarre game partly out of curiosity and partly to be a team player. It was evident that some members of the group were more in tune with its paranormal aspects and found it a plausible diversion. They were more accepting than I was. I am a skeptic, I suppose. How did or does one have faith in the supernatural when one's belief system had been shaken by an unexplained loss of a dear friend?

That was my dilemma: I still harbored guilt that I had not done enough for Amy before she died. Her decline had been rapid, and our bucket list items had not been accomplished. That's why I wrestled with how to be the best friend I could possibly be to Roxie, especially when she needed me, especially now. I struggled with how to properly convey my concern over her mysterious phone calls and frustration with Ben. I didn't want to get it wrong. This time, wrong was not an option.

◈

~30~

NIGHT NIGHT

Deidre	Tuesday 10:00 PM

Although we had all wondered where Ruth Ann was and giggled about the possibilities, it had been difficult to stifle a yawn and the urge to escape into my own dreams. The novelty of this adventure was wearing thin, as were my nerves. I was used to togetherness, but this was getting a touch too old. Besides, my mind felt like I was in an episode of *The Twilight Zone*. I desperately craved a hot shower, fresh clothes, and the comfort of the Lodge's bed.

We were totally confounded when we left the Ouija room and found our street clothes clean and neatly folded in our "dorm" room. We smelled them to make sure we weren't delusional.

"How the hell did this happen?" Roxie asked.

"Well, maybe Hazel did it," answered Mira.

We quietly changed into our regular clothes, placing the gowns on an empty sofa. The Ouija sat unattended on the table in the adjacent room.

"I wish the Ouija board would disappear. Good riddance," I said.

"And this handkerchief? Everyone reach into your pockets— mine is embroidered with my initials," Roxie exclaimed. "I repeat, *how the hell did this happen?*" We all looked in our respective pockets. She was right. Tucked inside our fresh clothing were dainty, embroidered, monogramed handkerchiefs. Each of our initials was sewn in colors that corresponded with the gowns we had worn.

"These are like the hankies I saw in the library," Joesie said. "But those were so old. These look like replicas—brand new and with our full monogram."

Eve seemed to float in from nowhere. "I see you found your little gifts."

I glanced up to ask how they had materialized but whoosh, she was gone. Not even a puff of smoke. We were dumbfounded and mystified.

"This is the last straw," I shouted. "If the waters haven't receded by tomorrow and Jimmy John hasn't worked his magic on those goddamn branches, I'm *walking* back!"

It was apparent we were all on edge. Joesie pulled on her cowboy boots again. Allison blinked incessantly; Mira was muttering to herself. Roxie was plumping up pillows as if she were getting ready to show the house. I pulled her aside.

"Too many out-of-body experiences for my liking," I said. I was already unsure of how I would explain our experience to my family, but if things continued at this rate, I knew there was no point trying. No one would believe me.

"Rox, this might not be the best time, but we need to talk," I whispered.

"Stop whispering. Are you talking about me?" Mira questioned.

"No, no." By this time some of us suspected that Mira was not herself. We didn't know if it was a result of the circumstances or something else. Allison had shared that she was off her medication. Joesie and I had decided to tread lightly where she was concerned.

"What is it?" Roxie asked.

"Well, I don't know where to start—it's about Ben. But maybe it can wait until we get back to the Lodge."

"What about Ben? What do you think you know?"

At this point, all eyes were focused on us in the corner. I pulled up a footstool and motioned for Roxie to sit close by me.

"I think, I think…" I stuttered.

Roxie blurted out, "You think you know about Ben and his 'special saleswoman?' Is that it?"

"Well, I have seen him around town with a younger woman and they seemed rather chummy. I know you have a lot of women on your sales team but she—I mean *they*—looked different together. And when I approached him one day at the café, he didn't introduce her and couldn't look me in the eye," I said.

"Are you projecting so you can have material for a new book?" Roxie asked with an arched tone.

"No, no. Of course not. I didn't know how to bring this up. I thought maybe it was my imagination, but when you started receiving those phone calls, then lamented he didn't call, and then you made some of those side comments, I figured something was up. This isn't easy for me either…" My voice was fading, but I did add that perhaps what I saw was innocent, but I feared it wasn't.

"Easy for you? What business do you have, making up stories? Who did you tell?" Roxie was clearly upset.

"No one. I assumed it would blow over," I said, trying to soothe her.

"Ha! Some blow over. More like I'm blown away. I wonder what I'm going to find when I get home?" Roxie mused, reminding me of her vision of Ben with another woman. I put my arm around her. She accepted it and whispered an apology for her rant then said, "What will I do if Ben leaves me?"

Allison crouched by Roxie's chair and murmured, "Do you want to talk about it? We're here if you need us."

Roxie was gripping the edge of the armrests. "No. Not now—maybe not ever. And you, my so-called good friend," pointing at me, "I may have to deal with this myself when we get back. Where the hell is Ruth Ann anyway? She needs to learn a thing or two about men."

I needed to retreat for my own sanity. How long had we been here? It felt like a decade. Grabbing a coverlet, I slumped down into my "assigned" area.

"Whoever heard of an inn that doesn't let you use their beds, or that has food appear out of thin air? You all can enjoy your *adventure*. I just want to get home. You all may believe in ghosts—but I just think this place is plain old *sick!* How hard has Jimmy John really tried to help us? If he was such a caretaker he'd be taking better care of us!" I exclaimed, Roxie's frustration seeping into me.

"Oh, stop whining. We're all in the same boat. Jimmy John will come to our rescue, you'll see." Mira now seemed to be the placater.

"Ha! Dream on! Wake me if Ruth Ann ever shows up," I said.

"We'll wait up for her," Mira and Allison said in tandem. Roxie remained sullen.

"Do as you wish," I pronounced moodily as I yawned and started to fade off.

⌒

I stirred in my sleep because I had to adjust the thin blanket that had slipped from my shoulder. Even the slightest sound or movement of fabric seemed to arouse me. It must have been the years of waking in response to the kids. First, it was nightly feedings, then pint-size nightmares and then—*then*, it was the slamming of the car door or the creaky front door hinges I adamantly would not oil. One time, my son had purposely left the kitchen door unlocked so he could sneak back into the house without us knowing. But his nighttime craving for a snack, after a forbidden outing, got the better of him. Caught in the act and having violated curfew, it was a gotcha moment. Did I feel a slight thrill at the capture? You betcha!

Having settled back into a somewhat hazy lull, my mind wandered back to the lunch we had scrounged around for earlier in the day. Half in, half out of a dreamlike state, I imagined wearing a flouncy little apron and panties, putting a small streak of raspberry jam on the side of my neck, and calling out to my husband. *So many memories of our life together.*

"Paul, can you come in here?" I was ready for action.

"Hey, in a minute, DeeDee." The Giants-Dolphins game was blasting in the den.

"Honey, you may want to come in *now*." I judiciously smeared a combination of jam and Nutella between my breasts. I left a little on my index finger for good measure.

"Hey, what's up?" he asked, stopping short and eyeing me provocatively when he saw what I was up to.

"Try this combination." I held out my finger, beckoning him in an inviting manner.

One thing I can say about my husband is that he is not dense. He got the picture right away. He sidled up, leaned tenderly towards me, and kissed my palm before sucking on the aforementioned digit. "Hmm... Tasty. Any other spots I should test?"

"Well, there *is* a spot or two. You might have to check them out. I'm not sure the raspberry jam and chocolate are a good combination." My breath was now shallow, and my senses heightened. Words were coming out in a halting manner.

"What'd ya think?" I pulled the hair away from my neck and exposed the deep red streak of jam. My neck and earlobe had always been a vulnerable area. And he knew it, too. For good measure I leaned over the counter to expose the concoction poised between my rising breasts. The action was not missed.

"Isn't this apron a little too tight around your neck?" he asked.

"Maybe a little—could you adjust it?" I turned around, moved the hair off the nape of my neck, and pressed my lacy panties into his bulging jeans. The kitchen counter had already been cleared in anticipation of our activity.

And then— and *then* I heard a slight moan. Was it me or had Allison emitted the same sound I was ready to release? Hard to tell. Jolted from my reverie, I glanced around and saw her stirring as well. A sly smile emanated from her youthful face. Our eyes locked in the dim moonlight and for a minute I felt in simpatico with her. Had we had a mutual dream again? Were our minds merging?

"Ugh, I must have drifted off, waiting for Ruth Ann," Allison whispered hoarsely as her eyes closed once again.

Could it be possible? What was she dreaming about? I needed a glass of water. I had to get out of this place, come hell or high water. I tried to readjust myself in the chair. I felt every lump and bump. My mind swirled. Images of all of us in our respective gowns invaded my previous fantasy. I imagined taking home my gold gown to show Paul and the kids. How would they believe me otherwise? Or did I really want to share this with them? Wasn't this a bonding experience that would be better being the group's secret? The aches in my bones only exacerbated my thirst. It was a toss-up between getting up to look for water or staying down and trying to recapture my sexual interlude with my husband. If only he looked like Jimmy John, the image would have been more vivid.

Thirst won out. I was now more alert, and I observed the others in assorted slumbering positions around the room. The moonlight from the window illuminated Allison's face. She was still smiling. *Lucky girl.* I felt my way towards the pitcher we had left on a side table. I could not explain the contrast between the sumptuous meal we had eaten with Eve, Charles, and Hazel with the meager findings in the kitchen. It didn't add up. Come to think of it, nothing did.

I stubbed my toe on the leg of the table, silently mouthed "shit," and realized from the pain that now enveloped my foot that this was real. I longed for my own bed, the comfort of the night-light in my bathroom, and the cool marble floor that would often help relieve the leg cramps that disturbed my slumber. I was actually homesick. I was embarrassed by a feeling I had not encountered since summer overnight camp. Was I regressing even more, going back to childhood? Did this place have more of an effect on me than I first thought? My imagination was running wild.

I heard a noise coming from the porch. I prayed it was Ruth Ann as I blindly stumbled back to my chair, longing for some answers and daylight.

∽31∾

MIDNIGHT

Ruth Ann	Wednesday 12:00 AM

Wanting to appear independent, I shrugged off Jimmy John's offer to walk me back to The Inn. I checked my watch as I approached the porch and was shocked to see it was almost midnight. The moon gave just enough light for me to find the steps. I held the wine Jimmy John had given me under my right arm as I went through the back door, feeling like a sneaky teenager.

I peeked into the parlor where the rest of the women were in their "assigned" places, resting or asleep—it was hard to tell. The grandfather clock chimed, making me jump. I lost my balance a bit and bumped the side of the arched doorway, making enough sound to awaken the dead. Had I ruined my chance of creeping "home" unnoticed? Feeling a bit like Cinderella, and happier than I had been in a long time, I tippy-toed toward my sleeping place in the parlor. I set the package down on the coffee table and tried to settle in, pulling the blanket up over me and feeling like I had actually made it safely back without disturbing the others. Roxie suddenly jumped out of her chair, exclaiming, "Ruth Ann, we've been worried sick. Do you know how long you've been gone?"

"And what are you wearing?" Allison asked, rubbing her eyes, and sitting up abruptly.

"Oh, this? It's J.J.'s. He let me wear his shirt because I was cold."

"Ahh, it's *J.J.* now, is it?" Allison added with a smirk. "And look at those bare legs."

"You didn't sleep with him, did you?" Roxie asked. I saw the expectation on Roxie's and Allison's faces, and knew I had to say something. How could I put into words all that had happened tonight?

"J.J. showed me his place. His cottage is really cozy, so much nicer than I would have envisioned for a single man. I really like him."

"You *did* sleep with him, didn't you?" Mira lamented, shaking her head.

I hugged the chambray shirt around me and pulled out the bottle of wine J.J. had given me. *No time like the present.* Deidre and Joesie stretched and yawned. I grabbed glasses from the kitchen, opened the wine, and poured for the ladies. Then I began to share my story, albeit with some parts left out. Those, I would save for my diary.

"Well?" Allison yawned. "Then what?"

"He took me for a walk. It was so beautiful in the moonlight, the mountains in front of us, the stars above, brighter than I ever remember."

"That is infatuation, my dear Ruth Ann." Deidre got up and looked out the window, retracting her statement. "Wow, you're right, Ruth Ann, it's a brilliantly clear night and the stars are gorgeous. Okay girl—go on with your story." Mira seemed resigned to the conclusion.

"We were walking along the path toward the cemetery," I continued. "J.J. told me about it. It's a family cemetery. He took my hand about five minutes into the walk. I felt so safe with him. He kept up a running commentary about the history of The Inn, Eve and Charles, and how and why he came to live here. The farther we walked, the closer he moved toward me, lifting me over the puddles. You would think he'd know this place like the back of his hand, but we veered off the path a bit and missed the cemetery.

I didn't want to see the anyone's final resting place again, anyway. Why spoil a nice evening with a visit to the dead?"

"Oh, Ruth Ann, maybe he avoided the cemetery on purpose. He probably just wanted to get in your pants," Mira chided.

"It wasn't like that, Mira. You all have to believe me. I felt like I was in a fairy tale, the way he kissed me. There was nothing dirty or sordid about it. I know he cares for me."

"He kissed you?" Deidre asked.

"Yes. We were standing in the shadow of his cottage. He turned, putting his arms around me, and stepped back a bit, holding my shoulders like he was considering something. Then he held my face in his hands. It seemed like an eternity as he stared into my eyes. Then he kissed me. I thought I would faint. You know how in romance novels characters swoon? Well, I swooned."

"Then what?" the "sisters" said in unison.

I took a deep breath, sipped from my glass, and continued, "He invited me in. I thought, why not? I deserve some happiness and it had been a long time since I'd been comfortable with a man. We stepped inside and were greeted by Baxter, his Siamese cat. He's tan, with dark-brown chocolate points on his face, ears, and legs—so handsome. Baxter rubbed up against my leg and when I reached down to pet him, J.J. picked him up, gave him a kiss, and put him in my arms. Can you imagine, a guy who likes cats? He was so gentle with him. We sat on his sofa and talked and talked, with Baxter in my lap."

"Enough about the damn cat, enough!" Roxie exclaimed. "What happened next?"

"Well, he gave me a tour of the place. He lit a couple of candles and used a flashlight to guide us. The cottage has two bedrooms, a bathroom, a sitting area, and a full kitchen. "

"He never showed *me* all those rooms," Mira lamented.

"His power was out, also. He showed me where he cooks, and all his exotic spices. Did you know J.J. went to school to be a chef? He promised to cook for me one day."

Deidre and Allison exchanged a knowing glance and sighed collectively.

"His room had a rustic look to it. His bed was made. Can you imagine, a guy who makes his bed? It had a forest-green comforter with a moose and some trees on it. He mentioned that it matched the gown that I was still wearing. He turned on a transistor radio for some music, and the tinny sound made me feel like I was in an old movie. We slow danced. We kissed. I think I'm in love."

"Now I'm interested and impressed," Joesie exclaimed. "My father insisted that all beds should be made with square corners. But, seriously, we do need to get out of here."

"Yes, we need to get out of this place," Mira said.

"J.J. promised he'd get us out in the morning," I explained.

"Lord willing," Roxie said.

"Lord willing? We need to get out of here, period!" Joesie exclaimed.

"And if we don't?" Allison piped up.

"Ladies, I am really, really tired," I yawned. "We all need some sleep. We'll work on getting out of here in the morning." After the dinner, J.J., the wine—I was drifting off to sleep, despite protests from the group, who no doubt wanted more details.

I yawned and managed to thank them for making me feel so comfortable, like real sisters, before drifting to sleep.

∾

❦32❦

FAREWELL TO
THE GUESTS

| Jimmy John | Wednesday 7:00 AM |

Alone. But not *lonely*, in my cabin. That was what my motto had always been. Others may disagree but I liked my life on the grounds of The Inn. Well—I *was* alone, until I stumbled across that character, Mira, and the lovely Ruth Ann.

The rag-tag group of travelers made me rethink my single status. I was content living in my cabin, looking in on Hazel daily, and maintaining The Inn at Raspberry Hill. This place was in constant need of attention. I was committed to retaining the grandeur that Eve and Charles had always maintained. Perhaps I should have been paying more attention to other things, like someone my own age. There was something about Ruth Ann that caught my eye. The local girls seemed preoccupied with their cell phones and the latest Kardashian trends. They forgot they lived out here in the "sticks," constantly bemoaning their fate, but chose not to do anything about it. And the way they dressed! Why, half of them exposed everything, leaving nothing to the imagination. Eve had really set the bar high for me when it came to modesty and style. I liked a different kind of gal.

Lots of books and my radio with extra batteries were at the ready as I never knew when those strong summer storms would come in. Always have to be prepared. That way, if I got stranded, I could occupy myself. Again, alone but not lonely.

I liked the way Ruth Ann seemed to nestle into my chest when I pulled her close last night. True, I don't have the bragging rights of most guys, but I knew a good kisser when I met one. We parted reluctantly. I didn't want her to get the wrong impression and knew the travelers would be leaving as soon as the roads cleared.

"Have you lived here long?" Ruth Ann had asked. She also seemed interested in my time as a chef. If she stayed longer, I could prepare a real meal for her. She was talking about some banquet food they'd had. I had cooked for the women and brought it to Hazel, but it was hardly a feast. Perhaps hunger had overtaken their imaginations.

I noticed Ruth Ann taking in the neatness of my cabin. She even nodded in appreciation of my made-up bed. She took a shine right away to my cat, Baxter. Baxter liked her, too. He was a good judge of character, not like Merlin. That cat was nuts. Baxter and Merlin hissed at each other when they crossed paths. I've tolerated him because Merlin seemed to calm Hazel down, providing companionship and comfort. *Hazel, Hazel, Hazel.* She was becoming so repetitive it was starting to drive me crazy. Devoted Hazel. She came to my rescue when I lost my parents. She tried so hard to make everyone feel welcome. A good soul.

Yet my cat and I could use some company. Perhaps when things return to normal, Ruth Ann could pay me another visit, or I could visit her. She reminded me Florida was nice in the winter. Maybe it was finally time to escape the freezing cold Berkshire winters and spread my wings again. There always seemed to be a pull to take care of something at The Inn. I could use a partner in life as well as a helpmate. Would Ruth Ann go for the idea? There were some preschools nearby. Maybe one would hire her?

I knew I was getting ahead of myself. I didn't want to get my hopes up that she would stay longer. She seemed pretty tied to her job and friends. We'd promised to keep up communication. I would like it if she wrote instead of texting—too impersonal.

Even an email would be okay. Call me old-fashioned, but I hate those things.

I was torn between placing more boards in the somewhat still-flooded driveway, clearing the pathways, and stalling them with an excuse for why they should stay longer. Truth be told, I only wanted Ruth Ann to stay. Some of the others were getting to be a pain in the neck, but I got it. They didn't intend to be here, so who would blame them? You would think they couldn't do without their cell phones for a day. That's one thing I liked about Ruth Ann. She seemed to be a real sport. While I was glad Mira had discovered my cottage, she was a bit too much. She was so intrigued by the cemetery. I wondered why. Most people forgot it was even here, but to me it was a sacred place. Regardless, I would be ready at dawn, with my chainsaw, to clear the way of any detour. Then they could be on their way.

After Ruth Ann left, I wanted to get some fresh air and survey the damage from the storm, so I parked myself on the hand-hewn bench I had made and placed near the cemetery. The air was rich with the pungent smells after a storm, and my senses were heightened. I read somewhere that the odor is ozone: more oxygen is in the air. I liked that idea. It reminded me of what I found so appealing about this place. *Strange.* Who would think to find refuge in a place that was clearly closed? Perhaps, they were desperate. Perhaps, they knew of our fine reputation. Or maybe something else I don't know about. At any rate, they were here, and I had an obligation to help them.

I had thought the moonlight would give me a chance to assess the damage last night, but the ground was too muddy. It would just have to wait. Still, the air smelled so fresh and I found comfort in the solitude of the hills. I've lived here most of my life. I can't picture being anywhere else. Also, I continue to feel an obligation to this family. After all, Hazel, Eve, and Charles had taken me in.

I'd have been fine if the storm had lasted a few more days. I am always prepared. I've cut wood for my stove, loaded up on lanterns and batteries, and have enough "vittles" for the time being. And there was always the lake behind my cabin—a nice fish would tide me over.

But the guests? I had better see to some of their needs. Aunt Hazel was not reliable anymore. I've taken on more of the responsibilities Charles used to oversee. After the storm cleanup, the contractors would be coming. Supervising them was just one more thing on my plate. Oh well, even though the rest of the women seemed antsy to escape from Raspberry Hill, I knew they'd appreciate my clearing the road. The "river" they described in front of The Inn had disappeared. All was clear. The travelers could soon be on their way. I heard some murmurs of their returning at another date. Not sure I want all of them to repeat their stay, but Ruth Ann—she was welcome anytime.

Soon it would be morning and I'll be checking on the road. Good thing I kept a supply of gas for the chainsaw. Yes, alone but not lonely. That's the way I've always liked it—until now.

⌒

At 7:30 the next morning, back at The Inn, I was about to start the chainsaw when I saw someone coming toward me. Ruth Ann. She looked more beautiful than ever. My heart was in my throat and I was at a loss for words. She gave a little wave. I gestured for her to sit next to me on the fallen tree that was now a convenient bench. I was hoping she would want to talk.

"Just came over to say goodbye," Ruth Ann said.

I felt self-conscious, being sweaty and bare-chested from clearing the road. Ruth Ann didn't seem to care. Her eyes were bright and her face expressive. It was clear she was glad to see me. She turned and looked behind her and I looked too. There was a bevy of women bunched together, watching our every move. I had the distinct impression that if I kissed Ruth Ann right then, they might've clapped. Ruth Ann motioned for them to give us some privacy, which they ignored. We resumed our goodbye chat.

"Ruth Ann, did you say your parents live nearby?" I asked.

"My mom. She lives a couple of towns south of here. My sister is in the next county. My dad and mom divorced after I started middle school. My dad remarried and has another family. I haven't seen him in over five years."

"That's got to be sad for you, Ruth Ann," I said, reaching for her hand. I couldn't help but notice that she had the softest skin and long piano fingers.

"Oh, it's okay. My mom's bitter, but I'm not. My dad had to get away from her. They were toxic together. He still has a relationship with my sister, but I was so young, we never really bonded. Frankly, I do feel badly that the years are going by and I have never reached out, but then, neither has he." She seemed at ease in the conversation.

"Well, this is what I was thinking. Maybe you'd like to come back, stay a while. There is so much we could do together. Maybe you could even contact your dad. I'd be glad to go with you."

"That would be nice. Every time I think about calling him, someone talks me out of it. He and I are a lot alike. We even look alike. He has the same brown hair, is thin like a runner, and is very pale—at least he was the last time I saw him. He's a lawyer in Pittsfield. Lots of business these days I hear. He's a public defender."

"That's a noble profession, wouldn't you say? He can't be too bad," I remarked.

"I agree. So, let's make a plan. I have to go back to Florida to set up my classroom, but I still have a couple of weeks before school is back in session."

I sighed, "That would be great, Ruth Ann."

"But J.J., what if The Inn sells? What will you do?"

I told her not to worry. Truth be told, I would never want to leave here. "I have roots here you know nothing about. But one thing is for sure. I'm staying here." I turned toward her and really wanted to kiss her but being sweaty and bare-chested, I wasn't sure how she'd receive it. I leaned toward her and gently kissed her cheek. Not only did she not pull away, but she also moved closer, turned my face to hers, and kissed me back—on the lips. Over her shoulder, our audience was indeed applauding, but I didn't care, and I don't think she did either.

"This isn't really goodbye. I'll see you soon," Ruth Ann said.

"Exactly," I replied.

I watched as she jogged toward her friends.

Wow! I think I have a girlfriend.

~33~

IMPRINTS-FAREWELL RASPBERRY HILL

We awoke to the sounds of a chainsaw. Not much doubt in our minds who was operating it. Having straightened our makeshift bedding, putting everything back the way we had found it, it was time to depart.

Even after the sumptuous banquet, we were still surprisingly hungry. Except for Ruth Ann, the rest of us were eager to leave Raspberry Hill, find a place to eat, and head back to the Abenaki Lodge. Well, that was *partially* true. We did want to go together back to the Abenaki Lodge, but leaving our newly found sisterhood would not be easy. It was more than closeness really; it was a serious, deep bond in which we shared our innermost thoughts and feelings. I wondered how each of us had been affected by our adventure together. Would I be willing, in the future, to share my deepest thoughts and decisions with them, and accept their input? I supposed our determination and time together would be true indicators.

Allison and Ruth Ann rushed outside to see if the road was clear. They came back in stammering and breathless. "You won't believe it. Oh, my God!" Ruth Ann declared. "Other than the small ruts from our tires, the driveway is completely clear. That Jimmy John is a miracle worker for sure."

"But what about the mud?" Allison asked.

"Let's use the boards J.J. put out," Deidre suggested. "Anything to get out of here."

"I agree," Joesie added.

Mira said, "Allison, you're the Girl Scout. What do you suggest?"

"With Jimmy John's help, we can put the boards under the tires, and we'll be free," Allison answered. We ran outside with our cell phones—I don't know why, actually. There had been a kind of peacefulness without them. And miraculously, we had service! Finally, after we had all listened to our messages, we headed back inside to gather our belongings before we left for good.

"Would you believe it?" I asked. "Ben called me to ask about the exterminator! My gosh, he couldn't even figure that one out himself. How in God's name does he own a real estate office? He is so good at selling houses but ask him a simple question about our home and its workings, and he is a such a doofus. He knows diddly squat! You can see he'd be lost without me to do the mundane things. Or would he? Men need women to tend to life's details."

"The dinner last night was so fabulous, and didn't Eve look ever so lovely?" Joesie added. "She is a delightful hostess, and I'm certain all of us want to thank her for this marvelous hospitality."

"Well, not so much hospitality, really," Allison chimed in, "but at least we did have a roof over our heads."

"True," added Ruth Ann. "However, we can't forget all of those beautiful gowns, and that glorious dinner. Someone should walk upstairs and find her so that we can all give her our individual thanks. And where's Hazel? We need to find and thank her, too. I hope we left enough money to cover their expenses. I'll look for her."

"You know, it is odd that Eve hasn't come down to see us. Surely, she must have heard us all moving around," said Deidre.

"I'll go," I volunteered. "I'll look for Eve. Maybe this time I'll be able to actually see the inside of her bedroom."

I walked slowly up the dark mahogany staircase. The wall next to it was lined with what appeared to be old family portraits. Women wore dresses bustled in the back, low cut in the front. "My gosh, it's 'my' gown in this portrait!" I called down to my sisters below. Other photographs showed mustached men posing in waistcoats. I descended the stairs more slowly than I had gone up them, barely a few minutes ago.

Seeing my somewhat shaken state, Joesie asked, "Roxie, what is it? You are so pale."

I didn't know what to say. I had knocked on Eve's door; there'd been no response. At the top of the stairs was a set of magnificent double doors, hewn from mahogany. As I approached them, I could see the carved angels embossed in them, their mother-of-pearl wings shimmering in the early morning sunlight. I had knocked gently on one of the doors, and receiving no response, knocked a little louder. Still nothing. At this point, I really needed to check on Eve and Charles, to make sure they were okay. I turned the knob slowly to open the door, calling "Hello? Hello?" I'd stopped short in the doorway, my mouth agape.

It was an elegant and beautiful room. I felt as though I had stepped into another world and stood, transfixed. The window, doorways, and moldings were all dark wood. The walls were lemon-yellow silk that at one time must have made the mouth water. Within the silk I saw small floral patterns in white and faded periwinkle blue. The focal point of the room was a massive, carved, canopied bed centered on the far wall. My God, it was beyond anything I had ever seen and believe me, I had seen plenty! How was I going to convey to my sisters all I did and did not see? I walked down the stairs and described what I saw.

"The wood, silks, and satins were unique. There was a rather large bed on the far wall. I'd sell my soul for a bed like that one. Anyway, Eve was nowhere to be seen or found. She just wasn't there…nor, for that matter, was Charles. Oddly though, the bed was covered in an antique bedspread with two heavy imprints, as if they had slept on it last night. I can't explain it, other than to say it was a bit eerie. I don't think we'll find Eve. She's not in her bedroom and she's not outside on the grounds from what I can tell. We'll have to find another way to say goodbye and thank you."

Deidre came over to me, patting my back as if to say she was supporting me. "I couldn't find Hazel either. This is a bit weird."

Allison went on to mention there was a guestbook on the table in the hall. "I'll write a note in there from all of us, thanking them. I'll include my address. That way, they can contact us if we need to pay for our stay or any extras. We can leave the book open to that page, and Eve will be sure to see it when she comes in from wherever she is," Allison added. We all agreed it was a good idea.

Ruth Ann turned to the last page and began writing the note. "Wow," she exclaimed, "The last date in this guestbook is over a year ago." She put down the pen and walked out the door, heading straight toward Jimmy John.

⌒34⌒

RELEASE

Having said our goodbyes to J.J. and strategically laying down some boards, we pulled out of the mud and waved our farewell to The Inn at Raspberry Hill. I looked over my shoulder for one last peek. There was Merlin, perched on top of an old Adirondack chair, watching us. His mouth was open, and it was obvious he was yowling but we couldn't hear him with the car windows up and the air conditioning on. He swished his tail. His long white fur shone in the sunlight. "I guess he's saying goodbye," I said to Deidre, giving a little wave to the feline.

"Good riddance, Merlin. Baxter too! I am heading back to my cat-free home," Deidre said.

"That's funny, Deidre. Because I'm tired of living alone and I'm going to get myself a kitten." This was the first time I had announced my plan.

"More power to you, Ruth Ann. I'm better off writing about cats than having one," Deidre said. "I might write a piece about the Magical Merlin and his human Hazel."

"Speaking of Magical Merlin, look! The streetlamps are on and it's daytime. Could the timers be off from the storm? Maybe the power is back on? But then, why is the house still dark?"

"Who cares? Goodbye, goodbye, goodbye," sang Mira from the back seat. Just as the car pulled parallel to the house, Hazel came into view. We all waved, and Roxie lowered the back window and yelled, "Bye, bye, bye!"

"Thanks, thanks, thanks!" she called back, waving.

We set out along Route 2, thankful to Jimmy John for clearing our way to freedom and telling us about the Seabreeze Diner. We were all famished and ready for breakfast. The way out of the valley was a series of climbs, corners, and dips—each move elevated us farther up the mountain.

Allison

I took my place behind the wheel of the damp, musty car. It felt so good to be in control again, even if it were only by literally being in the driver's seat. My mind was brimming with ideas of potential story lines and I was eager to settle into my own space back at the Abenaki Lodge to jot them down. Quite by accident, I had left my notebook on a side table at The Inn at one point. Deidre had picked it up and remarked that the illustrations were quite charming. I had never revealed to the rest of the group that I dabbled in drawing. I wasn't confident that my artwork measured up to my story lines. Still, maybe this experience would give me the support and confidence to do both. I was grateful for the group's interactions and encouragement.

Images of magical raspberries and shared dreams were, "ripe for the pickin'." *Oh dear!* I have been caught up in the group's odd sense of humor. I chuckled to myself.

"What's so funny?" Joesie asked.

"I can't help myself. This whole experience has been so bizarre. If I were to write down what we just went through, people would think it was fiction. Do you think the raspberries were to blame?" I asked Mira and Joesie, my car mates, who looked at one another and giggled.

"Who knows? Maybe we entered an alternate universe for two days. There are plenty of TV shows with whole seasons about experiences like we just had. Perhaps we should switch it up and write scripts for a network," Joesie posed. "We could include the mysterious effects of eating the raspberries and our other weird experiences."

Mira exclaimed, "Good idea! It could be a joint project for us, and we could have an excuse to meet around a table with real food provided by a commissary. The shared dreams—Roxie seeing Ben...So much to consider."

"What Kool-Aid are you drinking?" A voice floated over the jovial atmosphere. We had forgotten those in Ruth Ann's car were on speaker, a vestige of our "togetherness," no doubt.

"Let's just get to the diner, regroup, and figure out what we tell our families and friends. I don't know how to explain what we saw and heard," I remarked.

My family. I had not given them a lot of thought in the past few days. That was probably a good thing. Since we couldn't be in contact, my ex had had to be in charge and manage the kids. It was about time. I had grown weary of all my responsibilities. I wished that I had a partner who was more in tune with my needs. I didn't want to burst Ruth Ann's bubble, but it was harder to find a true partner than she thought. Perhaps Jimmy John was her destiny. Hard to tell after such a brief interlude. But who knows? Stranger things have happened, at least in stories.

Stories. I tried to focus on the road ahead, but crazy images of dancing raspberries kept reverberating in my mind. Maybe I could create a children's book in which a fruit salad would dance and sing. My ruminations were interrupted by a cry from the back. *When did Joesie and Mira switch seats? Had they leapfrogged while I wasn't looking?*

"Why are they following us?" Joesie asked.

"Who?" I wondered.

"The motorcycle riders!" Joesie announced. "It looks like they're following us."

"Hard to tell," Ruth Ann said. "This road is only two lanes. If they're going our way, they'd have to be behind us or in front of us and there's no passing."

"Now what? I can't wait to get back to the Lodge and what remains of the conference," Joesie said.

We dodged the fallen branches and storm debris on the road. Pools of water still lined the sides of the road. I was preoccupied with steadying the car as I had swerved at Joesie's exclamation.

We passed a few motels, trading post gift shops, many with American Indian motifs, and more than one restaurant. All were closed on this Wednesday morning. I took in the beauty of the mountains as we drove farther down into the valley. They seemed to rise up as we descended. Even in the full green of summer, I could imagine the splendor to come when the leaves changed this coming fall.

Deidre

I had sunk into the passenger seat of Ruth Ann's musty-smelling, rescued rental car. She had flown up from Florida for the conference and a visit with her mother. The interior odor was a bit stale. I promptly started sneezing. A muddy trail oozed from the door jamb. I half expected to see fish settled on the floor of the back seat. Any creature would have wanted to escape that eerie place. I certainly had. Try as I might to make the most of our "adventure," I was simply playacting. It was tolerable for one night, but two, not so much.

I turned and looked over my shoulder at Allison's rental car behind us, where Joesie was riding shotgun. I couldn't see her, but I hoped Mira was still in the back seat, eyes closed, a smile on her face, lost in her own world. With our cells back in service, we were on speaker with Ruth Ann's phone.

"What's up with Mira?" I asked.

"Dozing, I guess," answered Joesie. We all knew she hadn't slept much.

I felt somewhat guilty. I hadn't been able to enjoy roughing it, or to relish the strange experiences like the banquet, the amazing costumes, and Hazel's odd speech pattern. My reaction seemed to be different from the others.

I tried to imagine a story line but was too preoccupied with my own literary pursuits and the launch of my new book. I had invested so much time, energy, and savings into this book. I was determined it would not fail. Taking a deep breath and stealing a glance at Roxie, I grimaced as she was preoccupied with her cell phone once again.

I was still embarrassed about our argument over Ben. Perhaps I hadn't been as supportive as I should have been. At least Roxie had apologized. If Ben were involved with another woman, how would Roxie cope? How would I in that similar circumstance? I couldn't imagine working and living with a man who had betrayed me.

Mulling over each travelers' journey, I hoped we'd all emerged from our experiences together with a stronger bond. Ruth Ann had blossomed the most, like a tulip bud, slowly opening. Her stamen was vulnerable. I hoped Jimmy John would not break her heart. Maybe meeting him was just the experience she needed to open her heart to other possibilities. Come to think of it, I felt that each of us represented a different flower:

Joesie was a peony, complex with layers and layers. She had a tight core that was not easily accessible.

Roxie was of course the classic red rose, thorny, with dynamic color. Her flower might bend but her stem remained strong.

Mira was a "crazy daisy." I had been reluctant to reach out to her. Allison seemed to be the patient and supportive one of Mira. She tended to be more understanding and in tune with her mood swings.

Allison was definitely the sunflower, bright with possibilities. Her approach to children's stories was upbeat and demonstrated that despite adversity, one prevailed.

Ruth Ann could also be a forget-me-not, as if we ever could. Would Jimmy John?

And me? I pondered where I fit into this bouquet. Not a utilitarian carnation. Something more exotic, like an orchid. I thought I was more independent; I wasn't part of a bouquet. I realized that was egotistical, but I didn't care.

No longer simply someone's wife, mother, or loyal friend, I was now ready to be accepted for who I am: unique, delicate, but with stamina. I had been dormant too long and was ready to bloom again. Yes, I was an orchid. Note to self: research floral varieties when I get home.

Home. We had been away for several days, but it seemed like weeks. The pull and tug of the familiar versus the unknown called to me. I had tasted the unknown and realized I had much more to learn.

All the *had nots* rattled in my brain. I had not been a good enough friend; I had not been productive enough. The thought of spending two days away from the conference had not lowered my anxiety; it had raised it. I was a dilettante. That was the reality. A dilettante in life. All these thoughts had raced through my mind as we drove away from The Inn at Raspberry Hill. In time, I realized there were a number of things I *had* done.

I had pursued my dream of publishing a book despite taking a few detours along the way. I had lost a dear friend but gained five sisters. And what a brood we were! We had a number of things in common: the love of the written word and a commitment to support each other's literary endeavors. Along the way, I had to temper my impatience and tolerate my new sisters' idiosyncrasies. I wondered if they felt the same. The trick was maintaining a sense of humor. I had explained to my family that this trip was to be designated "my time" when in fact it had become *our* time. This detour led me to greater insights—to appreciate friendships and let life unfold at its own pace.

I tuned in to the chatter from the other car. Ours remained largely silent. Could this be another metaphor of how each of us had blossomed? We had created our own bouquet with our respective writings. Roxie was distracted. We seemed discordant. I wondered how a group like ours could pull together with our disparate needs. Some wanted to explore cemeteries, others were content to have explored the mysteries of a seemingly haunted house. I felt like I was caught in a spell.

The banquet had clinched my uneasiness. How could I have consumed so much rich food and still have felt hungry? I guess because I threw it all up. The handkerchiefs Roxie and Joesie found upstairs had only one initial, one for each of our first names. Then, handkerchiefs with two initials were in a box in the library, and again in the pockets of the gowns. Finally, the handkerchiefs with all of our complete monograms were in our freshly cleaned street clothes pockets. What was that all about? Surely, Hazel could not have embroidered all our initials so quickly.

"How would she have known our full monograms?" I asked the group. "Did you hear that, ladies in the other car?"

"Yes," they all chimed in.

Mira

"It's a predicament...." said the King of Siam in the musical *The King and I.*

Thoughts of my husband Avrom and son Elijah entered my mind but disappeared. All the years were erased. All the yearning, all the wishing for something I didn't have. *I was in his arms. Rico! Was the love of my life back?* I wondered if he had married and had a family but that would have to wait.

He twirled me around and put me down. Smiling, he said, "My God, Mira. I've thought about you every day for years. I won't let you go this time."

My arms at my sides, I looked deeply into his brown eyes and said, "I hear you!"

Is this real? With my upbringing, I should feel guilty…about the family I have with Avrom. *But I don't. This feels right.*

I opened my eyes, mesmerized by the motion of the car. It had felt so real, but I had some sense I might have been dreaming. I closed them again and immediately drifted back to Rico. I put my backpack in the Porsche and slipped into the front seat. I couldn't let him go. Not this time. *Please, dear God, let this be real!* What are the chances of our coming back together, in the Berkshires of all places? Was it meant to be? I just wanted him with me for the rest of my life. *Please!* I could tell him about Elijah, even introduce them.

I didn't know where we were headed but it was impossible to ask questions over the roar of the engine. I reached out to touch the hand on the stick shift and felt him tense, then relax. Was he nervous, too?

We pulled into an unpaved driveway, just barely wide enough for the Porsche. After a few turns, we came to a house that was unmistakably designed in the manner of Frank Lloyd Wright. I was in awe of the house and surroundings, especially the dramatic turn my life might take. I couldn't speak, in anticipation.

"C'mon, let's go inside," Rico said.

The floor-to-ceiling glass in the great room brought the outside in. I saw nature at its most awe-inspiring. Rico watched as I took in the splendor of the endless majestic mountains, adorned with all the colors of an artist's palette. Through the pine trees, I saw a doe, silently running into the safety of the nearby woods.

We headed outside and sat under the darkening sky. I leaned back to watch the evening stars make their light.

"Let's go get wet," he said. We both stripped. Rico whispered to me as he took my hand and we jumped into the warmth of the swimming pool. I couldn't believe I was skinny dipping with Rico! I sputtered, spitting a stream of water into his face, and fell into his arms. What seemed like hours later, Rico said, "I'm hungry. Let's go see what's in the fridge."

We headed into the kitchen. I opened my backpack and found a clean pair of underwear but nothing else in the way of clothes. My bottle of pills lay on the bottom; I ignored them. Rico slipped his hand into mine and walked me through the rest of his jewel of a home. He saved the master bedroom for last.

Allison's car bumped along the road. I opened my eyes to discover I was in the back seat. *What?* Joesie leaned over the seat and poked me in the side. Now I was fully awake, but irritated. "I was in such a happy place. Why couldn't you leave me in my dream?"

"Sorry," Joesie apologized. "Thinking ahead, to after the Washburn conference. What is the date of the Boston conference?"

"It's the week after Labor Day but before we schlep up to that Boston conference, please pack more efficiently, Joesie. I guarantee that women like Abigail Adams did *not* travel with such a cache of stuff."

"But, can we talk about this later?" I asked. "Avrom would be delighted to spend more time with Elijah."

⁓

～35～

MILITARY ESCORT

"Stop now! Gotta do it! Emergency, I promise," I shouted.
"I'll beep at the others before they get too far ahead!" Allison
said and acted quickly.

"What's the matter?" Mira lurched forward.

Holding my hands over my mouth, I stumbled out of the car.
Once I was done, I stated the obvious, "I hadda throw up! Whew!
Just in time! Woulda been all over your car. Thought dinner was
lovely, but boy did I have a sudden stomachache! Sorry, but I *really*
needed to throw up. Must've been those *bits and bobs* of Scottish *mashed neeps—not* mashed potatoes! They're really damned
turnips. Oh, my poor, aching belly!"

Allison asked if we could finally get going. I gave her a thumbs
up and we piled into our cars and drove on. "Uh oh, what now?"
Ruth Ann asked through the cell phone speaker, sounding
concerned.

"Gotta stop, please," I exclaimed.

"To throw up again?" Deidre asked.

"No! Look at that sign!" I responded weakly.

"What sign?" Mira asked.

"OMG! Just like the one out my window at the Abenaki
Lodge—another Church of Perpetual Harmony. You think it's a

special sect around here?" I asked. Two sets of shoulders shrugged in unison.

"Why do we have to stop?" Allison asked.

"*Please*, Allison!" I insisted.

"Okay! Okay already!" Allison spoke into the phone to the others, "We're stopping. Follow me." We all fell forward as she jerked the car over a curb and into the churchyard. I unfastened my seat belt and ran over to the sign and hugged it. Just then, the parade of motorcycles pulled up beside us. Now that we could see them up close, we could tell they were old, bearded Vietnam vets wearing leather boots and gloves. The backs of their jackets were emblazoned with embroidered insignia, indicating their service in the Vietnam War.

"Hey, ladies, you okay?" one asked with concern, noticing that we had gotten out of our vehicles and were standing by the sign. "Was that you getting sick a moment ago at the side of the road?"

"Oh yeah! Thanks. Why?" Joesie asked.

"Cause folks around here usually hug our sign when someone's dead or dying. Ya'll lost someone?"

"Yes, as a matter of fact, my dad died three weeks ago. Matter of fact, he was career army," I explained. Roxie pulled out her monogrammed handkerchief and leaned over, wiping away the tears running down my face.

"Well in that case guys, grab an arm and form a circle. Let's do a prayer for this young lady," one of the bikers said, pulling off his helmet. They formed a huddle around me, holding hands in prayer.

"Hey, y'all are just what I needed. Something to remember. Stay safe out there. Bless y'all and thanks so much." I had reverted to my Texas twang. *If that biker wasn't so scruffy looking, he would look just like my dad. Same height and build. There's something about when people who are close to you pass away—you seem to "see" them everywhere.*

"Where y'all headin'?" the lookalike asked.

"Seabreeze Diner," the six of us answered in unison.

"Oh, matter of fact, so are we. We'll make sure you get there safely. All military are family."

Roxie whispered, "If we 'matter of fact' a few more times in a row we'll start to sound just like Hazel."

"Stop," Deidre said. "Let's forget about Hazel and move on."

"Wow! What are the odds of two churches with the same exact name? Must need a lot of harmony around here," I commented.

Finally, back in our respective cars, we shook our heads in disbelief. "Thanks, Allison, for indulging me. The confusion of the past two nights brought home the reality of my loneliness," I said.

"Why are you so maudlin, kiddo?" Allison questioned.

"But we were together," said Mira. "Six women sleeping side-by-side."

"But not inside *my* head," I continued. "I've left friends strewn about like rose petals along the paths from home to home—so many moves I almost lost count. I have to keep looking at a list of addresses and contacts that gets longer and longer. Since the death of my dad, I can't seem to get organized."

We were on the road again with running commentary between the cars. Modern technology was great now that our phones were working.

"The last move, so much was lost or maybe even pilfered by the movers—like stolen memories. That's why I've kept this tangible memento of a raspberry bush cutting for Ruth Ann."

"For me?" Ruth Ann piped up from the other car. "Thank you!"

"Oh, she's blushing enough to make the temperature in the car go up," Deidre observed for those that couldn't see.

"Yes, maybe for your bridal bouquet someday, or a little cottage, or maybe even for your own inn. Who knows what's in your future? Just hope it's a happy one with Jimmy John."

"We'll see," Ruth Ann replied.

"Are we finally settled in, now?" Deidre asked, sighing.

"Yes, dear Deidre," Roxie assured her.

"Let's all take a deep breath. First, how's your stomach?" Mira asked, surprisingly calm.

"Better now, thanks," I replied.

"I want to drive in *peace*," Allison said quietly, taking a deep breath. "Can we keep the conversation light? No more true confessions for now."

"Guess that means I can't talk about cradles, cribs, or christenings? Okay, right, end of discussion," I piped in from the lead car.

"How's everyone doing? The GPS says we're almost there. I see our biker friends are making sure we make it to the diner," Ruth Ann said.

From the other car, Deidre piped in, "As my kids would say, *OMG!* I'm hungry! Can't wait to get to the diner that Jimmy John recommended. After that, hopefully we will be on our way back to the Abenaki Lodge and what remains of our conference. I wonder how many books The Bear Claw bookstore sold for me. I can't wait to find out."

Roxie

I looked down at the ubiquitous phone in my hand and wondered again why it was so important, after these past few days without it. And paradoxically, why hadn't I heard from Ben? Maybe he was tied up with the exterminator. There were no messages, emails, or texts but I did see his number in my missed calls log several times. I wonder what Ben's been doing and why he's so enigmatic all of a sudden? Is he up to something I should know about? On the one hand, I want to know, but on the other, I feel a bit disloyal suspecting him of anything.

He was usually so supportive of me and my endeavors, in business, decorating, or writing. But, for some reason, he was somewhat hesitant and a bit skeptical of my foray into writing with my sisters. Maybe in the car, I could talk to Deidre. She had been my rock for a long time, and I knew I must apologize again for brushing her off.

Having had a few days without the phone was not as bad as I had feared. In fact, it was refreshing not to have to talk, text, or do anything else with it. Yet, once we got service back this morning, my old feelings came back, and anxiety crept over me.

Ben has been my mainstay forever. There are those who think I am nuts, but I really did fall in love with him at first sight and first bite. My eyes were riveted on him; his were so blue and he had such an infectious smile. It was uncanny how rapidly we discovered our similarities, likes, and dislikes. Our conversations captured my interest from his first words, especially the discussion about real estate. I fell for him hook, line, and sinker. After a whirlwind romance of two months, we married. Sure, we'd had our ups and downs, but love always superseded any argument or differences. Besides, making up was the best part for us!

Our anniversary was coming up soon, number twenty-five. I had already searched for some first edition volumes on Abraham Lincoln to give Ben as a gift. How could I justify my worries, those elusive feelings appearing every now and then? I felt so guilty. I just had to believe everything was the way it should be. But with Deidre's suspicions, I couldn't just brush it off. We had had a constant loving relationship, starting from the very beginning. I needed to believe in *us*.

We had decided to start our own real estate company, which we built from the ground up. Ben has the greatest business sense. I have learned so much from him. He in turn learned about decorating from me.

When we were first married, we talked about having kids sometime in the future, but that future never came. We never resolved why I hadn't conceived but we accepted it. I pushed the thoughts of children to the back of my mind. Though I felt disappointed, Ben and I were content with each other and our lives. I'd like to think we still are. I was hoping to talk with Deidre about all of this. Perhaps she would quell my fears.

Roxie, the strong one, will forge on ahead!

⌾

～36～

THE SEABREEZE DINER

Ruth Ann	Wednesday 9:00 AM

We finally came upon The Seabreeze Diner, nestled in the shadow of the valley. It was open, with a few cars scattered in the parking lot. It was inviting, but its name made anything but sense in this landlocked valley. We settled into a large booth, glad to be away from The Inn at Raspberry Hill, although we were already nostalgic about our time there. The bikers filed in and sat together on the opposite side of the diner. We would be on the highway shortly, heading back to the Abenaki Lodge, and eventually to our lives, families, and normalcy.

The dog days of summer were upon the valley, but inside The Seabreeze, the air from the twirling fans was heavenly. We were cool and comfortable in the cushy booth. The nametag pinned to the waitress's pink-striped uniform announced her name as "Babs." She and the diner were a throwback to another era.

She greeted us with gusto, wiped her hands on a stained apron, pulled out her pad and pen, and asked, "Whatcha havin' ladies? Coffee? Five coffees and a tea, it will be." She paused then spoke to the air, her head tilted away in mock annoyance, "Always gotta have a different one in every bunch." Babs stared pointedly at Allison.

"Can you believe this?" Roxie asked, spitting and sputtering.

"What? What? What?" Deidre asked, making everyone laugh.

"Look at all these people on their cell phones," Roxie continued, her annoyance with Babs now transferred to something else. All our phones dinged with messages except Roxie's.

"Well Roxie, you were never too far from yours. It was usually attached to your ear," Deidre said.

"I can tell you one thing, you're not going to see it attached anymore," Roxie said solemnly.

"It's not even New Year's and already you're making resolutions." Allison said, obviously moving on from Babs' judgment. "All I want to do is take a shower."

"What did you do with Jimmy John's shirt? Did you keep it as a souvenir?" Joesie asked.

"Yes, for now. J.J. wanted me to keep it, but I plan to wash and return it to him," I answered.

"Oh, really. When?" Mira asked.

"He said we would keep in touch. I told him I had a couple weeks of vacation left before I had to go back to my school job. My cousin's wedding is in the fall so who knows, maybe he'll be my plus one."

"I, for one, am grateful to Jimmy John for clearing our path," Mira declared.

"Too bad we missed some of the conference," Joesie said. "But think of all that happened in the past few days—more for us to write about."

"We should write a book together!" Deidre exclaimed.

"That's a great idea," Allison said. "What do you all think?"

"Maybe. You never know," I remarked.

Roxie nodded and said, "I was supposed to meet Ben in New York City to celebrate our anniversary. We've almost made twenty-five years." She wiped a tear from her eye, cleared her throat, and sat up taller. Ruth Ann put an arm around her.

"I'm alright, girls. Freedom may be a wonderful thing," Roxie whispered. She glanced at her phone in her bag, and I assumed she was checking for service and bars on her cell. "Guess I won't be able to reach Ben until we're back on the road."

"You know, I would normally be upset that I missed some of the workshops, but after my time with all of you, I feel like I can go with the 'flow' a bit more," Joesie said, inciting snickers.

"We covered that topic," Allison said. "Hey guys, when's our next adventure? Let's see where there's a good conference next summer. A place with no mice, spiders, snakes, or caterpillars," she continued. "Only fireflies allowed!"

"Look, here's one in the newspaper. We could go to the Greylock Writers' Forum next summer," Deidre suggested, displaying a touristy local paper she'd folded in half to reveal the advertisement to us. "It's near Canyon Ranch." "Oh, that's here in the Berkshires. Lenox," I said. "We could catch a concert, make spa appointments…" my voice trailed off as I looked at the others to evaluate their interest. They all nodded in agreement. *Whew!*

"For sure. That would be great. Girls, why don't we have lunch together at my house in Florida when we get back?" Mira suggested. "We could talk about next year's writing conference. If you're not in Florida, you can join us by video call."

"What would be on the menu?" asked Joesie.

"Well, it would be more than the fish we caught," Mira said, tongue in cheek. "What do you think, Ruth Ann?"

"I like it!" I answered.

"I can start experimenting with raspberry dessert recipes," Roxie said. "I can use them in my next cookbook. Allison, maybe we could collaborate."

"My catering company could sponsor you," Allison added.

Deidre continued flipping through the pages of the local newspaper. Besides the ad for the writers' conference near Canyon Ranch, it also had discount coupons for mini golf, savings at restaurants, and other local articles. There was a story about a glass blower, a farm-to-table featured chef, and a list of various cultural events.

"Look, an article about Raspberry Hill!" Deidre froze, hand raised for attention. We huddled closer together as she read the article aloud.

THE OBSERVER
THE INN AT RASPBERRY HILL TO REOPEN
By Skye B. Blu

CHESHIRE—The Inn at Raspberry Hill will be taken over by Jimmy John Broadhurst, nephew of Eve and Charles Broadhurst. The new innkeeper, Broadhurst, plans to renovate The Inn, with a grand reopening before next summer's tourist season. Everyone's favorite "aunt," Hazel Broadhurst, sister of Charles, will stay on as the official greeter. The exact date of the reopening will be announced upon completion of the renovations.

Last year, a passerby on the Ashuwillticook Rail Trail witnessed a car careening into Cheshire Lake. The Massachusetts State Police reconstructed the accident scene. They determined that there must have been something in the road, a bear, or deer, perhaps, that caused the vehicle to lose control. By the time the police had arrived, the vehicle had sunk to the bottom of the weed-filled lake. A dive team eventually pulled the driver and passenger out of the water. CPR was performed, but it was too late. They were pronounced dead at the scene. The couple was identified as Charles and Eve Broadhurst of Cheshire, Massachusetts, the original innkeepers.

"Eve and Charles are dead?" I gasped as Deidre stopped short after reading the words that had left us sitting dumbfounded. I put my hand to my mouth, Joesie was tearing up, and Allison had a look of horror on her face.

"There must be some mistake. They fed us, took care of us—even talked to us!" Roxie exclaimed.

"The mounds," Mira said. "The two mounds in the cemetery. That's what they were? Eve and Charles!" Mira stood, arms raised, her tears spilling over.

"I *knew* there was something weird about that place," Deidre lamented. "But dead! They're really *dead?*" Somehow, Deidre read on:

Following the accident that landed the Broadhurst's vehicle in Cheshire Lake, The Inn had been listed on the market. The loss of the beloved innkeepers a year ago is still a fresh memory for young Broadhurst. He plans a memorial reading at The Inn's grand reopening next spring. Broadhurst noted that he is grateful for the investors who placed their faith in his ability to run The Inn at Raspberry Hill.

"Whatsamatter?" Babs interrupted. "You ladies need some fuel in you. Looks like you seen a ghost or something."

"You have no idea, I. . ." began Deidre.

"Truthfully, I'm not surprised after all the weird crap that went on," Allison interrupted.

"Not only that, but your pal Skye wrote this article," Deidre said, holding up the newspaper and looking at Joesie. "Imagine that."

We sat in stunned silence; the chattiness of our two-day ordeal now tabled. When someone did speak, it was about everyday things: the menu, the trip back home, the weather. No one mentioned that when the power came back on that The Inn had remained dark. Each had tried to make their whereabouts known, but the cell phone service was too spotty. No one mentioned people by the names of Eve and Charles, who had cared for us at The Inn at Raspberry Hill, while we were waylaid there.

"Ya gonna order some of our waffles or are you guys omelet people? I have toast and jam, too. Local jam if you like," Babs continued. "Raspberry jam?" she asked as she set down Allison's tea.

"Absolutely not, Babs," Allison said, shivering slightly, preparing her tea. As she took a sip, I could see her brown eyes tearing up above the cup and glowing like they held a glorious secret. She seemed resigned and accepting of Eve and Charles' deaths.

Each of us dutifully ordered our breakfast so as not to ruffle the feathers of the impatient Babs. Frankly, I was glad for the interruption, as the implications of the article shook me to my very core. How bizarre this all was! I almost wanted to go back to The Inn. I didn't know how to feel. I felt a strange pull toward The Inn. Maybe I could say a proper goodbye to Eve and Charles, or at least visit their graves. But I also wanted to leave it alone, never go back. I felt full of love for my writing sisters but also drained. I needed to talk to J.J., but that would have to wait. I was confused and a little miffed that he hadn't revealed the status of The Inn, and worse, that he hadn't told us that Eve and Charles were dead. The Seabreeze's screen door creaked open, and ironically, in walked Jimmy John.

"Ladies," he announced, wearing a big grin, "I see you found your way."

I stood and glared at him. My hands were on my hips in a posture I had never before assumed. I was so upset I could feel the heat rising in my face. But the longer I looked at him, the more I softened. He appeared freshly showered and shaved, his dark hair curling at the nape of his neck. He was wearing a light blue t-shirt. The sleeves broke at the middle of his bicep, revealing his sexy, athletic physique.

"I don't know if I'm mad or sad or both. Why didn't you tell me about Eve and Charles? And furthermore, you're keeping The Inn? Wow! When were you going to tell me?" Jimmy John looked crestfallen at my anger. "I think I have good reasons to be angry, J.J."

He gently put his hand on my arm and led me away from the group. He took my hand and said, "Let me explain. I didn't want to spill the beans. Ruth Ann, please. Look, I was told by my lawyers not to say anything. Eve and Charles had a large mortgage as they had added whole-house air conditioning and other upgrades to the old place. Plus, I needed investors and wasn't sure if they'd take me on as a junior partner. Besides, I'm here because I needed to see you one more time."

"I have a lot to think about. I've only known you for a few days. Give me some time to think," I said.

"I'll call you, okay?" Jimmy John asked.

I watched as Jimmy John left the diner.

Mira

I sipped my coffee. The reality of our adventure was slowly seeping from my right brain to my left, where I could perhaps make sense of the whole thing. Joesie was up taking pictures of the diner, sneaking in photos of us too, I'm sure. We were in total shock. We tried to speak at the same time, cutting off each other's words before they could become phrases.

Ruth Ann walked back to the table as Jimmy John left with his breakfast. Our food had arrived in the meantime, and we ate in relative silence. Roxie stared into space; her cell phone ignored in her purse. Deidre asked Ruth Ann if Jimmy John had provided any explanations.

"Well, what did he say?" she asked, clearly annoyed when Ruth Ann didn't respond. Her head was in her hands and she looked pensive as though pondering all that had happened.

"Another example of the faulty Y chromosome," Joesie opined.

I was suddenly restless and got up to go to the loo. *Wow! Eve's still affecting me,* I thought at my use of the British term. Babs pointed me to the little hall past the booths and I waved at the bikers as I went by. Coming back from the loo, I passed the screen door and glanced outside. I saw a blue Porsche with what looked like Florida plates. To my surprise, our blue-haired Skye jumped out.

"Thanks for the ride," Skye told the man. Then, she waved to me through the door and said, "Where have you been? Your group never came back to the conference."

"The storm," I explained. "We went off the road and stayed at an inn up the way."

"Oh yeah, I know that place—The Inn at Raspberry Hill—even better after interviewing the investors."

"We just read your article," I said. "What a coincidence!"

My brain suddenly disconnected from my body as I watched a tall man with black curly hair, graying at the temples, unfold himself from the Porsche. Feeling like I was floating, I walked out of the restaurant. I watched as he took off his sunglasses and squinted as if to get me into focus. Immediately, I realized he was the man who paid our bill that first night at the restaurant.

"Rico?"

"Mira!"

"That's my sweater!" he said, smiling as I ran into his open arms.

Ruth Ann

Babs refreshed the coffees and asked, "Where's your friend goin' with Rico?"

"Who's Rico? What just happened?" Joesie asked.

Babs answered, "Everyone around here knows Rico by his reputation. He's a big shot real estate developer, and he's quite a player." We turned to see Mira in a tight embrace. The man opened the passenger door and she slid in. Before we could say a word, the Porsche was gone.

"I guess she knows him," Allison said. "Even off her thyroid meds, she wouldn't be hugging a stranger."

"Thyroid meds! I thought it was something else," Deidre interjected.

"Wait," I said, "I have a text from her…"

I read it aloud, "Don't worry. I'm with Rico, the love of my life. Will make my way back, eventually. Plans up in the air. Lots to figure out."

"Oh my God, Mira. What are you doing?" I asked.

"Is she crazy?" Deidre asked.

"What a detour this has been," Allison said. "The storm, Eve and Charles, you and Jimmy John, Mira leaving us. Wow! A lot to take in."

"Now your ride's gone," Joesie said to Skye.

"I'll be okay, no worries. You have room for me now?" Skye asked, ignoring Babs as she slid into Mira's former seat.

"Everybody get their Evite®?" Skye asked.

Joesie wagged her finger at her and motioned Skye to be quiet. "It's supposed to be a secret," she whispered.

"What are you talking about?" Roxie asked.

Joesie held back the impulsive Skye with a look as Deidre broke the news, "I'm sorry, my dear friend. It's about Ben."

"Ben?" she gasped.

"It's not what you think," Deidre explained to Roxie.

"Ben's been planning your twenty-fifth anniversary party in New York City and was trying to keep it from you. We're all invited. I didn't know myself until our Evite® came through when my phone came back on. Now I get it. The woman I saw him with was the event planner. He didn't hire me because you and I are too close. Plus, he wanted someone familiar with New York City."

"That's a relief," Roxie said. "But wait—what do you have to do with this, Skye?"

"Roxie, I was hoping Ben had a chance to explain but he's been calling you and calling you but wasn't able to get through. He kept getting your voicemail," Skye explained. "We've been communicating with one another."

"What in the hell for?" Roxie asked before etiquette kicked in. She backed up and explained, "It was the storm. None of our cell phones were working. He could have left a message, but he didn't."

"Oh, that makes sense," Skye responded. "But there's more."

"Spit it out," Roxie exclaimed. "What else?"

"I've been working on my genealogy. There is a simple saliva test you can take. My mom was a single parent. She never told me anything about my birth father, so I've been digging. I started researching when I was fourteen, but it got too hard—emotionally—since my mom admitted going to a sperm bank," Skye said, her blue eyes teary. "Then I took a DNA test."

Roxie stared hard at Skye. She couldn't help but notice the resemblance. "Are you trying to tell me Ben may be your father?"

"Not maybe—he *is*."

"How do you know?"

"DNA doesn't lie. Ben's matched mine. We connected a short while ago."

"No, it *doesn't* lie," Roxie said, as her Palm Beach tan faded at the news. "I don't know what you expect me to say right now."

"Roxie, I know you're in shock but now you have both Ben *and* Skye. Wow, you're so lucky, Roxie. I wish I knew what had happened to *my* baby. I feel as though I still don't have the truth," Joesie lamented. "At least now, Roxie, you have a stepdaughter."

"I guess Ben and I have a lot to talk about when I get back," Roxie said. None of us had a chance to respond to this bombshell, as Babs interrupted with, "Where ya stayin' at?"

Joesie answered in a soft tone, "We were just passing through," and saved the rest of us from having to fabricate a more believable story or worse yet, from having to reveal anything about our stay during this detour.

After all, we *were* just passing through.

❧

EPILOGUE

The Inn

My shutters wobbled and floors creaked, as doors and drawers opened spontaneously. I groaned under winter's rage. But despite the punishing weather, Jimmy John had done his best to keep my meandering driveway and all my exits clear of snow for the workers to come and go. His pickup truck was well equipped with an all-terrain package and plow on the front. He would zip up his snowmobile suit, pull a woolen hat down over his ears, and set out with gloved hands to conquer the winter.

Workers showed up daily, sanding my floors, painting my walls, bringing in furniture, updating my wiring. I was annoyed with all the comings and goings but had to concede that they were making me feel revitalized. Sounds are intrinsic to any place. I, The Inn at Raspberry Hill, was no exception—but not everyone welcomed the sounds. When my floor creaked or shutters opened or closed "spontaneously," the workers noticed.

"This old place is haunted," affirmed the electrician, Butch. "I can't wait to get this job done."

His sidekick, Brett, did not agree. "I don't believe in that crap. Every time you hear a noise, you smell a ghost."

"I don't care. You won't see me spending one night in this place," Butch replied. "Too scary!"

"Stop being a sissy," Brett teased. "I'd stay here if I could afford it. With all the work we're doing, this place will be restored to its original beauty."

"Brett, I'm being serious. Listen to me. One day when I was on the roof, I swear I heard two people talking—a real conversation—I couldn't make out what they were saying but it was definitely a man and a woman speaking. Do you know what? No one was here but me. I almost fell off the roof," Butch said, looking sheepish at the very thought of his own fear.

"Get out," Brett chided. He put a furniture drape over his head in a ghost-like fashion.

"Look out, Butch. There's no such thing as ghosts 'cept maybe me dressed up for Halloween."

"You'll see, you old disbeliever. How 'bout that time the hammer fell down off the shelf?"

"That was weird, I agree. But ghosts?" Brett answered. "Ghosts make great storytelling but that's about it. Get back to work. The quicker we finish this job the sooner we'll be outta here.

Now months later, my main house and grounds were almost ready for the grand reopening.

Jimmy John considered the type of guests he would soon be welcoming. They would come to an old inn like me for the experience. They were not your Motel 6 or five-star people. These guests will want everything: an old-time experience with modern touches. They will marvel at my newly varnished mahogany staircases and capture my essence, taking photographs of me from various angles. I boasted four-poster beds and sideboards with ornate mirrors hung above. Yet, my guests of today will expect all the modern conveniences. Jimmy John had seen to it that high speed internet was available, and the guest rooms will be stocked with comfort items.

The loneliness that had encapsulated me had lifted. I was back in tip-top shape. Eve and Charles rested peacefully out back; the mounds now topped with granite headstones. Jimmy John remained largely unaware that ghosts had visited me.

Hazel spoke of Eve and Charles often, as if they were still alive, but that was Hazel. Jimmy John was too much of a realist to entertain thoughts akin to the paranormal. When a creak was heard or a door mysteriously opened, there was always a real-life explanation. Besides, the whole ghost thing would scare away the guests.

Jimmy John would do what he was meant to do. Now that he had raised enough capital to make me shine, and was the proud manager/junior partner, as well as head chef. He was perfect for the job. His family legacy to serve would be realized and he would carry on the family tradition of innkeeping. His new gourmet stove would cook up hearty but healthy meals, and guests will come back year after year for his shepherd's pie and wholegrain crusty bread—at least, that was the dream. But an inn was a big responsibility as I know well. Oh, but to do it right, Jimmy John would need his own "Eve" by his side. Images of his brief encounter with the lovely Ruth Ann warmed me.

Hazel sat in the foyer, reminiscing about last summer when she had approached the front room and waved goodbye to the six travelers as they got into their vehicles and drove away after that terrible storm. She had been a bit dejected but soon tottered back to her cottage mumbling "gone, gone, gone."

The presence of Eve and Charles had brought life back into me and Hazel had played along. Poor Hazel. She had known for a long time that her brain was playing tricks on her. She easily forgot things and repeated herself all the time. Jimmy John wanted her to retire. "Go somewhere you don't have to take care of others," he'd insisted. But Hazel stayed to have another go at serving guests. Her take was that it was so kind of Eve and Charles to have helped with the travelers.

Now, Jimmy John awaits the arrival of guests, and perhaps the return of Ruth Ann.

I'll be watching.

Book Club Discussion Questions

1. How did you relate to the major themes in the book (i.e., female relationships, love, mystery)?

2. Which characters did you empathize with or relate to the most/least and why?

3. Which scenes have stuck with you the most?

4. How did The Inn as a character work in the novel?

5. What did the raspberries symbolize to you?

6. Why do you think Hazel repeats words three times?

7. Did you relate to the Ebb and Flow chapter? Is there an experience you wanted to relay?

8. Did you think that the magical realism is possible?

9. What was one thing about the plot you wanted to know that wasn't answered?

10. Did the locations (Hudson Valley and The Berkshires) pique your interest? Do you want to visit?

(Continued on next page)

11. What unexpected detours have you taken, and would any of them make a great novel?

12. What experiences have you had that might be otherworldly?

13. What would attract you to a collaborative creative project?

14. What do you think was the glue that held these five authors known as "The Inkslingers" together?

15. Do you have any lingering questions to ask the authors?

ABOUT THE
AUTHORS

Group Acknowledgments

The Inkslingers are a group of women with varied personalities. Through laughter, tears, and words of encouragement, they have bonded, meeting life's challenges. They took the opportunity to create a noticeably unique work, where their distinctive styles could merge on the page. Their numerous emails back and forth, along with multiple Zoom sessions, are a true testament to their perseverance.

They would like to recognize Ann Mallen who, due to unforeseen circumstances, was unable to remain in the group. They thank her for her initial ideas, involvement, and support.

They wish to thank Penelope Love, Todd Monahan, Jamie Cox, and Rolf Busch of Citrine Publishing for their continued support and advice throughout the editing and publishing process.

Additionally, The Inkslingers extend their heartfelt thanks to our beta readers, Susan Goldstein, Patricia Grimes, and Suzanne Magee, for being our ardent supporters and making what could be a difficult job easy.

The Inkslingers believe their collaborative book, *Detours*, has taught them valuable lessons, reinforced their communication skills, and promoted harmony within the group. Despite the normal vicissitudes of life, they were able to share graduations, weddings of their children, and the births of grandchildren. Through it all, they have maintained their friendship and love for one another. They are all daughters, wives, and mothers; but most of all, they are forever sisters.

Biographies and Acknowledgments of The Inkslingers

Rosemary Gensler fell in love with the power of the word when she was seven years old, writing her first essay. She has written many pieces since then, culminating in her memoir, *I Refuse to Say Moo*. She has also published stories through the Kravis Center in Florida, where she was an original member of the Writer's Circle. Her works have been read on NPR in Florida, where she presently resides and writes. She and her late husband are the parents of three, and proud grandparents of nine. Rosemary looks forward to the continual learning of the written word and seeing more of her work in print.

She'd like to thank her family for always being at the ready to support her in every way and for inspiring her to become the best version of herself. Julie Gilbert, longtime mentor and friend, pushed her to continue to rewrite and rewrite once again. Without friends to have helped her realize the meaning of inspiration and friendship, she would be lost. Most of all she wishes to thank her

Inkslinger sisters who embody the true meaning of the word "sister" and are the best ever!

Phyllis Hoffman knew she wanted to write before she could read. She remembers trips with her cousin and their grandmother to The Public Library in New York. At the time, she wished she could read *all* the books.

She owes whatever talent she has to all the teachers who encouraged her to write—and to her father who thought she could write "the great American novel." Phyllis has a Master's degree in Special Education. She was chosen as one of President Bush's Points of Lights for her volunteer service. Phyllis was honored by The Executive Women of the Palm Beaches Foundation, the Cystic Fibrosis Foundation, and Jewish Family and Children's Service.

Her book, *Butterfly Girl*, is the story of her journey with

her second daughter—an amazing woman with special needs. Phyllis is married, has three children, five grandchildren, and various grand-dogs and cats.

Marion Susan Phillips was raised in rural New Jersey's nearby waterways and Appalachian foothills. Her high school essays won her the appointment as senior yearbook editor and finalist in *NY Herald Tribune* Student Forum. She gardened and fished with her father, whose neighboring immigrant parents' and assorted relatives' tales continue to inspire her writings.

She was awarded two graduate degrees; became founding member of the Working Writers' Forum and Cinema Society;

had essays published in magazines and read on Florida public radio; presented a paper regarding childhood hearing loss following maternal rubella; and co-wrote funded grants enabling Appalachia-NY State Child Project and Maryland federally funded ESOL program.

Marion thanks her husband, Leslie, for opening new worlds, dancing the Tango, and chauffeuring her to airports for writing projects' destinations. On Historical Society stage, she directed military war-wives and volunteer actresses, all portraying wives' remembrances—alas, script survived, camera failed! She is also the author of a nonfiction book capturing the authentic voices of U.S. war-wives.

Nancy S. Sims is the author of a short story collection, *Verbal Snacks,* and novella, *The Pillow.* She is one of the charter members of the Kravis Center Writer's Circle, and excerpts of her writings have been showcased there, and on a Florida NPR station. She is an ardent supporter of the literary arts as demonstrated by her involvement in her community as a book fair consultant, workshop facilitator, and tutor. Her leadership positions have included: President of the Jewish Community Center in Palm Beach County, Board Member of the Jewish Federation, and Chair of their Community Relations Council during the aftermath of September 11, 2001. Nancy serves on the National Jewish Book Council, where she has been a past judge.

She wishes to thank her family, and those—past and present—who have encouraged her many interests. She is indebted to Julie Gilbert of the Kravis Center for being a mentor. Most of all, she is grateful for the experience of meeting like-minded writers like The Inkslingers who believe in the transformative power of the written word. She is the mother of two children and resides with her husband in Florida.

Ellyn Horn Zarek is a writer from Massachusetts and an alumnus of UMass Boston. She was named Best Fiction Writer of the Year in 2016 by the Palm Beach Book Festival for her novel, *Far Town*. She has had several short stories read on NPR and is a *Chicken Soup for the Soul* contributor. In addition, she has been a member of the Kravis Center Writer's Circle since 2005.

Ellyn has entertained audiences with readings of her original essays at the Palm Beach Institute for the Entertainment Arts. She is proud to have served two years in AmeriCorps, and to have taught English for International Language Homestays. She is on the board of both The Cream Literary Alliance and Kayla Cares 4 Kids.

Ellyn wishes to thank her parents, William Francis Horn (1922-2000) and Jeannette Ford Horn (1923-2017), and son Scott (1976-2005), who were major supporters of her writing. She thanks her husband, Jeff, daughter Mary Ellyn, and son Bradley for their continued encouragement.

She would also like to extend her thanks to authors and mentors Julie Gilbert, Donna Carbone, and John Boles. To those in The Jane Austen Thursday critique group, and The Cream Literary Alliance, Ellyn thanks you for your inspiration. Ellyn lives with her husband and Miniature Schnauzer, Daisy, and calls Florida home.

∽

www.InkslingerAuthors.com

PUBLISHER'S NOTE

Thank you for reading *Detours*. To help other readers find this book, here are suggestions for your consideration:

- Write a customer review wherever books are sold.

- Gift this book to friends, family, and colleagues.

- Share a photo of yourself with the book on social media and tag #detoursbytheinkslingers.

- Bring in The Inkslingers as speakers for your club or organization.

- Suggest *Detours* to your book club and local library.

- Recommend *Detours* to the manager of your local bookstore.

- For bulk orders, contact the publisher at 828-585-7030 or email Orders@CitrinePublishing.com.

- Connect with the authors at www.InkslingerAuthors.com.

We appreciate your book reviews, letters, and shares.

14 DAYS

Massapequa Public Library
523 Central Avenue
Massapequa, NY 11758
(516) 798-4607

Made in the USA
Columbia, SC
17 June 2021

40339105R00174